ACCLAIM FOR THE WORKS OF MICHAEL CRICHTON:

"Michael's talent outscaled even his own dinosaurs of *Jurassic Park*. He was the greatest at blending science with big theatrical concepts...There is no one in the wings that will ever take his place."
—Steven Spielberg

"Crichton keeps us guessing at every turn."
—*Los Angeles Times*

"[Crichton] marries compelling subject matter with edge-of-your-seat storytelling."
—*USA Today*

"Crackling...mysterious..."
—*Entertainment Weekly*

"One of the great storytellers of our age... What an amazing imagination."
—*New York Newsday*

"Crichton writes vividly."
—*Washington Post*

"Compulsively readable."
—*National Review*

ODDS ON

MICHAEL CRICHTON WRITING AS JOHN LANGE™

Odds On
Scratch One
Easy Go
The Venom Business
Zero Cool
Drug of Choice
Grave Descend
Binary

#1 *NEW YORK TIMES* BESTSELLING AUTHOR

MICHAEL CRICHTON

WRITING AS JOHN LANGE™

ODDS ON

BLACKSTONE
PUBLISHING

Copyright © 1966 by John Lange
Copyright © renewed 2005 by Constant c Productions, Inc.
Copyright © assigned 2013 by Constant c Productions, Inc.
to the John Michael Crichton Trust
Copyright © assigned 2013 by the John Michael Crichton Trust to CrichtonSun LLC.
All rights reserved under International and Pan-American Copyright Conventions.

CrichtonSun™, John Lange™, and Odds On™ are trademarks of CrichtonSun, LLC and are used with permission.

No part of this book may be reproduced or used in any manner whatsoever without the express written permission of the copyright owner except for the use of brief quotations in a book review.

This is a work of fiction. Names, characters, places, incidents, notes and bibliographic citations are products of the author's imagination or are used fictitiously and are not to be construed as real. Any resemblance to actual events, locates, organizations or persons, living or dead, is entirely coincidental.

Printed in the United States of America

ISBN 979-8-200-98754-2
Library of Congress Control Number: 2022950456
Fiction / Mystery & Detective / General

Version 2

Blackstone Publishing
31 Mistletoe Rd.
Ashland, OR 97520

www.BlackstonePublishing.com

www.MichaelCrichton.com

FOREWORD
by Sherri Crichton

It is such an honor and pleasure to see the John Lange books freshly and newly published by Blackstone, to reintroduce these books to fans and also present them to a whole new generation of readers.

My husband, Michael Crichton, put himself through Harvard Medical School in the sixties by writing pulp fiction novels. He wrote them as John Lange and Jeffery Hudson before he was published under his own name with *The Andromeda Strain*.

The John Lange books are adventure stories, and you can start to see in them the genius that would, only a few years later, become so apparent. While later in his career Michael made a point of separating his identity from these novels, I suspect he had a lot more affection for them than he showed.

The books are set in the late sixties and seventies and were his tribute to Ian Fleming's James Bond novels and to one of his favorite Alfred Hitchcock films, *To Catch a Thief*; the books are about secret treasures, heists, archaeology, unlikely heroes, seductive and at times treacherous lovers, classic villains, and much more.

I look at these John Lange novels with great affection as I

picture Michael studying medicine day and night and writing these fun books over school breaks and holidays. Becoming an author was his dream—not being a doctor—and the John Lange novels truly are a testament to his exotic imagination, places he dreamed of visiting, and above all, they show the birth of Michael as an author.

In an interview from December 2000,
Michael shared details of the beginning of his career
in the sixties. His comments reveal how he went
from John Lange to Michael Crichton:

I was one of those kids who seemed to know very early what I wanted to do. I was driven to writing. I did a lot of it starting around the third grade, when I wrote this enormously long puppet show that had to be typed up by my father with carbon copies so that all the kids could have their parts.

At that time most of the third graders were writing a page, and I had written this very long thing. But I just wanted to do it. I don't know how to explain it any differently.

When I was thirteen or fourteen, I had visited a place in Arizona called Sunset Crater Volcano National Monument; I thought it was extremely interesting and relatively unknown. I complained that people didn't have more knowledge about this place, and my mother and father told me, "Well, why don't you write an article?" I said, "I can't do that." And they said, "No, no, the *New York Times* accepts articles in their Travel section from all kinds of people." So I wrote an article and they published it.

ODDS ON

I'd read that only two hundred people in the United States were able to support themselves full time writing books. I thought to be one of two hundred people in the entire country seemed a very difficult group to join. And six thousand doctors graduated every year. That seemed much more doable. But while I was in medical school, I began to write to pay the term bills. I wrote under a pseudonym because the grades you got in those days were very dependent on the evaluation of your teachers, and I was quite convinced that if they knew I was running off to write books, they would think less of me.

The names I chose were John Lange and Jeffery Hudson. John Lange, I drew from my own first name, which is John, and I thought of these books as James Bond thrillers, fairy tales for adults. I associated the books to Andrew Lang, who was an author of Victorian fairy tales, and Jeffery Hudson, who was a little person from the court of Charles I of England and a great adventurer. I thought it would be very entertaining for me to have the name of a little person since I am six nine.

The book I wrote under the name Jeffery Hudson, *A Case of Need*, was optioned for a movie and eventually made by Blake Edwards. It made my life very strange because I was sometimes going to California to talk to the screenwriter, then I'd come back and put on my whites to be in the hospital. There's a bizarre difference between being an impoverished student and then having these periods where I got into limousines and drove around Hollywood. It made me a little crazy. Yet, even when *A Case of Need* won the Edgar

Award for Best Mystery and I had to go down to New York to accept the award, no one in the medical school ever found out, which was odd. It showed me how self-centered the institution of medicine really was.

Eventually, I was going to write a nonfiction book, which ultimately was published as *Five Patients*, and I had to go to the dean to get permission to skip certain classes to do this book. He said, "Well, writing a book is very difficult. Do you realize how difficult it is? Have you ever done anything like that?" And at that point I finally thought it was okay, and I said, "Yes, actually, I've written several books."

My next novel to be published was *The Andromeda Strain*; I wrote it in secret, and when [director] Robert Wise bought it to make it as a film, it got publicized that there was this kid in medical school who had sold a book to the movies for a lot of money.

My picture was on the wire services. The story was officially out. Everybody knew. But looking back on it, it was a very free time.

ODDS ON

CONTENTS

Saturday, June Fourteenth 1

Sunday, June Fifteenth 12

Monday, June Sixteenth 25

Tuesday, June Seventeenth 45

Night, June Seventeenth 63

Wednesday, June Eighteenth 94

Thursday, June Nineteenth 124

Friday, June Twentieth 158

Afternoon, June Twentieth 173

Saturday Morning, June Twenty-First 188

Afternoon, June Twenty-First 199

Night, June Twenty-First 209

Sunday Morning, June Twenty-Second
    (12:00–1:00 a.m.) 217

Morning, June Twenty-Second
    (1:00 a.m.–12:00 noon) 224

Afternoon, June Twenty-Second 253

"There are three kinds of lies: lies, damned lies, and statistics."
BENJAMIN DISRAELI

SATURDAY, JUNE FOURTEENTH

LE PERTHUS, FRANCE

The dynamite, neatly bundled in "Happy Birthday" wrapping paper, lay casually on the back seat. Miguel had thrown his sport coat over it some hours before, and so, as he drew up at the end of a line of cars waiting to pass Spanish customs, he gave his package no thought. It was perfectly obvious and perfectly safe.

He killed the engine of his Simca and lit a cigarette, feeling the midmorning heat settle around his car. It had been miserably hot the whole damned day. The drop had been scheduled for 6 a.m. in Marseilles, but as usual there was a snag, and then, when the bastard had showed up at nine, he wanted endless identification. And to top it off, he was annoyed that Miguel didn't speak French. Miguel spoke excellent English, as well as German and Swahili—and, of course, Spanish. He had been born in Mexico, raised in Texas, trained and tempered in the American army. He had made his fortune in Europe after the war—a modest fortune, but decent enough. In the late forties and early fifties, his business had been money—still was, in Yugoslavia, Turkey, and Egypt—and afterward, it had been watches and cameras. The Japanese had put a big dent in that game by taking away demand for German and Swiss stuff; the market had never been the same since. Miguel had shifted his attention to guns, but even that was breaking down as rebels got scarcer, and legitimate sources for armaments opened up. For the last six months he had sat around in Beirut doing nothing except hustle girls and smoke hash, and then finally Bryan had contacted him. Bryan was a good man, cautious and perfectly straight, but Miguel wished he had been given the whole story. He didn't like smuggling for no reason. Bryan had said the reason was damned good, and that Miguel would just have to wait, and although Miguel had argued like hell, Bryan hadn't budged an inch.

So now he was waiting.

He looked down the long line of cars to the Spanish customs officers in their green-and-red uniforms and funny black hats. Luckily, they weren't checking trunks. Miguel had chosen this border crossing particularly because it was hot and crowded, and he was hoping for a perfunctory check. Usually the Spaniards were careless—unless they had been tipped off.

Miguel had taken precautions against that. The Marseilles contact, a fat bastard stinking of garlic, had helped stow the dynamite inside the trunk of an Opel, and, without being asked, Miguel had mentioned that he was driving it into Spain. The Frenchman would assume that Miguel was taking it anywhere but Spain; he might alert the Italians or the Austrians, but it didn't matter much. Miguel had driven east from Marseilles to Cassis, checking constantly to be sure he wasn't followed, and then had left the Opel and started back in the Simca. He hadn't stopped for lunch, thus insuring that he would reach the border at the hottest part of the day.

Slowly, the line of cars inched forward.

The car had been Bryan's idea. It was leased to Miguel,

ODDS ON

registered in Paris, with red "TTA 75" plates, indicating he was an American tourist. His passport—his real passport—was American, so everything was on the up-and-up. That was the way Bryan liked it, always truthful whenever possible. Miguel smirked. Bryan was overcautious, unable to bluff. He wondered what the Englishman would do if he knew Miguel was crossing the border with the stuff practically in sight on the back seat.

Not that Miguel believed in taking chances; he didn't. He was supposed to be a tourist, and he had gone to great pains to enhance that impression. His clothes were new, sporty, and, even by his own relaxed standards of taste, rather vulgar. The car was cluttered with road maps, tourist literature, guidebooks, and loose boxes of film, the result of a week-long tour through southern France. During that week, he had been a genuine, rubbernecking, picture-snapping tourist; now, both he and his car looked authentic. The impression was unmistakable and impossible to falsify.

The last of the cars ahead of him passed through customs. Miguel pulled up and handed his passport through the window. Without glancing at it, the inspector handed it to the man in the little glass booth, who stamped it perfunctorily. It was returned, and Miguel handed the inspector the green card, proof of registration and insurance. The inspector didn't seem too interested.

"Cigarettes?"

"No," Miguel said.

"Liquor?"

"No."

The inspector nodded. "Where are you going?"

"Barcelona, then Madrid." He was careful to pronounce the names awkwardly.

The inspector returned the green card and waved Miguel through.

Miguel drove slowly along the winding road, passing the rolling green hills, the occasional red-roofed farmhouses, the wheat fields. He would spend the night in Gerona, celebrate his passage with a good roaring drunk, and drive to the hotel in the morning. Bryan had said it was a fancy hotel with lots of broads. The meeting there would be a little dividend on the project, a nice change.

LONDON, ENGLAND

Bryan Stack listened to Jane sleeping quietly beside him. She breathed regularly, with the peaceful exhaustion of a totally relaxed and satisfied woman. He pushed a strand of her dark hair from her face, and looked thoughtfully at her aristocratic nose and cheekbones, the sensual full mouth. Well, she ought to have fine features; she was Lord Averett's only daughter. He smiled to himself. If the old man only knew.

He slipped out of bed, groped in the dark for cigarettes, and went to the window. Through the dark drops of rain which rattled against the windowpane, he could see the blurred, dark-green patch of Hyde Park below, completely deserted. He wondered how he was going to tell her. He should have said something weeks ago, but it was always so difficult to find the words.

"Bryan?" Her voice was sleepy.

"Sorry," he said. "I thought you were asleep." He looked back at her, naked beneath the white sheet, which clearly revealed the twin mounds of her breasts and the slow curve of her full hips. She stretched lazily.

"I *was* asleep," she said. "It's warm in this room. Why don't you open the window?"

"It's raining."

She sighed. "Summer in England. Light me a cigarette, would you? Thanks." Her eyes caught his in the brief glow of the cigarette lighter. "Is something wrong?"

"Of course not."

She studied his face in the darkness, trying to read his features, to fathom the expression. She knew Bryan was a master of expressions; his face, handsome and excitingly cruel, was his stock in trade.

"You're leaving me," she said.

"Yes."

"Where is it this time?"

"Italy," he lied.

"I wish you wouldn't, darling."

"I know." He wanted to add that he didn't have any burning desire to go, but that wouldn't be strictly true. Bryan Stack was a slightly disreputable man of action, and he always had been. He lived for tension—and his women lived for the aura of excitement which hung about him.

"Will it be dangerous?"

"I can't be sure. Probably." Spain would be a hell of a place to pull a stunt like this, he knew. Police states were always tougher. Still, it all looked good on paper.

"Gone long?"

"A couple of weeks."

Jane sighed. She had waited for him before, many times. She had waited longer than two weeks. She would manage. She stretched again, and felt her muscles begin to tingle with the first faint hinting of desire. She ran her eyes over his naked body, sitting at the edge of the bed at her feet. She knew every inch of that body, every bulging muscle, every scar. She loved it, and she needed it. Whenever he was gone, she was restless as an alley cat, roaming the streets and bars like a common whore, occasionally taking stray men who looked as if they might be able to satisfy her. They never could, and they only increased her longing for Bryan. He was the genuine thing—a man who could hold her, excite her, drive her into such a frenzy that she no longer knew who or where she was, and then ease her gently back into the world. He did it with such strength, such confidence.

"When do you leave?" she asked.

He hesitated. "Tomorrow morning."

She nodded calmly, expecting that. He'd already arranged it. Bryan always left in a hurry, always came back to her with unexpected abruptness. That was his way.

The tingling had increased perceptibly. She now felt her thighs growing warm, the area between her legs heated. She scratched her shoulder, wondering if it was a passing urge which would leave, and she waited. It did not leave her, but built in intensity. She raised one leg and kicked off the sheet, enjoying the way he looked down her exposed body.

"Bryan," she said. "I want you. Now."

He smiled in the darkness. "I thought you'd had enough."

"Have you?"

Without answering, he lay down beside her and kissed her, biting her soft lower lip. His hands, strong and assured, ran down her neck, across her breasts, and slowly down her flat stomach. He kissed her ear, and she felt a sudden thrill which made her grind her hips into the sheet and spread her legs. Then he began to kiss her breasts, stroking them gently with his tongue until the nipples were tense and firm. She moaned softly; her body was taking on a life of its own, and she was losing the power to control it. She felt the muscles in her abdomen tighten as his hand slipped between her legs.

She moaned as he came into her, felt her hips churning, driving, wanting him. She wondered briefly if he would come

ODDS ON

back to her, but then all thoughts were blotted out in a rising overwhelming surge of passion.

CAMBRIDGE, MASSACHUSETTS

It was very quiet in the basement of the computation laboratory. Steven Jencks listened to the muffled sound of activity in the glass-walled rooms around him. To the left, secretaries and graduate students pored over computer printouts or arranged programs; to the right was a single room containing the card-sorter. It was in operation now, shuffling through data input cards and dropping them into a row of slots.

The main computer, an IBM 7090, was upstairs on the ground floor. Jencks had been up there a short time before, watching as the computer ran through its programs. Though he had seen it at work a dozen times before, it never failed to amaze him; he could stare for hours as the lights winked on the control consoles, and the memory reels whirled back and forth, imparting the knowledge stored on magnetic tape.

It was an expensive machine. Computer time cost hundreds of dollars an hour, and he had had to buy the full hour, though his actual program would require only a minute or two of machine time. The rest of the money would pay for the technicians who fed in his raw data and program cards, which the computer then transferred onto tape. The computer worked only with taped instructions and data; punch cards were too slow for it.

Since he had access to a card-punching machine, Jencks had supplied the card file ready to run. The technicians had been surprised, and grateful. But Jencks had not spent twelve exhausting hours with the big machine which cut little rectangles into the computer cards out of any feeling of sympathy for the technicians. He had done the dull work because he wanted no one else to see it.

His project was a specialized one, and might cause comment.

A technician named Allerton, a young PhD candidate with heavy glasses and a mop of black hair, came up as he was finishing his Coke. "Dr. Jencks?"

"That's right." Jencks was not a doctor of anything, but there was no point in explaining.

"Your output should be coming off in a few minutes."

They went upstairs and watched as the 7090 reeled off pages of computations, which were written with incredible speed onto broad sheets of green paper. The paper fell in folds into a wire basket on the floor.

The output typewriter paused, making a rapid click-click-click as it waited for the next program to be run through. Because computer time was so expensive, one project after another was handled by the machine with barely a pause in between.

"Yours should be next," Allerton said.

As he spoke, the typewriter began again, racing across the page with blurring speed, hammering out row after row of numbers. Jencks's eyes hurt as he tried to follow it. After about a minute, the typewriter stopped, and began its click-click-clicking once again. Allerton ripped off the continuous strip of paper, separating the printout from the large blank sheaf above the typewriter. He picked up the thick wad of printed output and handed it to Jencks.

"We made two copies," he said. "Is that enough?"

"Fine."

"You want your data cards?"

"Yes, if you can find them." He kept his voice casual, indicating no concern. In fact, he was very concerned; he wanted every trace of his project removed from the computation lab.

"I think I know where they are," Allerton said, and went off.

Allerton had seen the program and had watched the output with some interest. He knew that Jencks had run through a simulation; he didn't know what it was about, but he understood its general nature well enough. It was the CRIPA program, used to test the best way to combine a series of separate jobs leading to some final goal. Industry used it to build intricate things like jet planes and submarines. In fact, the CRIPA program—standing for Critical Path Analysis—was first used on the Polaris project. The idea was to find out which jobs were most likely to hold up the entire construction schedule, and to make sure those jobs were done on time, in smooth order.

Jencks had fed some kind of data into a CRIPA program. Allerton didn't worry about what the data specifically referred to; after all, it was just a bunch of numbers, perhaps even a hypothetical experiment, like Professor Forte's simulation of paths for subatomic particles.

Allerton found the cards and brought them back to Jencks in a narrow cardboard box almost three feet long. "Here you are."

"Thanks," Jencks said, slipping the box under his arm. He picked up his briefcase, which now contained the computer printout.

"Good luck with your problem," Allerton said, as Jencks left.

"I may need it," Jencks replied truthfully.

Without hurrying, he walked outside and caught a cab to Logan Airport.

Three hours later, he was watching a New York cabbie put his luggage in the trunk. Jencks slipped into the back seat, his briefcase at his side. "Kennedy," he said.

The driver sighed. "Got a time problem?"

"No," Jencks said. He never had a time problem. He ran his

life serenely, with proper allowances, with careful planning, with consummate skill. He had been blessed with a fine memory and a quick mind, and he had used both to his advantage. Steven Jencks was a professional gambler, and a very successful one. He reached into his pocket for the telegram which had arrived in New York that morning, just prior to his trip to Boston. He found the cable along with the receipt for his hotel bill and a wad of newly purchased traveler's checks.

AGREE FILMING SCHEDULE MEET LOCATION
ACCORDING PLAN PROPS ARRANGED
BRYAN

It was succinct. It showed that Bryan was a man after his own heart, a man who got right to the point and didn't play silly games.

But what about their third man? Bryan had assured him that the man was good and could be trusted. Jencks preferred to reserve judgment until he had met him. The fellow was a smuggler, and smugglers had a tendency to play both sides of the fence (Jencks smiled at the pun) and to hop out of the heat at the first opportunity.

The cabbie drove through the tunnel and headed east toward the Belt Parkway. Jencks returned the telegram to his pocket. He would dispose of it later; perhaps he could flush it down the toilet at the airport.

"Goin' abroad?" the cabbie asked.

"Yes," Jencks said coldly.

The cabbie ignored his tone. "Europe?"

"No, Africa."

"Africa. No kidding. Whereabouts in Africa?"

"Timbuktu."

"I don't know where that is," the cabbie admitted. "You a salesman or something?"

"A white hunter," Jencks said, thinking that it was almost true.

The cabbie laughed. "All right, mister. A guy can tell when he's being kidded."

"Sometimes," Jencks said, "but only sometimes."

SUNDAY, JUNE FIFTEENTH

CANNES, FRANCE

Peter Merritt Ganson IV walked shivering out of the water and threw himself down on a striped beach mattress on the Carlton beach. From the water, Jenny waved gaily and called to him.

"Bitch," he muttered under his breath. He rubbed himself briskly with a towel, watching the goosebumps form. The water was too cold. He had said so, but she had insisted, knowing that it would annoy him. Peter didn't like ocean water to be any colder than a warm bath. That was why he preferred his parents' home on St. Thomas to any spot on the Mediterranean. There was no getting around it, the Mediterranean was cold most of the year.

But no colder than Jenny, he thought irritably.

Two weeks before, he had been dreaming of this summer vacation with Jenny. As he sat in his little room in Eliot House, overlooking the traffic on Boylston Street, he had planned an idyllic two months on the Continent. His dreams had carried him through three weeks of exams at the end of his junior year, but now they seemed totally wrecked.

She continued to refuse to sleep with him until they were

ODDS ON

married. It was the same old line she had used for months in Cambridge, and he still could not soften her, though God knew he'd tried.

When she had agreed to meet him secretly in Paris, he had assumed she intended to sleep with him. After all, it was ridiculous for two people to travel together for eight weeks and never go to bed together, wasn't it?

Separate rooms, good-night kisses. Christ.

He felt cold water on his back, and looked up to see Jenny shaking her hand over him. "Thanks," he said.

"My, you're cheerful today." She dropped down on a mattress next to him and began to comb her dark blond hair.

"You can't blame me."

"I don't blame you. I just don't understand why you take this attitude, as I've told you before. You act like you're being cheated, and you're not. I wish you'd stop being such a bore about it."

"I'm sorry you find me boring."

Jenny sighed, looked up at the sun, and said nothing.

"Maybe we shouldn't travel together anymore," he said, chewing his lip. It was a nervous habit.

"Whatever you think best."

He looked at her quickly and realized she was serious. She would be perfectly happy without him and would probably visit family friends in Switzerland or Amalfi. The thought sent a cold shiver down his spine. He let his eyes travel from her face to her body. As always, it tempted him—the firm, large breasts, the small, supple waist, the long, slimly muscled legs. Jenny was a big girl, almost 5'8", with the kind of expansive exuberance typical of girls from the western states. In Jenny's case, the state was Texas. Her father was in the oil business, and though she once complained about how hard it was to make money in oil these days, she also complained that if she hadn't gone to Wellesley, she would have been able to keep her Porsche at school.

Peter had flown out to her home in Midland, Texas, over Christmas, and had met the old man. Big Jack Cameron. A hearty, informal, somewhat coarse bull of a man who smoked Havana cigars, handed out St. Christopher medals to his friends (he wasn't Catholic) and had big, beefy hands and red cheeks. Jenny always called him "Daddy." Peter always called his own father, who was in banking, "Father," or—in rare moments of intimacy—"Dad." It was, he reflected, the difference between Massachusetts and Texas.

Jenny wore a black one-piece bathing suit, a nice one with a deep-plunging neckline which showed the full globes of her breasts, but somehow the fact that it was one-piece and not a bikini represented all his problems in his eyes.

Jenny rubbed herself briskly with the towel, and lay back on the mattress. She bent one leg, and Peter looked at the slim knee, the tapering thigh, and the lovely smooth line of her calf. Damn it all!

She raised her head and ran her fingers over her chest just below her collarbone. "Am I peeling?"

Peter tried to concentrate on the peeling and not the breast. "I don't think so."

She smiled, showing her dimples, and he thought again how deceptively angelic she looked, "I hope not. Pass me the suntan cream, will you?"

"Want me to rub it on?"

"I'll do it," she said, taking the tube. "Thanks anyway."

He lay back and stared at the hot sphere of the sun through half-closed eyes. She never gave him a chance, never an opening, never an opportunity. It was always like this, and he had a feeling it would continue—unless he could do something to

ODDS ON

change the entire situation. Perhaps a change of scenery. Cannes was pleasant, but too familiar. They had each been here before.

Abruptly, he recalled the leaflet he had glanced through at the travel agency the day before. He needed someplace new and isolated, someplace elegant, yet out of the way. That hotel might be the answer. He tried to remember what the brochure had said: three hundred rooms, four dining rooms, hairdresser, shops, nightclub, swimming pools, and tennis courts. An isolated, complete little luxury community on the Costa Brava.

It was worth a try.

"I'm tired of Cannes," Peter said. "Let's go somewhere else."

She looked over at him, shading her eyes from the sun. "Are you serious?"

"Yes."

"What do you have in mind?"

"Spain."

"Too far," she said, closing her eyes and lying back.

"We could make it in two days."

"The Costa Brava?" She opened her eyes and looked at him with new interest. And excitement? He couldn't be sure.

"Yes," he said. "I know a place."

"It's a thought," she said. "Why don't we talk about it later? I want to sleep for a while."

"Okay. We'll talk about it later."

Suddenly feeling much better, he lay back in the sun and relaxed.

———

Jenny Cameron did not sleep, though she pretended to. As her bathing suit dried and the sun beat down on her, she was filled with a vague but powerful desire. She shifted uncomfortably, and rolled over on her stomach. She wanted a man; it had been months now since the last time, and she was growing increasingly convinced that Peter would never fill the bill.

Her father had put his finger on it last Christmas. After he met Peter, he had said to her privately, "Get yourself a man, Jen. You'll tear this kid apart someday."

She hadn't taken Daddy's advice. She had hoped Peter would relax in Europe, once he was away from the grinding snobbery of Harvard, and become natural. Peter was good-looking, and he appealed to her, whenever he was able to forget that he hadn't made Porcellian, despite his good family, his English-tailored clothes, and his new Jag. It was a nice car, an XKE in British racing green, but Peter's attitude toward it was typical; he insisted on calling it a "Jag-u-ar," in the British manner. It was sad. Apparently, Peter was not going to relax, and that was too bad, for it meant that she would have to find another man, and she knew from experience that the men who could satisfy her were few and hard to find.

Now Peter wanted to go to Spain. Did he think that she would climb into bed just because it was a Spanish bed, and not a French one? If he did, he was being foolish, and he would soon learn it. On the other hand, perhaps he might finally loosen up in Spain, under the influence of a different environment. Almost without realizing it, she felt her thighs begin to rub together, slowly, up and down. She stopped herself with an effort. She would give him one last chance, she decided, in Spain.

GERONA, SPAIN

Miguel drove fifteen kilometers out of town, and pulled off onto a dusty dirt track. He followed this for about three kilometers, until he came to a grove of pine trees at the edge of the road. He pulled into the grove and parked. For acres in every

ODDS ON

direction, there was nothing to see but fields of yellowish wheat, waving gently in the hot breeze. No one was about; it was, after all, Sunday in a deeply religious country. He got out of the car and opened the trunk, removing the small, empty suitcase that was no larger than an overnight bag. That empty suitcase might have caused trouble if the customs people had checked, but he was prepared with a story. He had bought it to carry all the souvenirs he planned to buy.

He opened the suitcase and laid it out on the ground. Then he placed the package containing the dynamite inside, padding it with newspaper. The blasting caps and batteries were removed from the underside of the dashboard and added; then the small cannister of tear gas. Finally he packed something of his own—a small automatic pistol and two clips of ammunition. Satisfied, he snapped the suitcase shut and locked it. It was heavier than hell, but he would carry it himself and nobody would be the wiser.

He checked his watch—11:30. Another hour to the hotel, an hour and fifteen minutes if he got lost. He had plenty of time. He would drive slowly, in deference to his headache, the result of his drunk the night before with that girl. The one with the big boobs and the rolls around her stomach—he had forgotten her name. Hell, why should he even try to remember?

BARCELONA, SPAIN

The landscape of Spain, bone dry and dust brown, spread 20,000 feet below. It was vast, rugged, majestic, and monotonous—rather like Nevada, Jencks thought. He stared out the airplane window and tried to ignore the other passenger at his side. It wasn't easy.

"Been in Spain long? I've been here six years, myself."

Jencks had changed planes in Madrid, making connections for Barcelona. And he had found himself seated next to this idiot—a heavyset, sweating fellow dressed in a seersucker suit. The man's collar was damp, his jacket limp, his balding head beaded despite the air conditioning.

"No. I just arrived."

"You're American?"

"That's right."

"I thought so. From your accent," the man explained. "What brings you to old *Español*?"

He's been here six years, Jencks thought. Six years my ass.

"A little pleasure. I'm on vacation."

"Wonderful place for a vacation. Marvelous, I can tell you. When I first came here, I traveled all over. All over. Marvelous. My name's Alan Brady, by the way."

He held out a sweating hand.

"Steven Jencks."

"Steve, good to know you. How about a drink?" Brady clutched Jencks's hand determinedly.

"Fine."

The hand was released in order to press the call button for the stewardess. Brady's arm was thrown across Jencks's shoulder. It was damply hot on his neck. "I'm an agricultural engineer," Brady said. "What's your line?"

"That sounds interesting. What exactly is an agricultural engineer?"

The stewardess came, a coldly pretty girl. They ordered drinks, and Brady leaned into the aisle to watch her leave. "That's what I do," he said, nodding toward her buttocks. "I cultivate. I sow and reap." He smiled. "Sow and reap."

"Pleasant. Where do you live?"

ODDS ON

"Seville. Ever been to Seville? Marvelous place. But you were saying . . ."

"I've never been to Seville."

"No, I meant your business."

"Ah. I'm an industrial designer. Automobiles."

"Automobiles! Marvelous. I'm a great fan of automobiles. Have a Ford Galaxie over here myself. Wouldn't be without it, I can tell you."

"Air conditioned, I hope," Jencks said, looking out at the landscape.

"Well, of course."

"Aren't taxes rather prohibitive on an American car?"

Brady frowned. "Not really. How long have you been designing automobiles?"

"Ten years. My specialty is taillights." As soon as he said this, Jencks felt instinctively that it was a mistake. This man was not a fool, though he was trying to appear so. He reacted to Jencks's statement with nothing more than the slightest narrowing of the eyes, but it had clearly been absorbed.

"They're integral to the design," Brady said.

The drinks came.

"Well, cheers." Brady threw his back with a single gulp. "One thing I'll never get used to about Europeans. They drink hard stuff like it was deadly poison—sip at a time, twice yearly. Know what I mean?"

"I haven't traveled much."

"Well, you've picked a good place this time. Where are you spending your vacation? In Barcelona itself?"

"No, outside."

"I can recommend Torremolinos. Perfect weather, good people—if you don't mind Germans, which unfortunately I do—and lots of snatch. You'll want to watch your Barcelona girls, by the way. They can really clap it to you!" He let out a hearty guffaw, and slammed his hand down on Jencks's shoulder. The drink sloshed all over Jencks's trousers.

"Oh, damn. That's terrible of me. I'm always doing this sort of thing, really inexcusable." Brady whipped out a handkerchief and dabbed at Jencks's clothing, pushing up against him in a gesture of impulsive contrition. For the briefest instant, Jencks wondered if the man were queer, but when Brady straightened and sat back in his own seat, he knew better.

"Really sorry about that," Brady said, pulling at one heavy cheek. "I'm awful damn clumsy."

You'll have to do better than that, Jencks thought. Much better, very fast.

Brady smiled, hot and uncomfortable. He loosened his tie. Jencks said nothing, just stared. Brady's smile tightened, and he suddenly stood up.

"Jesus, I've gotta take a leak. Why don't you order another round? On me—it's the least I can do." He walked aft, toward the bathroom.

Jencks did not watch him go. He reached up and patted his breast pocket. It was gone. Quite neatly done, almost perfect. He sighed, and looked out the window. This was a very disturbing turn of events, but not because of anything Brady might discover—there was nothing—but because something Jencks had said or done had obviously prompted suspicion.

That was quite upsetting.

He reached up, pressed the call button, and ordered another round of drinks. Idly, he wondered how Brady would return it to him. Probably with another display of finesse that just fell short of perfection.

But why?

He reviewed their conversation, and found nothing in it that suggested anything unusual. He shrugged.

Brady returned. "Much better," he said, dropping down. "*Much* better. Are the drinks coming?"

"Yes." Careful, Jencks thought. Just a touch of sullen irritability, but not enough to make him suspect you know.

Brady extended his hand again. "Jesus, I really am sorry. Shake on it?"

Despite himself, Jencks smiled. He did play it well. "Sure."

"No hard feelings," Brady smiled, and slapped his hand on Jencks's knee. "That's what I like about Americans—forgive and forget."

"Right," Jencks said.

Twenty minutes later, the stewardess announced in Spanish, French, and English that the plane was about to land in Barcelona—"Barthelona," with her Castilian accent. The weather was clear; the temperature on the ground 32 degrees Centigrade.

"How much is that?" Brady asked.

Before Jencks could answer, the stewardess announced it—90 degrees Fahrenheit. Brady groaned.

The plane circled and came down. It taxied to a stop, and the passengers stood to collect their hand luggage. Jencks was shrugging into his raincoat when Brady nudged him and pointed to the floor.

"That yours?"

Jencks looked down. A small leather wallet lay at his feet. He picked it up.

"Yes. My passport. How do you suppose that happened?"

Brady shrugged. "Must have dropped it somewhere along the line."

Jencks slipped it into his breast pocket. "I guess so."

They went through the airport, and out into the taxi

ranks. "Going into town?" Brady asked. "Maybe we can share a taxi."

"All right," Jencks said. On the way in, he pretended to be fascinated with the view, not wishing to talk to Brady. The heavy man did not seem disturbed, however; he maintained a steady stream of chatter, discussing the city, its history, current position and problems. He seemed quite knowledgeable.

When they reached the center of town, Brady said, "Which is your hotel?"

"Arycasa," Jencks said.

Brady gave brief instructions to the driver in terrible Spanish. Jencks frowned, and Brady said, "I have a bad ear for languages. Always have. You should have heard me four years ago."

Four years? Six years? Jencks said nothing.

"I can't afford a place like the Arycasa, myself. I'm going to the Regente."

Jencks could see it coming. He did not want to meet for a drink. "I wish we could meet somewhere along the line," he said, "but I'm going to be rather busy here."

"Thought you were on vacation."

Jencks allowed himself a slight smile. "I'm meeting a girl."

"Oh, you devil!" Brady pounded Jencks's back.

Mercifully, they came to the hotel, and Jencks got out. He shook hands, collected his luggage, and went inside.

———

His room was pleasant, though Jencks was not in the mood to appreciate it. He paced up and down, trying to establish his next move. He examined all his alternatives—checking out of the hotel, leaving Barcelona, tailing Brady, breaking into Brady's room and searching it. He needed more information before he could know how to act, but the question was whether to seek this information or play it straight. He finally chose passivity, and went down to the desk to inquire about the Picasso Museum.

The Picasso Museum in Barcelona is not mentioned in any official tourist literature of the Spanish government. Picasso, a Communist since the Second World War, once wrote a pamphlet entitled the "Dream and Lie of Franco." He had not returned to Spain since he was Director of the Prado Museum in Madrid in 1937, and witnessed the bombing of priceless art treasures by Franco's planes. But he had been born in Malaga, down the coast from Barcelona, and had spent much of his early life in the city.

The museum is on a side street. It was built to house the collection of Picasso's friend, Jaime Sabartes, the poet. It is a pleasant building, a remodeled town house with a sunny central atrium and spacious galleries. Jencks walked through casually, playing the tourist, never glancing over his shoulder.

It was not necessary. The skinny little man who was following him was painfully inept.

He spent an hour in the museum, then went to a waterfront restaurant for a seafood lunch. He could see the little man leaning against a lamppost across the street, reading a newspaper. After an excellent meal of mussels and crayfish fried in garlic and butter, he took a taxi to the gothic quarter, and spent another two hours wandering among the old buildings, which contained government offices. He was careful not to lose his man until he entered the cathedral, and then slipped quickly out a side door. He went directly to the street and took a taxi to the Hotel Regente.

It was not far, on the Rambla de Cataluna. He bought a copy of the *Times* and sat in the lobby, waiting. Twenty minutes later, the skinny man walked briskly in and headed for the elevator. Jencks watched the numbers. The elevator stopped at the fifth floor. He got up and went over to the reception desk.

"Excuse me," he said, "I am looking for a friend who is staying here. He just arrived today—Mr. Alan Brady."

"American?"

"Yes."

The man consulted his file. "We have no American who arrived today. Are you sure?"

"I met him on the plane from Madrid," Jencks said. "He is a very big man—" he gestured with his hands, enlarging his own waistline "—who is hot all the time." He mopped his brow.

The clerk frowned for a moment, then smiled. "Oh yes. You mean Monsieur Bernet."

"Bernet? He is French?"

"Yes. He arrived three hours ago. Is that the man, *señor*?"

Jencks appeared puzzled. "Perhaps. What is his room number?"

"521. You can call on the phones over there." The clerk pointed to the house telephones.

"Thank you," Jencks said.

He walked to the phone, dialed nothing, and spoke for several moments for the benefit of the clerk. Then he left, feeling very strange indeed.

MONDAY,
JUNE SIXTEENTH

COSTA BRAVA, SPAIN

It was hot. The damned car was like an oven, Bryan Stack thought as he climbed out. He slammed the door, then remembered that he had forgotten the binoculars. Reaching through the open window, he plucked them off the passenger seat and walked away from the road, up a hill covered with scrubby underbrush. You could tell the sea was near—the air had a salty sharpness, the ground was sandy and soft, and the wind was fresh and cool. The low, thorny bushes scratched his legs, and he swore loudly, yet he was determined to see for himself.

This whole idea was Jencks's, and it had taken more than three days of drinks and discussion in a stuffy room of the Great Russell Hotel on Russell Square to convince Stack. Jencks had come equipped with blueprints and photographs, and it looked good—almost easy—on paper. But things had a way of becoming more difficult when plans turned into reality. Stack wanted to see with his own eyes before he became involved any further. If it wasn't right, he would pull out; Jencks would be annoyed and Miguel bewildered, but that would just have to be. Because for a thing like this, the police wouldn't merely slap your hand and send you on your way. You'd die in a rotten, stinking Spanish jail.

He came to the crest of the hill and looked down. White and shining, the Hotel Reina lay spread out before him. It was a high structure, L-shaped, built on the tip of a rocky promontory. It was, in fact, built on a small island connected to the mainland by a short suspension bridge. This was a particularly wild and deserted section of the Costa Brava, miles from any town—Gerona and Bagur were the nearest, both of them inland, neither very large. The Reina, proud and shining, stood alone—cut off from civilization and completely self-sufficient. Bryan remembered Jencks's words.

"It's like a luxury liner, fully outfitted. Three hundred rooms, barber shops, a casino, hairdresser, nightclub, four restaurants, stores, and shops all lumped together in one luxury hotel, miles from anywhere. It's the new thing on the Costa Brava, and several hotels are about to be built copying it; it has been open one year and has been incredibly successful. The jaded rich flock there to live for a week or two just as they would aboard the *Queen Elizabeth.* There's black tie for dinner; dancing; two swimming pools; lots of drinking, skin diving, and water-skiing. You get the picture."

Bryan had understood immediately. It was almost too good to be true. No, it *was* too good to be true. It had to be. Somebody must have thought of this before.

He had said this to Jencks, and Jencks had replied, "Bullshit."

Now, with the hot Catalonian sun beating down on him, Bryan surveyed the Hotel Reina through the binoculars. He followed the road to the suspension bridge, noting that it was sturdily constructed; then to the traffic circle, with a fountain and palm trees in the center (there must be an underground garage, he decided); then to the hotel itself, modern and tall,

ODDS ON

with glass window-walls and individual balconies for each room; then over to the swimming pool. He could see only one of the pools. The other must be salt water, hidden from his view behind the hotel itself.

The center of activity seemed to be the pool. Deck chairs surrounding it were all occupied, several of them by women in bikinis. He could not see any more than the mere fact of the bikinis—it was impossible to judge figures at this distance. He thought of Jane with sudden longing, and realized that he was growing more attached to her with each return to London. With a slight twinge, he realized that this was the first time he had ever missed her while he was abroad. It was, he knew, a sign that he was slowing down.

Bryan Stack had been slowing down for some time. He had begun in a burst of glory, attending Eton and Oxford, and had a good war record operating the Resistance station "Epinephrine" in southern France. He had gone bad—if that was the word for it—after the war, when his modest but comforting family fortune was lost, and he discovered that his education and service record didn't mean much in postwar England. For a while, he had looked for a job, but after six months gave up the search to do freelance work "borrowing" paintings from private collections in Spain and Switzerland. He went on to try his hand at hoofwork in divorce cases for eminent clients, and eventually was asked privately to handle a particularly rough embassy job in Lisbon which called for an accidental drowning on a pleasure yacht. Success there led him to other things—stealing papers from a Polish diplomat's office in Vienna, planting false evidence to facilitate the removal of a Russian attaché in London, and similar tasks. His work paid well, was never official, and never openly acknowledged—except that once, when he was caught pinching stuff in Brighton, he was released without questions—but spoken to rather roughly afterward. It was his own fault; the Brighton maneuver had been ill-conceived and insufficiently planned. Stack believed in planning, practice, and more practice. The older he grew, the more faith he put in preparation rather than muscle.

Well, he thought, this would be a job that would take planning. If it were to be successful, the timing would have to be nearly perfect, the coordination superb. It would require finesse and coolness, but the stakes were high and the rewards immense.

He returned to his car and drove down to the Hotel Reina. He would have a nice swim before lunch and then spend the afternoon practicing with his flash cards.

TANGIER, MOROCCO

Like a giant white whale, the Lincoln Continental crept through the winding streets on the outskirts of the Casbah. Jean-Paul, at the wheel, kept his palm on the horn as veiled women in black and men in striped *galabahs* scurried for the sidewalk. Even so, progress was slow; the streets were clogged with people talking, buying, and selling. On the sidewalk, vendors squatted beside their wares, arguing with the customers standing around them.

The car passed two horse-drawn carts laden with dried red peppers and grain in burlap bags. The air was momentarily pungent with the smell of spice. He honked again at an old man balancing a crate of chickens on his head.

"Must you continue to do that?" Miss Shaw asked irritably from the back seat.

Jean-Paul rolled the toothpick he had been chewing to the corner of his mouth before answering. "It is all they understand—the horn."

"But it makes *such* a frightful racket. Do try to be more sparing. Moderation in all things, my boy."

Jean-Paul sighed, and glanced at the dried-prune face of Miss Shaw in the back seat. At least five times a day, she repeated this dictum to him. This time, however, he could see that she was genuinely upset; her jowls, liberally covered with powder, were quivering unhappily.

"I will try," he promised. It didn't matter much now. They were already at the Grand Socco, the main square where most of the Arab bartering took place. There was a fountain in the center of the square, and a colorful mosque to one side; around the perimeter were shops and open-air stalls where everything from fruit to fan belts and aged tires were displayed. It was a hectic, busy scene, but soon they would reach the broad, well-policed avenues of the modern town—the European quarter of Tangier.

"That's a good boy. Now where did I put that newspaper? Oh—here it is, right next to me. Fancy."

They drove in silence for several minutes. Jean-Paul glanced briefly at the neat shops along the Boulevard Pasteur as they went by. Tangier was not the same, he thought. Before 1956, when it had been a free port, the city had been a pleasure. In those days, you could do anything, get anything, trade anything on the streets of the town. He remembered with fondness the little stalls of the money changers, and that fine "nightclub," which the proprietor, an Egyptian political refugee, had stocked with such superlatively sexual hostesses. Now it was all reputable banks and clean, antiseptic floor shows. The fire and excitement of the town had vanished.

He turned right off the main street and stopped before an appliance store. The window displayed refrigerators, irons, and washing machines.

"We're here, are we?" Miss Shaw asked. "Good. I shan't be a minute."

She waited while Jean-Paul fumbled in his shirt pocket for a cigarette.

"The door, stupid," Miss Shaw snapped. "Don't forget yourself."

He jumped out and opened her door. As Miss Shaw stepped out, she said, "And be sure you wear your hat from now on. I didn't buy you that uniform for nothing."

Jean-Paul nodded and slipped back behind the wheel. Inwardly, he was angry. The little woman could treat him like dirt when it suited her; she had the icy, sharp imperial tongue that the British of her generation had perfected before the Empire fell apart in their hands. He thought about Miss Shaw, asking himself for the hundredth time what made her tick. He was never able to understand. Nearly seventy, but sprightly for her age, with a quick mind behind that absurd, dumpy little body, she was a complete enigma to him. She had been ever since she had hired him two weeks before.

He lit his cigarette and smoked slowly, calming himself. He preferred to be calm, to take things slowly, to be relaxed.

Jean-Paul was French-Algerian, twenty-eight-years old, somewhat handsome in a slim, rangy way, and a gigolo. He did not think of himself in those terms, of course. He preferred to regard himself as a soldier of fortune, a romantic drifter, a man of good taste but flexible. He was tall and well-built, for a Frenchman, and had worked, in his time, at many jobs: construction worker, circus acrobat, nightclub bouncer, and escort. He had two great loves in his life, Scotch whiskey and young women, but he had found from experience that to afford the Scotch, he often had to forgo the young women. Fortunately, he was a flexible man.

Before he had met Miss Shaw, he had worked for a black-market money operation in the Casbah. His job required him to carry large sums in a money belt through the cramped, dark alleys of the Arab section. It was a dangerous job, one he would not normally have undertaken, but it paid very well. And he had been lucky—only twice in three months of courier work had he confronted a grim face and a glinting knife at the end of a narrow street that stank of urine. The second time, he had nearly lost a hand, but he had caught the bastard and squeezed the information out of him. It was an inside job, of course; Jean-Paul had returned to his employer's office and confronted the culprit.

The poor fellow was still in the hospital.

But essentially, Jean-Paul disliked violence and hard work. Whenever possible, he preferred to make his money easily, with the soft touch, the gentle hand. He had been more than pleased to accept Miss Shaw's offer. It was precisely the kind of job he most enjoyed.

Miss Elizabeth Shaw left the appliance store, and Jean-Paul opened the door for her. It was tiresome, this routine of opening doors, but Miss Shaw was less demanding than some he had known. At least she had no perversions. He flicked on the ignition and the big engine rumbled to life. This car was a wonder to him—it was like a boat, so big and soft riding.

"The port," Miss Shaw said. "Don't hurry, we have plenty of time."

Through the rear-view mirror, he watched her unbutton the top buttons of her blouse and slip a flat package wrapped in gray paper into her enormous, heavy bosom.

"You're taking it to Spain?" he asked.

"Of course."

"Is that wise?"

"Don't be silly, dear boy. Of course it's wise. Do you imagine for one minute that any impertinent Spanish customs officer would *dare* suggest that I be searched, that I . . . *disrobe?*" She said it with great indignation, almost horror. It was an act, he knew, but a good one. Jean-Paul knew that Miss Shaw could puff herself up like an angry bird if the occasion demanded it, and that the effect was invariably scathing. No Spaniard would brave her proper British wrath.

"How much did you get?" he asked.

"Almost a kilo of very good stuff. My God, it's heavy," she said, feeling her breasts. "I would rather put it in my purse, but occasionally the Spanish become nasty about purses. A friend of mine had an unpleasant experience some months ago." She wrinkled her leathery face at the distasteful recollection. "It was a tip-off, of course, but still . . . I don't care for it myself," she continued, patting her bosom mildly, "you know that. But others like it, and I feel that we should make ourselves useful. Don't you agree?"

"Certainly," Jean-Paul said, wondering who "others" were. His attention returned to the traffic, which was heavier as he approached the port. Carefully, he maneuvered the giant car with its aging British gentlewoman passenger, her five large suitcases, and her two pounds of marijuana, down to the boat. In three hours, they would reach Algeciras and Spain.

ORGON-SUR-PLAN, FRANCE

Peter Ganson pulled off National 7 just east of Avignon, and parked in front of the inn. He cut the motor of his Jaguar XKE and listened for a satisfied moment as the deep-throated growl died away. Then he turned to Jenny.

"Not much to look at, is it?" he said, nodding at the building. The inn was small and painted a rather sickening pink.

"Who cares? I'm tired, and the food is supposed to be good."

ODDS ON

"It's right on the road. The trucks will keep us awake all night."

"Maybe they'll keep *you* awake. I'll shut the windows in my room and won't hear a thing."

"It's too hot to keep your windows shut."

"I'll sleep nude."

Peter groaned inwardly at the thought of Jenny nude between crisp sheets. "Look," he said, "why don't we share a room?"

"No," Jenny said, then added, "not tonight."

HOTEL REINA, COSTA BRAVA, SPAIN

They met according to plan at precisely 8:15, in the bar of the hotel. It was a large room with subdued lighting and a heavy-duty appearance, which indicated its importance to the social life of the guests. The decor and furniture were modern, and in one corner a guitarist played softly. Miguel had already been there for half an hour, eyeing a woman who sat alone at a table demurely sipping her drink. She was slim, darkly tanned, and tough looking in a sophisticated way. After an appropriate interval, they had begun to exchange glances of increasing frankness, and Miguel would have asked her to join him in a drink if Bryan hadn't been coming. He relaxed on his stool—the girl could wait. His first concern was the project. Although he had given it considerable thought in the last few days, he still could not guess what was going on. One idea had occurred to him, and he didn't like it— kidnapping or assassination. Various high government officials vacationed here, as well as important people from Barcelona who drove up for the weekend. Miguel knew Bryan had been mixed up in political things before, and it disturbed him. Any kind of politics disturbed him, because he felt no interest or concern, no dedication. Miguel was not a fanatic about anything but money.

Bryan came into the bar wearing a light blue sport coat and an ascot showing little ducks on a navy-blue background. He looked very cool and very British. His short-cropped gray hair and sharp, aquiline features gave him a distinguished appearance. Miguel thought with approval that his friend might be a lawyer on a holiday or an executive taking a few days off from a business trip.

Bryan sat down on a stool next to Miguel without looking at him, called the bartender, and ordered a vodka gibson. He let his eyes run casually around the room as he drew out a cigarette. Then he began to pat his pockets, a look of consternation crossing his face.

Miguel whipped out his lighter, beating the bartender. "Allow me."

"Thanks." Bryan accepted the light with just the right mixture of formal gratitude and dismay. He seemed to be thinking that it would have been more proper for the bartender to light the cigarette; now he would have to engage this fellow in polite conversation. "You speak English?" Bryan asked, with reserve.

"Yes, I'm American."

"Really? How interesting." He did not seem interested at all as he raised his glass. "Well, cheers."

"Cheers," Miguel said, raising his own.

The two men looked at each other, a silence falling between them. Bryan appeared embarrassed. "Not many Americans on the Costa Brava these days," Bryan said finally.

"Not many Britishers, either."

"True," Bryan said. "I've noticed that."

Another silence. The bartender was still nearby, drying glasses with swift, practiced movements.

"Have you been here long?" Bryan asked.

"I arrived yesterday."

ODDS ON

"It's a long way from the United States, isn't it? Did you fly to Madrid?"

"No, I came through France from Paris, by car."

"Ah, that's a lovely way to do it. Good trip?"

"Fine, thanks."

The bartender moved away to take care of new customers.

"No hitches?" Bryan asked, the forced friendliness gone from his voice. He was all business now.

"Not one."

"Where is it now?"

"In my room, in a suitcase."

"Locked, I hope."

"Of course it's locked. I'm not an idiot."

"Good." Bryan sipped at his drink.

"Well, are you going to tell me what the story is?"

"No," Bryan said smoothly. "For that, you'll have to wait for the third member of our little party."

"The mastermind, eh?"

"More or less."

"And when is he due to arrive?"

"Tomorrow," Bryan said, finishing his vodka. "And we will meet in his room as scheduled. You'll get the details then. Have you been working with the flash cards?"

Miguel was growing angry. He was being treated like a child. "Listen, if you think I'm going to sit around here without the slightest idea—"

"That's exactly what I think. Keep your voice down."

"I don't like it," Miguel said, sulking.

"You will."

Miguel shook his head. "Just tell me one thing. Is it political? Because if it is, I'm not—"

Bryan stood to go. "No, it's not political. You needn't worry

35

about that." He started to leave, then turned back. "Just one thing. At the meeting tomorrow night, don't be funny, and don't call him 'the mastermind.' He won't like it."

Bryan left the bar.

Miguel swore to himself, ordered another gin and tonic, and allowed his attention to return to the girl. With disappointment, he saw that she had been joined by a Spaniard. She was listening to him with obvious inattention, watching her cigarette smoke curl up toward the ceiling.

Miguel liked her. She looked like a hot number. He called the bartender over.

"The lady in the corner," he said. "Who is she?"

The bartender shrugged inside his starched white jacket. A discreet bastard. Two hundred pesetas should overcome his scruples. He pushed the money across the bar. "Buy yourself a drink."

"Maria Theresa Gonzales," he said, and added in a conspiratorial tone, "but that is not her real name."

"No kidding. And what is her real name?"

"I don't know."

"Not very good at your job, are you?"

The bartender shrugged again, a deferential, hesitant movement. So it was another two hundred pesetas. Well, Miguel was not interested. He had time, and he was confident that very shortly he would know a great deal about that girl, no matter what her real name was. She seemed the type worth knowing.

BARCELONA, SPAIN

Steven Jencks stared at the plans and blueprints spread out on the bed of his hotel room. To one side, neatly folded in a heavy envelope, was the computer output. He had spent three hours

ODDS ON

reexamining the plans and the output. He had found nothing wrong—every possibility, every chance and contingency, had been considered, weighed, and evaluated.

Except for Mr. Alan Brady-Bernet.

Jencks sighed. He had spent most of the day sightseeing, admiring the view from Tibidabo hill, looking at the Gaudi Cathedral. The skinny man had been close behind. Late in the afternoon, it had started to rain, and Jencks had returned to his hotel to think.

No answers. The plan itself was perfect, but Brady-Bernet was a new factor, a complete unknown. There was nothing he could do but wait and see what happened. Jencks was certain of only one thing—the fat man did not know, could not know, what was planned. That was absolutely impossible.

He glanced at his watch—10:30. It was time to meet the man with the launch. Undoubtedly, it would be an exhausting and suspicious encounter. Jencks sighed again, found the two packets of money, and slipped them into his jacket pocket. Then he went outside, and walked down the Ramblas toward the waterfront. The skinny man picked him up a block from the hotel.

Jencks ignored him. There would be plenty of time to lose him later.

The Ramblas was a street that never failed to fascinate him, though he could not say he enjoyed it. It was the main street of Barcelona's port section—broad and lined with cafes and bars. In the center, dividing traffic, was a wide strip of pavement along which people strolled, taking the night air, stopping to buy books and magazines from the stands. As always, the crowd was young, gay, and boisterous; boys laughed and shouted, while girls pushed away roving hands with small giggles.

The cafes were a study in themselves. At the north end of the street, near the Plaza Cataluna, they were clean and elegant, and patronized by the rich, international set. As you approached the water, they became smaller, dimmer, and less respectable; the whores sat about, waiting for customers or talking in a bored way to other whores. Eventually, the cafes became waterfront bars, bawdy and raucous, blaring rock-and-roll music with a heavy sexual thump into the dark.

Jencks turned left off the Ramblas onto a narrow street, walked one block quickly, turned left again. He entered a bar jammed with sailors and their girls and waited for his tail. The skinny man arrived moments later, and Jencks dropped back in the shadows. The place was noisy, crowded, chaotic. The skinny man looked around, did not see Jencks, and went to the bar to speak to the bartender.

Jencks slipped out the door. He walked to the end of the street and entered another bar, where he waited ten minutes, drinking ginger ale. All around him, the sailors and pimps shoved and argued. He kept his eyes on the door. The skinny man did not show up. When Jencks was satisfied, he went outside and returned to the Ramblas, caught a taxi, and drove north to the Plaza de Cataluna, then west on Avenida Jose Antonio to the Plaza de España, and back toward the waterfront on the Calle Marques del Duero. At the intersection of Ronda de San Pablo, he stopped, changed taxis, and returned to the Ramblas.

He walked down another narrow street, brightly lighted by red and green neon signs advertising restaurants, snack bars, dingy nightclubs. There were several strip joints. The air smelled of sweat and fish; several furtive men approached him, an offer on their lips, but he pushed them aside and continued on, threading through a maze of streets which grew increasingly dark and deserted. Finally he stopped before a nightclub which had no name; the sign blinking on and off said simply "Nightclub." He pushed open a battered wooden door and went inside.

ODDS ON

It was very dark and smoky. A nonsmoker, Jencks noticed that first. His eyes stung, and he stood for a moment, trying to see around him. He made out the shape of a high bar to the left and little tables to the right. There was no music; the only sound was quiet talking among the dozen people in the club.

He stepped to the bar and ordered a glass of sherry. When he looked around, he saw an overweight blond woman in a tight skirt and sweater standing next to him, her breast against his arm. They didn't waste any time in this place. He looked at her face, which was old and hard, rather masculine; she was caked with makeup, through which two mean eyes surveyed him. She noticed his interest and moved closer. He smelled cheap perfume.

"Where is Barry?" he asked in Spanish. He did not speak much Spanish, but he could get along.

The woman shrugged and split her face into a lascivious grin. Her teeth were stained from smoking; her breath stank. He turned away from her and grabbed the bartender's sleeve.

"Barry?"

The bartender, a thin, dissipated-looking man, stared curiously at Jencks, then pointed to a dark corner of the room. Jencks saw a slim figure sitting alone at a table. He walked over.

"I am Barry," the man said, waving Jencks to a seat. He seemed very tired. His motions were slow and weary. "We speak English, yes?"

Jencks nodded and sipped his sherry. Spain was the only place in the world where he could drink sherry.

"Let us get down to business," Barry said, placing his palms carefully down on the table. His face was heavy, puffy, expressionless. "You have an important job, and you need a boat."

"Yes."

"When?"

"Saturday night."

"And what do you want done on Saturday night?" He spoke slowly, as if the words were heavy, and hard to lift up through his throat.

"I want you to carry a package a short distance down the coast."

"A package." Barry sighed. "So complicated. What is it, exactly?"

Jencks shook his head.

"My friend, each shake of your head costs you more money, because secrecy from you means risk for me. Understand?"

"Too bad," Jencks said.

"Where, exactly, on the coast?"

"You will pick up the package at the Hotel Reina, and take it down to Palamós. You will deliver it to a man in the Pension Anna in Palamós. That is the extent of your job."

"Expensive," Barry said.

"Of course," Jencks said. "How much?"

"It depends upon the details—"

"It does not. How much?"

Barry sighed, and ran his fingers pensively across the table-top. "Three thousand dollars."

"I'm looking for a dependable man, not a pirate."

Barry shrugged.

"I'll give you a thousand. Five hundred in cash now and five hundred in Palamós."

"Twenty-seven hundred. No less."

"The economy is booming," Jencks smiled, "but this is absurd. Fifteen hundred."

Barry said nothing. He snapped his fingers, and the bartender brought him another drink. "I like you," he said, "and I am good to my friends. Twenty-three."

ODDS ON

Jencks leaned back in his chair. They both knew, now, that they would finally settle on two thousand dollars. It was a sum Jencks had come prepared to pay, and he was satisfied. Within fifteen minutes, the ritual was over, and the men shook hands perfunctorily. Jencks passed Barry an envelope containing eight hundred dollars in old bills, mostly twenties. Barry accepted it without counting the money, and they proceeded to discuss the details.

Barry would receive a signal from the hotel late Saturday night, and would draw close to the water-skiing pier. His boat would be muffled according to Jencks's specifications—the alterations would be cheap and relatively simple. Shortly before 1 a.m., he would be given a package, a small suitcase, which he would ferry to Palamós and deliver to a man waiting in a particular hotel room. The man would pay twelve hundred dollars in bills of small denomination.

Barry said he understood it all, and Jencks got up to leave.

"Oh, one last thing," he said, smiling disarmingly. "This package will be locked, and treated in certain special ways. The man in Palamós will not pay if there has been any tampering."

Barry held up his hands, a pained look crossing his face. "Please, my friend—"

"We know, too, that you have a large family. A brother in Bilbao, a sister in Madrid, and a son at the university here. A nice boy, I understand."

Barry's face hardened, his eyes narrowed. "You have made your point."

Jencks nodded, satisfied that this was so, and left the nightclub. Outside, the air was cool and fresh; he felt tired. He walked to the nearest cafe and used the telephone.

"Reese here."

"Cafe Montaldo. Ten minutes."

ODDS ON

"Okay."

He hung up and walked along the Ramblas, now at the peak of late evening activity. The pimps were out in full force; he felt as if he were swatting flies as he made his way to the Cafe Montaldo. It was a big place, open to the air and brightly lighted. The decor was nondescript modern, but the clientele were easily pegged—international, vaguely rich, noticeably bored. There were women in floor-length gowns and immaculate hairdos, men in dinner jackets. There was a sprinkling of dungarees and riding clothes. Jimmy Reese was already there.

He was a young man with a boyish face and an athletic body. Jencks had met him in Reno and had formed an immediate friendship based on mutual interest. Jimmy Reese was a con man, a jet-setter, a man with a passport which he never renewed. There was no sense to it, he had explained—whenever it came up for renewal, it was always so densely covered with entry stamps and visas that he felt it was wiser to start fresh. He was a man who was always on the move, and he was perfect for Jencks's needs.

"You look tired," Jimmy said. "Problems?"

"No. It all went smoothly."

They ordered two coffees, and Reese had a glass of cognac.

"Tell me a story," Jencks said. The cafe was crowded; there were a dozen pairs of ears nearby.

"George is working on a novel, and this is his idea. It's about smuggling, and the hero receives the stuff—it's LSD, or something like that—in Palamós, drives immediately to Barcelona, and catches the morning plane to Rome. He delivers it to a doctor there and makes a good deal of money. But he never opens the package and doesn't know what's inside it. That's part of the twist."

"But if the hero's disreputable, he shouldn't care."

ODDS ON

"I imagine he doesn't."

"Sounds interesting," Jencks said, "though it needs development. What I wanted to see you about was this." He reached into his pocket and withdrew another envelope, business-sized and bulging with twenty $50 bills. "It's a short story that you might look over. I think it has possibilities, but you know how it is. I'm too close to it. Oh, and speaking of Rome, the next time you're there I want you to look up a friend of mine. He's very interesting. Here's his card."

Reese took it and looked at it thoughtfully. "It doesn't list office hours."

"He's available almost any time. Even Sundays."

"Sundays?"

"That's right."

"Must be a hard worker," Reese said. "The opposite of me. I never work on weekends. In fact, I've been planning a special little trip this weekend to the Costa Brava. I'd like to stay three days, but I may have to come back here Sunday morning for a little party. Private reception."

Jencks smiled. "Hard life. Tell me more about George's novel."

"You know how it is with George. Lots of talk so far, and not a word on the page. George is big on talk. This time, though, I think he may have something—he'd better, he needs the money—because he told me he has a firm offer from an uncle in Italy who's in publishing. Lots of world-wide contacts. Anyhow, he's going to get an advance of a thousand dollars."

"Does that satisfy him?"

"It seems to."

"I'm glad," Jencks said, finishing his coffee. "I've got to be off," he said. "Try and contact me soon, after you've read the short story. I'm very interested in hearing what you think of it."

43

ODDS ON

"You going to be staying in Barcelona?"

"Well, actually I have to go to Italy myself next week. A little business. I'll be at the Hotel Florian in Milan."

"The Hotel Florian? Isn't there a Hotel Florian in Rome, too?"

"Yes," Jencks said, "I think there is."

"Well, I'm sure we'll get together," Reese said, "one way or another. Milan, Rome—what's the difference?"

"None," Jencks said, laughing. "None at all."

He left the cafe, still chuckling to himself. Reese was a very bright boy.

TUESDAY,
JUNE SEVENTEENTH

HOTEL REINA, SPAIN

Annette Dumarche, assistant manager of the Hotel Reina, pushed the yellow card across the reception desk to the new guest. At the same time, she observed him carefully.

"Just sign here," she said, "and if you'll leave your passport, I'll fill in the rest."

"Of course." The man signed smoothly: Steven F. Jencks. He pushed his American passport across the desk and looked up at her. "Is that all?"

"Yes," she said. He was an unusual man, she thought, with a face that seemed both ugly and handsome at the same time. His features were coarse, thick; his nose was large and bulbous; his hair a nondescript curly brown. But his eyes indicated strength and great intelligence, and his stocky body was undoubtedly powerful. What was his occupation? The damned American passports never listed it, just the way they never listed city of issue.

"Where was this passport issued?" she asked, thumbing quickly through it. Mr. Jencks was a well-traveled man, whatever job he held. Perhaps he was some sort of salesman.

45

"Los Angeles," he said.

"Fine." She wrote quickly on the form. "The boy will bring your bags. You have room 205." She hesitated. "It doesn't have a view of the ocean, I'm afraid. We're practically filled at the moment, and—"

"That's perfectly all right," he said, smiling.

She thought that was odd. Most of the Americans were disappointed if they didn't receive a room looking over the sea. They were a fussy bunch, almost as bad as the French, but this one seemed genuinely unconcerned. She looked at his well-cut clothes, trying once more to decide his occupation. He wore a tasteful, conservative suit of dark gray, obviously custom tailored to fit his broad-shouldered body.

The bellboy came up to the desk, and she handed him the key. "Mr. Jencks," she said, "room 205." The bellboy nodded and led Jencks to the elevator. She watched them go, noticing his easy, well-coordinated walk. He had every appearance of a professional athlete, and she smiled. Annette Dumarche liked her men that way.

She was Swiss, as was the manager, Mr. Bonnard. The syndicate which had built the Hotel Reina had been fussy about the staff, and had stipulated that both the manager and assistant manager be Swiss, the *maître d'hôtel* French, and the concierge Scandinavian.

Annette had been with the hotel since its opening a year ago, and, looking back, she had to admit it had been a pleasant year. Her only real complaint was the shortage of men; she found the staff repulsive and most of the guests the same. On the average, a suitable man arrived at the hotel once every six or seven weeks, and that was not really satisfactory. At thirty-one, she was at the peak of both her desirability and her desire, and these brief, infrequent affairs were insufficient for

ODDS ON

her. Sooner or later, she knew she would have to quit this job and return to Geneva to find a husband. She did not particularly wish to become an honest woman, but she earnestly desired to become a satisfied woman. Marriage seemed the only solution.

But for the time being, she thought, there should be no problem. First that handsome Englishman yesterday, and now Mr. Jencks with his broad shoulders and commanding eyes. Either of them would do. She was certainly ready for someone; it had been more than two months since the German had left—the one who made ball bearings. He had been excellent for her, though a trifle cold and conceited.

"How is it going?"

She looked up at the pudgy form of Mr. Bonnard. "All right. Mr. Jencks just signed in and did not mind receiving 205."

Bonnard nodded absently. "He came alone?"

"Yes."

"I don't understand it," he said, shaking his head. "Over the past year, we have rarely had single guests of either sex. Yet within the last week or so, three single men have checked in. First that Spaniard, then—"

"Mexican," Annette corrected, remembering the passport, which had said clearly: "Birthplace Mexico, D.F., Mexico."

"Yes, Mexican. All right. Then that British fellow, the dignified, mean-looking one, and now this American. And we have a fourth man coming, named Gordon, due sometime late today."

"Well?"

"It strikes me as strange, that's all."

Annette said nothing. She knew perfectly well what was bothering Mr. Bonnard. The syndicate had stipulated a number of girls to satisfy single men when the staff lists were drawn up.

ODDS ON

The syndicate, a collection of fourteen worldly businessmen, thought of everything. Mr. Bonnard had tried to follow their instructions, but had changed plans after six months in view of spontaneous amateurism among the employees. The professionals had been fired, and the amateurs had each received a short talk from Mr. Bonnard, in which he laid down the ground rules of the game.

Behind the entire system was a pragmatic theory of hotel management, a theory which Annette understood well, though Mr. Bonnard had mentioned it to her only once, shortly after the hotel had opened.

"Single men on vacation," he had said, "need unattached women. That is, they need *preferably* unattached women. If none are available, they will begin to chase the wives of other guests at the hotel. That must be avoided at all costs." He was right, of course, particularly in the case of the Reina, which was isolated from any large city. This was a self-contained community, and the girls had to be supplied somehow.

"What's the latest on the lady in 313?" he asked her.

"That's no lady," Annette said. The woman in 313 was a potential source of trouble—a slim, dark-haired flirt, who had been at the hotel for nearly a week and had been seen talking earnestly with nearly every male guest in the Reina. The chambermaid thought that Miss Gonzales was probably doing more than talking but nobody seemed sure. Mr. Bonnard, amazed to find such an unexpected source of potential trouble, kept track of the woman—at least twice a day, he asked about 313.

"Nothing new," Annette said.

The discussion was interrupted by the arrival of two new guests. They were both young, both clearly American. The boy was slim, rather reedy, with a pimple on his chin and blond

ODDS ON

hair that was too long, though he was handsome enough in a vain and immature way. The girl at his side was tall, lushly proportioned, and beautiful. She wore her blond hair medium-length, her face had a scrubbed look, her eyes were soft powder blue beneath long lashes. It would have been an angelic face were it not for the lips and eyebrows, which indicated clearly to Annette that the girl was a bitch, and probably a sex tease.

"Good morning," said the boy. He seemed uncomfortable alongside the girl, "My name is Ganson. I believe you have my reservation."

His accent was flat, northeast United States, and his manner faintly condescending. Annette disliked him at once. She flipped through the book, and said, "Yes, that's right. A double room for one week."

The boy's face reddened.

"No," said the girl at his side. She spoke softly, in a slow drawl. They're as unlike each other as can be, Annette thought. What are they doing together?

"I'm afraid you've made a mistake," the girl said smoothly. "The reservation was for two single rooms. On different floors," she added, smiling sweetly.

The boy fumbled for a cigarette, not daring to look at either of the women.

What a pair, Annette thought.

"Yes," she said finally, "we have two free rooms. But I'm afraid neither of them face out onto the sea."

"Well," the boy began, "I don't think—"

"That will be just fine," the girl said. "I'm sure it will be marvelous."

"Listen, I—"

"Oh, Peter, shut up. You can be such a bore at times. We've

49

come all this way, so we might as well stay a few days. I think it's charming." She handed Annette her passport and turned to the boy. "Of course, you don't have to stay if you don't want to."

Silently, the boy reached for his wallet and produced his passport. Annette took out the yellow forms and began filling them out in the names of Jennifer Cameron and Peter M. Ganson.

"And tell me," said the girl. "I notice you have a hairdresser. Could I make an appointment for today?"

"I think so, yes."

"Wonderful." She patted her hair with one hand. "My poor hair is such a filthy mess after all this traveling."

"Of course," Annette said, pushing the forms across the desk. "Now, if both of you will please sign these, I'll have someone show you to your rooms."

"You're very kind," the girl said, signing briskly.

The boy said nothing. The bellboy came and escorted them to the elevator.

As they walked away, Peter said, "I'll just come along and make sure your room is all right."

"I'm sure it's fine."

"Well, you can't tell—"

"Peter."

"I'm only trying to be helpful, for Christ's sake."

"Shall we meet for lunch?"

They stood in front of the elevator, waiting for it to come down.

"All right," he said. "Why don't you come down to my room and—"

"I'll meet you in the dining room in half an hour."

The doors opened. They stepped inside.

ODDS ON

"Well," the boy whined, "I wish you would—"

The doors closed, and the lobby was silent.

Annette sighed and turned to Mr. Bonnard, who had watched the entire proceedings impassively from a seat behind the desk. She admired Bonnard for his ability to be unobtrusive; it was a quality which surpassed discretion, and which she felt must be inborn. Certainly, in the manager's case, his physical appearance helped him. He was medium height, medium weight, average age, with common brown hair and common brown eyes, passive features.

"What," she said, "did you think of that?"

"I don't like it. There's going to be trouble."

"Why don't they part company? I kept wondering that."

"It is beyond me," Bonnard said wearily. "Do you think they will stay a week?"

Annette shrugged.

"I hope not," he said, as if thinking aloud. "I sincerely hope not."

"You sound as if you expect one of them to take a leap from a balcony," Annette laughed.

Mr. Bonnard regarded her gravely. "We can laugh when they are gone, not before."

———

Maria Theresa Gonzales awoke at the sound of a knock on the door. She rolled over onto her back as the waiter in his starched uniform entered with coffee and two boiled eggs. She glanced at her watch, the only thing she wore when in bed. It was 11 a.m. He was right on schedule.

"*Buenos dias, señorita.*" Always polite, this boy. She had taken him, once, but he was disappointing. Though young and

ODDS ON

strong, he lacked all sense of discipline. He was like a bull in a china shop, as the English would say. Rampaging, excited, worthless—it was a shame.

"*Buenos dias,*" she replied, in her best Castilian accent. The boy left the tray on her night table and departed.

She tossed the covers aside and stood, yawning in the morning light which streamed into the room through thin white drapes. Those drapes always amused her. They seemed somehow reminiscent of diaphanous veils and an exotic life far removed from the Iberian asceticism she had known in her childhood. But then, she thought in those terms anyway. She was once known, after all, as Cynthia Sahara, "the girl with the cyntillating navel." She had torn the hearts and breath from the chests of men in London, Hamburg, and Monte Carlo. She smiled to herself as she recalled the smoky, dark rooms and the hot lights on her bare body, and barely visible to her, the audience, the wet gleam of a thousand shining eyes . . .

She walked into the white-tiled, spotless bathroom and stepped under a brisk cold shower. For a moment, she relished the stinging stream of spray, then dried herself quickly with a rough towel. It was her morning ritual—a cold shower and hard rubdown. Her days began in this swift and unsensual way, as if to heighten the contrast with what usually followed.

Pink from the towel, she stepped before the full-length mirror and surveyed her naked body coldly. Though she was no infant, her figure was still supple, muscular, and exciting. If anything, her dark face with her clear, almond eyes had grown more sensual with the years; that, no doubt, was the legacy of experience—a kind and degree of experience, part sordid and part luscious, which few women in the world had ever enjoyed.

ODDS ON

And her body, long and inviting beneath her fine-featured face, remained wholly satisfactory. The small, firm breasts showed no sign of sagging; the narrow, almost boyish hips had not begun to widen and grow soft. Her legs were still as slim and strong as when she was sixteen, receiving her first man, and her stomach was still perfectly flat.

She touched her navel gently. It was true, what the press agents and copywriters and gossip columnists had said—her navel was too large and too obvious when she moved. Experimentally, she twisted her hips in the shifting motion which had invariably produced wild cheers from the audience. Her navel moved clearly, as if tracing the complex contortions of her body. It was sexual almost to the point of obscenity. That was nice.

Her tan was dark, almost purple-brown, the result of both a naturally olive complexion and long hours at the pool. She was proud of the fact that it was an all-over tan, acquired from sunbathing in the privacy of her terrace. She liked the all-over tan, which made her body look healthy and inviting, and unblemished by strap marks and white sections. To accentuate the effect of smoothness, Maria carefully shaved her body every day, all over. It was a matter of vanity, she realized, and self-indulgent sensuality she derived from feeling the sharp edge of the razor on her skin. But she liked it, and anything she liked, she invariably did.

As she combed the straight black hair which fell below her shoulders, she thought of the night before. Essentially, it had been dull. That beastly Zaragoza industrialist had eluded his wife once again and had pounced on her table, scaring off the dark American at the bar. The American was too pudgy for her taste, but he had a look of boyish evil that she found interesting. Besides, she did not yet know him, and that would never do.

ODDS ON

Perhaps he would be at the pool this morning. If so, she would strike up an acquaintance. She never had trouble striking up an acquaintance with any man.

Maria Theresa walked to the night table and sipped her coffee. She would wear her best bikini today, the brief one in Italian racing red. She predicted that it would take half an hour.

—

Miguel lounged on a canvas deck chair and watched the sunlight play on the surface of the pool, which was slightly ruffled by a breeze blowing in from the sea. Although it was nearly 11:30, few guests had come out to enjoy the sun; no more than a dozen people beside himself were there, and no one was swimming. Apparently the clientele of the Reina slept late—or perhaps they merely stayed up very early. He wouldn't know. He had gone to bed before midnight, leaving the girl in the corner to have it out alone with the Spaniard.

Bryan appeared at the far end of the pool, a book in hand. They exchanged brief, impersonal nods, and Bryan seated himself in a stiff-backed chair near the diving board, his back to the pool and to Miguel.

Miguel leaned back and turned his face up to the sun, closing his eyes. Bryan was playing it very cool, maybe too cool. Or perhaps he just didn't like Miguel, though that hardly made sense—Bryan had asked him to take the job in the first place. Still, Miguel was sure that Bryan could have explained the whole business the night before if he had wanted to. The delaying tactic was a dodge, a diversion, or perhaps something worse—a double cross. Miguel didn't like it.

Of course, he reflected, it was possible that Bryan didn't

ODDS ON

know the situation or didn't know it fully. Considering the strange and ridiculously secret nature of the proceedings thus far, it was entirely possible. The American brain, whoever he was, might not have cut Bryan in any more than necessary, and Bryan didn't want to admit it.

Another possibility occurred to Miguel. Maybe Bryan was afraid of the third man. Miguel smiled. That would be interesting to see—a man who could intimidate Bryan Stack. But in his time, Miguel had seen many men as tough as Bryan, and tougher men, meet their betters.

He heard a splash and looked up. Someone was in the pool, a girl. He could see her dark head bobbing up, then ducking down again. She began to swim, using a slow, smoothly efficient stroke. Reaching his end of the pool, she stopped and stood in the waist-deep water. It was the girl who had been in the bar, he saw, wearing a flame-red bikini. She smiled at him, and he felt a slight ache in his stomach. Then she began to swim back to the diving board.

After a few moments, she returned to his end, holding on to the pool lip with one fine, carefully manicured hand. She looked directly at him, and he smiled, about to address her in Spanish until he remembered his orders from Bryan.

"Good morning," he said in English.

"Good morning," she replied, with a slight British accent. "You should try the water, it's invigorating."

"I intend to, but not until a little later, when the sun is warmer. Will you have a drink with me while I wait?"

She shook her head. "Too early. Can you make it a lemonade?"

"I think so."

"Fine."

He stared at her, fascinated, as she climbed the short ladder and walked dripping across the concrete toward him. Her bikini was brief and very sheer; through the fabric, the twin points of her nipples showed clearly.

"One layer of cloth," she announced, sitting in a chair across from him. She did not seem annoyed by his stare, but merely amused. "I prefer it that way. It dries more quickly, and you feel less encumbered in the water. I find clothes encumbering in all sorts of activities. Have you got a cigarette?"

He passed her the pack, and signaled to the waiter, ordering a beer and a lemonade. "I saw you in the bar last night," he said noncommittally.

"I saw you, too, and spent most of the time wishing you would come over and take me away from that terrible man."

"I thought he might be your husband."

She smiled. "Are you always so cautious?"

"Usually."

"Nothing ventured, nothing gained."

"Curiosity killed the cat."

She laughed then, showing very white teeth. Her lips were light pink, no doubt the result of lipstick, but the effect was stunning with her deep tan. He noticed her wide, sloe eyes, and wondered what mixture of blood coursed through her veins.

"Are you Spanish?"

"Not exactly. I'm one of those people who's hard to place. According to the records, I'm half Moroccan, one quarter Spanish, and one quarter Portuguese. Don't ask me who accounts for which part."

Miguel nodded. With variations, it was a fairly common Iberian heritage. The Arab blood explained, to some extent, her dark complexion and her fine, hard features. The eyes would be mostly Portuguese, and the temperament—knife-edged and

ODDS ON

moody—would be Spanish. Altogether, a ticklish and rewarding combination if ever he knew one.

"Do you disapprove?" she asked.

"I'm half Mexican," he said, as if that were sufficient explanation. She seemed satisfied.

"What are you doing here?"

"Just relaxing. In the States, I sell bed frames. Out of Cincinnati, Ohio. My name's Michael Sands. My friends call me Miguel."

"My name is Maria Theresa Gonzales. My friends call me Cynthia."

"It's a strange nickname."

"I got it when I was working in London."

"What do you do?"

"All sorts of things," she smiled. "I can't seem to hold a job."

"And you learned English in London?"

"Yes. I have lots of friends there."

She crossed her slim legs as the drinks came. They sipped for a moment in silence.

"And what are you doing here?" he asked, finally.

"The same as you, just relaxing." She did not offer any more, and something in her manner indicated to Miguel that he should not probe.

"Do you think," he said, "that you could relax over lunch with me?"

"Very straightforward, aren't you?"

"I'm only here for a week."

"Let's make it dinner," she said. "In my room. I've been here long enough to know what the kitchen makes well, and I can promise you . . . a memorable meal."

Damn! Miguel thought. Damn, damn, damn. It was cruel tricks of fate like this that could drive a man berserk. "I'm sorry, but I have a dinner date. Could we make it tomorrow night for dinner?"

"Tomorrow for lunch would be better. About twelve-thirty?"

"Your room?"

"Of course. 313."

"I'll remember," he promised, finishing his drink. He stood. "I think the sun's hot enough for me now. Coming in?"

"Certainly." She rose lithely and arched her back in the sunlight, pushing forward her breasts. "You see? All dry. It really is a wonderful suit."

"It really is," Miguel agreed, thinking that he would much rather spend the evening with her than alone in his room, eating dinner over the charts and plans that Bryan was bringing at six, prior to the big meeting. It was all arranged, and probably for the best, but he could not help thinking how terrible was the plight of a man torn between the conflicting desires of greed and lust.

———

Bryan Stack finished dinner in the large dining room, which was furnished with high-backed chairs padded in red leather, with red draperies on the glass window-walls. The draperies had been drawn back to allow diners to watch the sun setting over the rocky coast; the view from the dining room, which was located on the fourth floor, was magnificent. But now the sun was gone and the sky was dark blue, seeping into black.

He scribbled his signature on the dinner check, adding his room number, and left. He wanted to take a walk before going to the meeting, and he wondered how he could arrange to run into the receptionist. She seemed the most likely candidate.

ODDS ON

He took the elevator back to the lobby—a broad, square space with a floor of black and white marble and a large stairway that spiraled up and emerged near the desk. He looked over there quickly, but the girl had gone, probably to eat dinner. Disappointed, he walked outside to the swimming pool.

The pool was rectangular and quite large; though he was no judge of distance, he guessed it was 25 meters long. It was deserted now, in the fading light. A tired Spaniard swept cigarette butts from the concrete deck and another cleaned the pool floor with an underwater suction vacuum cleaner. He circled the pool and went around the hotel, past the tennis courts, now being sprinkled with water. The sprinkler, an automatic spraying device, made rhythmic phitt-phitt noises as it slowly rotated. He came to the saltwater pool, located on the seaward side of the Reina. It was a pool as large as the first and just as deserted. To the left, a flight of concrete steps had been cut into the rock leading down to the pier, where the single motorboat which was used for water-skiing was tied. A sign in Spanish, English, French, and German warned bathers against swimming in this area.

Walking further around the island, he came to another set of steps, which descended to a small rocky cove. A short distance out in the water a simple platform bobbed. Here was another sign, again in four languages, with the flag of each language next to each translation. It advised swimmers that the bottom fell sharply away, that children should not be unaccompanied, and that injuries should be reported immediately to the hotel physician. A small appended notice stated that aqualungs could be hired from the management.

All very nicely arranged, Stack thought. From beginning to end, the Reina was a carefully run and meticulously planned establishment. He listened to the water gently lapping and sucking at the rocks below; it was a hypnotic, lulling sound.

"How do you like it?"

He looked up sharply, startled. It was the girl from the desk. In the growing dark, she seemed strikingly beautiful, with long chestnut hair, very little makeup, and a lightly freckled complexion. She was dressed in a white silk shirt, open at the throat, and a simple gray A-line skirt. She would have appeared unsophisticated were it not for the frank blue eyes and the high patent-leather black heels.

"I like it fine," he said. "But what brings you out here? I thought I had it all to myself."

"I always come around at this time, to make sure everything is ready for the next day. You have to watch the staff here; if you slack off, so do they."

He smiled. "You sound like the manager."

"Assistant manager."

That explains a lot, he thought. The intelligent face, the direct manner were not the sort of things you'd expect from an empty-headed receptionist. She had a gentle accent and Bryan decided she must be Swiss. The Swiss were the best hotel people in the world. "I thought managers and assistant managers and vice presidents stayed in their offices and did paperwork."

"We try to avoid that," she said. "We like to know who's here, who checks in and out. It's better to keep in touch with reality, and the guests are our reality. If they don't like something, we don't like it either—we can't afford to."

"You eat the same food as the troops, I suppose?"

"I don't think it's a hardship."

"No," he agreed, thinking back over dinner. There had been a vast selection of *hors d'oeuvres,* all excellent, and the menu

ODDS ON

had contained a good variety of regional specialities, something he approved of. Basic, continental, big-hotel cuisine, which drifted somewhere in the never-never land of semi-French and pseudo-American cooking, with blandness as its only distinguishing characteristic, did not appeal to him. But neither, for that matter, did Spanish food, which called for liberal doses of olive oil. The Reina struck the perfect balance. He told her so.

"The chefs are mostly French," she explained, "and very good. We had trouble finding them. We have one Spaniard from Madrid, and he cooks with butter, not olive oil. He was hard to find, too. But we think food is important."

Stack caught a whiff of her perfume, a light scent of lily of the valley. Food seemed suddenly very unimportant. He caught himself—no sense in getting interested.

He offered her a cigarette, and lit it for her. "Have you been here long?"

"A year, since the hotel opened."

"Interesting work?" He hated himself. She was obviously a nice girl. That made it harder.

"Usually. Sometimes it gets a bit frantic. We've had some strange guests, I can tell you."

"You'll have to do that. Will you join me for a nightcap?" Not very smooth, he knew, but it had the ring of authenticity he wanted.

She gave him a cool glance. "I'd like to," she said, "but not tonight."

"Perhaps tomorrow?" He was pushing, and that was dangerous—she might become frightened.

"Yes. Thank you."

He smiled. "I'd introduce myself," he said, "but you already know my name."

ODDS ON

She smiled back. "Annette Dumarche," she replied. "Please call me Annette."

"Bryan.

"Tomorrow, Bryan," she said. "But I'd better finish my rounds now. Good night."

"Good night."

She walked off. It was now quite dark. He watched her, and then finished his cigarette, looking up at the lights of the rooms above him. Hundreds of lights, hundreds of rooms.

He checked his watch. Time for the meeting.

NIGHT,
JUNE SEVENTEENTH

Precisely at 8:45, the waiter delivered a dry vermouth on the rocks to Mr. Jencks in room 205. He found Jencks at the writing table, scribbling a letter on the Reina's engraved stationery. Jencks rose, took the drink, and tipped the waiter twenty pesetas. Thinking how foolish Americans were with their money, the waiter left.

Steven Jencks did not touch his drink. He went directly to his briefcase, unlocked it, and took out three envelopes. The first contained aerial and ground-level photographs. The second was filled with scaled-down copies of blueprints. The third was the computer output. He placed the contents of each envelope on the bed, returned to the desk, and then drank his vermouth slowly. It was, he reflected, the perfect drink. "The drink of diplomats," it was called, because it looked like vodka or something stronger and yet was sufficiently weak so that it could be drunk all night without loosening a tongue. At the same time, it had sufficient alcohol to produce sociability, or, in Jencks's case, fluency of mind and speech. He did not believe in crutches, but the evening ahead would be difficult, and he wanted to be sure he explained the entire proceeding to the two men with complete accuracy and absolute simplicity. In particular, the computer output, so complex and formidable-looking, would present a problem; Bryan and Miguel would take one look and conclude prematurely that it was beyond their comprehension. Yet it was essential that everyone understand what the figures represented. It was essential that everyone be confident. Without solid assurance on the part of each man, a project of such delicacy as this could fall flat on its face.

At five minutes to nine, Bryan entered without knocking. The two shook hands and sat in chairs at opposite ends of the room. Jencks knew that Bryan was studying him, though he appeared casual as he lit a cigarette. Bryan probed people, hunting for weakness. He did it constantly, automatically, with everyone he met. Jencks felt no resentment.

"Still look good?" Bryan asked. His voice was calm, but Jencks knew what was behind it. It had been arranged that Bryan would arrive five minutes before Miguel, and to anyone in Bryan's position, such an arrangement smelled either of failure or a possible double cross.

"It looks fine," Jencks said. "We'll go over it all when Miguel arrives. But I wanted to talk to you alone first."

Bryan blew a stream of cigarette smoke toward the ceiling. His face was impassive, waiting. "Okay."

"Tell me something about Miguel. Not his background, you gave me all that, and it was perfectly satisfactory. Tell me about his personality." Jencks glanced at his watch. "For three minutes."

Bryan nodded, then frowned as if confused or unsure of how to begin. "Well, as nearly as I can tell, he's a good man. He is unimaginative, as you wanted—he still doesn't understand

ODDS ON

even the basic outline of what is planned, though any fool would have guessed by now. He's solid, direct, uninspired, and very capable in his chosen field. Not chicken, but nobody's hero. The funny thing is that because he lacks imagination, he has extraordinary guts. I remember once hearing him describe how he outwitted Egyptian customs in '59, and I don't think I'll ever forget it. He was carrying forty thousand U.S. dollars to change on the market, and it made a sizable bundle. He suspected a squeal, so he knew that they would search him, but he walked right in with it anyway. In a Rolleiflex camera case—he simply removed the camera, after weighting the case with strips of lead. He flew into Cairo, and at the airport they took him aside and searched him, all right. But he was careful to bring in a certain amount of traveler's checks, all neatly recorded on his currency control form, as was his loose change in drachma. When they searched him, he put up just the right amount of fuss. Indignant at first, then slightly interested, and finally benignly amused, since he was just a tourist and obviously not smuggling anything. He acted as if it would make a good story for his friends back home, and a bad story for the Egyptian reputation. You know, searching innocent tourists.

"Anyway, they took him into one of those bare little rooms with no furniture except a large table, and they began checking him, setting everything out on the table. They checked the lining of his jacket, his suitcase, opened some of the rolls of Rollei-size 120 film, and let him through. They never bothered to open the camera case. He's that way."

"It sounds foolish," Jencks said. "He could have stuffed the money inside the camera itself."

"Maybe, but that's not the way he works. I told you, no imagination. He assumes that even a close check won't be

65

ODDS ON

thorough, that they'll just search exotic places, not something out in the open. To him, the purloined letter is the most effective approach, and he's right if you have the stomach for a sustained bluff. Miguel can sit in a room staring at his camera while cops slash up his jacket lining; I couldn't."

Jencks nodded, pleased. Miguel was sounding more and more like the perfect man for the job.

"He's a pro," Bryan said, "and he has a definite philosophy about his work. He thinks smuggling is a state of mind—that's his way of putting it—and he acts accordingly. He also knows that the smuggler is at an advantage in any search situation. No matter how accurate or reliable the tip they've received, the officials are still reluctant to follow it up, still basically on the defensive. Particularly with tourists, and Miguel is a consummate tourist.

"He told me, in reference to this Cairo business, that he was worried for about half the session. But midway through, when he was standing stark naked in the room, they decided to give him the finger, and—" He broke off, seeing Jencks's puzzled look. "Something wrong?"

Suddenly Jencks laughed. "You mean a rectal examination," he said.

"Yes, of course."

"Sorry. It means something else in American slang—'giving someone the finger,' I mean." Jencks showed him.

Bryan nodded. "Two fingers in England," he said.

They both laughed. "Anyway," Bryan continued, "they gave him the examination, and checked his mouth as well. At that point, Miguel realized he was safe, because he realized the customs people had no idea what they were looking for. They were working blind, and he knew that he'd make it. And he did."

ODDS ON

Jencks nodded and finished his drink.

"The strange thing about Miguel is that personally, he's precisely what you wouldn't expect. He's obnoxious, limited, given to cheap sarcasm, and easily hurt. He was bloody annoyed that I wouldn't tell him anything last night and seemed to take it as an insult. He drinks too much, never talks too much, and as nearly as I can determine, will go to bed with anything in skirts. I've never seen a willing woman that he's turned down, except for those rare occasions when he can't scrape up enough energy or enough money. He's already moved in on a woman here; I saw him with her at the pool this morning. She's rather a looker, and I don't know what she sees in him, but I'm no judge of these things."

"You gave him the scenario?" Jencks asked.

"Yes, this afternoon. He had dinner in his room and presumably read it then."

Jencks looked up sharply.

"Oh, don't worry," Bryan said. "He read it, all right. Business is business to him, and money is all."

Bryan sat back and stubbed out his cigarette. Jencks, who never smoked, felt his eyes begin to burn and went to open the glass door leading onto the balcony. The cool breeze felt better; he took a breath and exhaled slowly.

Bryan observed him carefully. He respected Jencks deeply, as he respected any fine mind. Jencks's photographic memory, of course, was a good part of his quickness. Bryan knew the way Jencks read—with lightning speed, as if he were merely glancing at a page. Strictly speaking, that was true; Jencks didn't read, he memorized instantly, and seemed to bypass the process of assimilation.

Jencks was an impressive man. Bryan wondered about his vices and weaknesses. He never smoked and only occasionally drank. Women? Bryan didn't know of any, though the man was certainly virile and energetic. Jencks didn't talk about his women, or his past—he spoke only of business, and Bryan could recall just one exception. That had been in London, when they were first considering the idea, or rather, when Bryan was considering Jencks's idea.

It was after a long evening of hammering out the problems and possibilities, and Jencks had apparently felt the need to speak of something else. They had gone around the corner to The Helping Hand, a large and boisterous pub off Russell Square; the clientele was mixed, ranging from beefy laborers to long-haired, mournful students to prim executives from the City, who looked unaccountably lost. Over whiskey macs, Jencks had told Bryan of his early life on a farm in Massachusetts, of dropping out of high school, and his eventual decision not to go to college. One incident stuck in Bryan's mind.

When Jencks returned from Korea with a brilliant record and an unscathed body ("I just played the odds, it was easy"), he had knocked around New York and Boston, doing various odd jobs. Then with a little money saved up, he had gone to Reno with a system of odds he had devised. Knowing that a spectacular win would cause attention, he had kept his earnings modest and kept his tables in his head. He never carried a slip of paper to check against, and for several years he managed to milk the gaming rooms at a fairly steady profit of 2.4 percent. By now he was a comfortably rich man, visiting the casinos and gambling spas of the world twice yearly. Bryan thought Jencks was probably worth close to a million dollars.

There was a knock at the door, and both men looked up.

ODDS ON

"Come in," Jencks said.

Miguel entered the room and shut the door behind him.

"Face the door," Jencks snapped. Surprised, Miguel turned and stared at the pine door.

"Now describe the room."

"Twin beds, one of them with three piles of papers arranged in a row. Closet door open, with three suits inside—brown to the left, blue in the middle, gray to the right. Pair of brown pants on a hanger next to the gray suit. Desk bare, except for a fountain pen with the point exposed and two sheets of paper. Bathroom door closed, door to balcony ajar about a foot. Suitcase open on the stand next to the door with the clothes unpacked except for two pairs of socks; briefcase of black leather, closed, near the desk. Will that do?"

"Okay." Jencks stood as Miguel turned around, and they shook hands. "Sorry," Jencks said, "but I had to make sure."

"I do my homework," Miguel replied, thinking of the days he had spent thumbing through the flash cards of room interiors, looking at the pictures for thirty seconds and then testing himself to see how well he had remembered the details. "Is there anything to drink?"

"No," Jencks said. "Have a seat. Smoke if you want." He returned to his chair and sat facing the other two men and the bed with the three piles of papers. He was interested in Miguel, whom he had never seen before. Medium height, and pudgy in an almost cute, boyish way. A devilish face, perhaps, but not sinister and apparently incapable of really serious crime. He was very different in appearance from both Bryan and himself, but that was all to the good.

"Let's get right down to business," Jencks said. "A meeting of this sort is highly irregular in a luxury hotel, and I don't think we should prolong it any more than necessary. Besides,

69

it will be long as it is." He turned to Miguel. "Did you bring the scenario?"

Miguel threw it down on the bed. It was a mimeographed little booklet with a red cover, on which was written: A HARVEY B. MANLEY PRODUCTION. Inside, Jencks knew, was a title page which read "The Missing Marquesa—a half-hour television film." Following the title page would be a page listing characters, then a page of scenes and props. Then the script itself began, with explanations of action, dialogue, and notations of short, medium, and long shots in capital letters in the left-hand margin. To the casual reader, it would look just like a real television script; to the more interested reader, who actually began to read, it would be a script of such exhausting banality that he would not progress beyond the first few pages. But one-third of the way through, the script ended abruptly, replaced by a detailed outline of the entire procedure, following the process step by step from beginning to end.

Jencks liked the idea of calling it a "scenario." He had treated the whole project as a scenario, but not in the Hollywood sense of the word. In the sense used by the Rand Corporation and the Hudson Institute—meaning, little stories of hypothetical actions which followed a given premise to its logical conclusion or conclusions in order to see what might happen . . . if. The Rand Corporation, of course, used scenarios to advise the State Department on international strategies, but the principle was widely applicable. Jencks had used it.

In a way, it was a natural outgrowth of his interest in statistics. Early in his life, Jencks had discovered that he had an aptitude for abstract thinking and mathematics in particular. This, coupled with a fascination with uncertainty, probability, chance, the odds, had led him into an informal study of statistics, which he later applied to gambling.

He had begun by reading simple texts on basic statistics—frequency distributions, means, and modes. He had progressed rapidly to correlation and regression, tests of significance, and finally, multivariate procedures using electronic computers. But in his studies he had read a number of books which applied mathematics and statistics to everyday life, and they had greatly impressed him. One was a slim volume entitled *Multivariate Procedures for the Behavioral Sciences,* which discussed the use of computers in predicting and explaining "human" situations. Another was Thomas Schelling's *The Strategy of Conflict,* a book concerned with how groups in opposition can and should react to each other. There had been an interesting example in that book of how a man might react to the knowledge that a burglar was in his home—what he might do, and what he might want to do, all expressed in purely mathematical terms.

That example had given him ideas.

But the book which had made the greatest impression was one by Herman Kahn, *On Thermonuclear War.* In it, Kahn, a statistician and physicist by training, had objectively outlined what could happen in the event of an all-out war, and how the effects might be minimized. The cold, often brutally logical thinking in that book, the buttressing of facts and opinions with mathematical evidence, the absence of sentimentality, had all appealed to Jencks. While reading it, he had decided to look for other uses for statistics besides war games and gambling. This project was the inevitable result.

He turned to Miguel. "You read the scenario?"

"Yes."

"Questions?"

"Many, many questions."

"Fair enough. But I think it would be simpler if I review

the plan in detail, from start to finish. Maybe I'll answer your questions as I go along. If I don't, interrupt me. All right?"

Miguel nodded. Bryan lit another cigarette. The atmosphere in the room was coldly serious.

"That basic idea is simple enough," Jencks said. "We are going to rob the Hotel Reina."

As the plan unfolded, Bryan watched Jencks with increasing amazement. The man could make a fortune as a salesman, he realized; the pitch Jencks was now giving was superb. He spoke with authority and conviction.

"One of the most important considerations is one that most people would never think of—why rob a luxury hotel? What's in it for us? There will be a few women here with valuable jewels. The guests will probably have a reasonable sum of cash with them. But most of the money here is undoubtedly in travelers' checks, and they're safe from theft. Supposedly.

"As for the hotel safe, it will contain any large amounts of cash which guests have brought, some jewels, and perhaps the payroll of the employees. That third sum is negligible—Spanish chambermaids and waiters don't make enough money to buy you ice cubes for a week. So on the surface, robbing this hotel doesn't seem to make sense. That is one of our principal advantages.

"I have, however, made a preliminary estimate of the total wealth at our disposal. There are three hundred rooms in this hotel. On weekends, with the two-day crowd coming up from Barcelona, every room will be filled. Let us say, as a low average, that the occupants of each room are carrying $2,000 with them in some form or another, not counting jewels."

Miguel looked surprised.

Jencks said quickly, "That's an *average*, don't forget. For every rich American carrying ten grand, you can have four others

ODDS ON

with no money at all." Miguel nodded and Jencks went on. "With three hundred rooms, that comes to $600,000. Jewels are hard to estimate, but let us say a minimum value of $100,000— it is probably twice that figure. In any event, the total minimum potential of the Reina is $700,000. And I think we will find, in actual practice, that it is closer to a million dollars."

Miguel lit another cigarette. They were talking about big money, and big money meant big risks.

"A great deal of that million will be in traveler's checks, perhaps as much as two-thirds or three-quarters of it. Technically, this money should be useless to us, not worth stealing. In fact, as you both know, it is perfectly good money if we are willing to lose a percentage in unloading it. I have made arrangements for all the traveler's checks we steal to be flown from Barcelona to a man in Rome. This man is an excellent forger and completely trustworthy. He will take the checks to Egypt and Turkey and dispose of them on the black market, where nobody bothers with things like passports and signing checks on the spot. He will change the checks for whatever currency he can get, preferably French francs and German marks. His services will cost us money. The exchange will cost us money."

"How much?" Bryan asked.

"Thirty percent."

"Of the gross take, or the net?"

"The gross."

"How fast will he work?" Miguel asked.

Jencks smiled. Bryan had been right, the man knew his business.

"The same day we take the checks, our man will get them in Rome. He will spend forty-eight hours in Cairo, and twenty-four in Istanbul. Within five days, all the checks will be converted, and the cash back in Italy. By that time, American Express and the other issuing banks will already have put out stop orders for many of the checks, but we'll be moving too quickly and too far underground for that to matter to us. Undoubtedly, some of the black-market people will find themselves with useless checks; lots of shop owners and small banks in the Middle East will come up with the others. But we'll be all right."

"Jesus," Bryan said, "it's going to cause a hell of a panic. Six hundred thousand dollars worth of forged traveler's checks in Europe."

"Too bad," Miguel said, grinning.

"The cash we find here," Jencks continued, "is cash. No problem there. The jewels are more difficult. It is impossible to say what they'll be worth, or how we can best get rid of them, until we see exactly what we have. But on general principles, I'm opposed to breaking down large stones."

The two men nodded in agreement. Too expensive, too much money lost. If you had a good fence, you could sell the stones intact and come out much better.

"All right. I think you can see now that the job is worth doing. All that remains is to show you how it is to be done. I'll tell you right now that it's complicated. It has to be."

He walked to the bed and picked up the pile of photographs and spread them out on the other bed.

"Actually," he said, "in planning this operation, three major difficulties presented themselves. The first was handling the money. The second was stealing the money. The third was escaping. On reflection, the second and third problems appeared to be related; in other words, the way we stole the money would directly affect our chances of avoiding a cozy Spanish jail. So the problem of the actual theft becomes critical." He pointed to the photographs.

ODDS ON

"These are views of the hotel taken from various viewpoints. You can study them later, but I want you to notice this one in particular." He held up an aerial view looking down on the hotel, its island, and the bridge connecting it to the mainland. The two swimming pools, the traffic circle, and the terrace on the fourth floor with its circular awnings and chairs were all clearly visible.

"In order for our robbery to succeed, we need isolation—at least, temporarily. This hotel is incompletely isolated. Therefore we must do two things: cut the telephone lines and blow the bridge."

"Who blows the bridge?" Miguel asked.

"I do," Jencks said.

"You have experience at this sort of thing?"

Jencks gave him a withering look. Quickly, Bryan said, "With the bridge cut, how do we get away?"

"We don't. That's the beauty of it all. We sit right here with the rest of the robbery victims. Our traveler's checks will be forged and distributed along with the rest. We will complain to the police along with the rest and bitch to the Consulate along with the rest. And we don't touch our money, which will be deposited in Venezuelan banks, for at least a year."

"Gutsy," Bryan said, "and very risky."

"As a matter of fact, it is the least risky way of all. Because we are going to provide one final diversion. We are going to make it appear that the thieves escaped *before* the bridge was blown."

Bryan sat up in his chair. This was new; it had not been discussed in London. "Is this the computer's idea?"

"The computer doesn't have any ideas. It only evaluates my own, but I'll come to that. The basic plan I have in mind is this: at 12:40 on Saturday night, a taxi will pull up in the

75

ODDS ON

traffic circle, apparently called all the way from Bagur to collect passengers. The cabby and the doorman of the Reina will exchange pleasantries; it will be a slow time of night. At 12:48, all the lights in the hotel will go out, and the ensuing confusion will be immense—screams, noise, panic. The doorman will hurry back into the hotel to find out what happened. As he goes, he will hear both doors of the cab slam shut, and the car will roar off. At 12:50, the bridge will be blown up."

"The cabby shuts the doors himself?" Bryan asked.

"Right."

"Stolen cab?"

"Stolen plates."

"What if the doorman doesn't hear the cab door slam and see it leave?"

"The chances are better than even that he will. But if he is too preoccupied with the confusion to notice it, he will recall it later—because in the clear light of Sunday morning, that cab will be gone. And anybody can put two and two together."

"Very nice," Miguel said.

Bryan nodded.

"This is really an essential part of the plot. We must make it look like an outside job, otherwise we're finished. If we ran away, it would be as good as a confession, and we'd never get out of the country. If we stayed here, but the police had any reason to suspect that someone in the hotel was responsible, they would run massive checks on everybody, and they would discover, among all the respectable businessmen and vacationing movie stars, three somewhat strange individuals with shady backgrounds. It would be all over.

"But given strong clues which clear everyone stranded on the island, and given the apparent idiocy of any thief remaining at the scene of a crime such as this, they will free everybody with only the most brief and soothing interrogations. They will feel that they must be nice to us, since we are foreigners robbed by a band of native hooligans. We'll get kid gloves treatment." Jencks smiled. "But we'll bitch like hell anyway, and rightly so. I'm going to be robbed of fifteen hundred dollars."

"Nine hundred dollars," Miguel said.

"Six hundred pounds," Bryan said.

"Rich bastard." Miguel laughed, and lit another cigarette.

"Now the robbery itself," Jencks said, "is very touchy. It will take place over a period of one day, Saturday. We will be robbing all day long. That is another unusual feature of our operation."

"I don't understand," Miguel said. "I read that in the scenario, and I didn't understand it then, either."

"It's really very simple. A person staying at any large hotel has his own private credit card—his room number. He can sign for anything and has no real need for money until he comes to check out and pay the bill. Therefore, people in hotels tend to be careless about their money. Certainly they don't bother to carry it with them, since they change clothes several times a day, what with swimming and sunbathing, and since they simply don't need money. They leave it in their rooms. And, except for the hottest part of the afternoon and late at night, they are rarely in their rooms."

Suddenly the flash card routine became clear to Miguel. "You mean we go into the rooms, don't disturb anything, and take money all day long?"

"Exactly. I doubt, during the course of a day, whether anyone will even bother to check if his money is still there. In the event that he does check, robbery will still be the last thing to occur to him. After all, the room has not been ransacked; nothing is out of place. Any sane man will think he has misplaced his money. Besides, most of it is traveler's checks, and who would want to steal them?"

"Very, very nice," Miguel said, in genuine admiration.

"What about keys?" Bryan asked.

"The problem of keys threw me for a while. Hotels vary in their locks; some small hotels have a single master key for all doors; some have one key for each floor. For several weeks, I couldn't get any information on the Reina."

"But you finally got it?"

"Yes. It's rather tricky. The doors do not have individual locks, as I had feared. They use a kind of zigzag system. Each key opens doors for one floor, on alternate sides of the corridor, skipping one each time."

The faces were blank. Jencks saw it, and explained again.

"My room is 205. The next room over, on my side of the corridor, is 207, then 209. The other way it's 203 and 201. Across the hall, the room facing mine is 206, and all the numbers on that side are even. Okay?"

"One side is even, the other side is odd. Okay," Miguel said.

"Now, my key, the one to 205, will also open 208 and 204 on the opposite side of the hall, and 201 and 209 on my side. My key will open 200, 201, 204, 205, 208, 209 . . . Get it?"

"It skips numbers 1-3-1-3," Bryan said. "That makes sense. It means that a man who forgets exactly where his room is won't open the wrong door by accident. On his own side of the hall, he can't open either door adjacent to his, nor can he open the door opposite his."

"I still don't get it," Miguel said. He showed no embarrassment, and Jencks appreciated that. A man who could say he didn't understand, without pride or false humility, had his respect.

"I'll draw a sketch," Jencks said. Rapidly, he drew two columns of numbers, connected with a zigzag line.

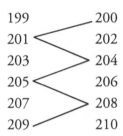

Miguel saw it instantly. "Two keys for each floor," he said. "Five floors—ten keys. Is that it?"

Jencks drew from his pocket a key chain, with ten shiny silver keys.

"Quick work," Bryan said. "How'd you manage that?"

"Preparation," Jencks replied, as if that were sufficient explanation. He went on. "On Saturday, you will each take five keys. Over the course of the day, you will examine the rooms which are worth examining."

"What do *you* do?" Miguel said. He wanted to add, "Sit on your ass?" But he didn't.

"I will be busier than either of you," Jencks said. "And you'll be very, very busy."

"We search all the rooms?" Miguel asked.

"No," Jencks said, "not all. In the first place, it is humanly impossible. In the second, it is not worth the trouble in many cases. Our job in the next few days—the three days between now and Saturday—will be to find out which rooms to leave untouched. This means that we must meet the guests, as many of them as we can manage."

ODDS ON

"And select the most juicy rooms?" Miguel asked.

"No. Select the least juicy. We will work to eliminate rooms, not include them. Understood?"

Heads nodded.

Jencks went on. "When precisely we search the rooms during Saturday is a matter of individual judgment. In general, the best times will be noon to two and four to six, with a final period between nine and eleven. In the early morning, people will either be sleeping late or the maids will be making the beds. In the afternoon, many people will rest before going back outside about four. Between six and eight, they will be dressing for dinner. Those are times which should be avoided."

Bryan scratched his short hair impatiently.

"Problems?" Jencks asked.

"Yes. What are you going to be doing all day?"

"I'll set the charges for the bridge and the telephone and power lines. I'll jam the elevator and provide a few other distractions of that sort. And I'll hit the safe."

"I was going to ask you about that," Miguel said. "The scenario doesn't allow very much time for—"

"That's right," Jencks interrupted. "But it will be adequate. You see, the hotel safe cost me ten thousand dollars."

For a moment, there was silence in the room, and then the two men grasped what Jencks had said. Finally Miguel spoke.

"You mean you have the *combination*?"

"That's right."

"Sweet Jesus," Bryan said. "How did you manage that?" First the keys, he thought, and now the combination. Jencks was a master, there was no doubt about it

"Don't ask. Ten thousand dollars isn't much money, but in

the right places it works wonders. And the fact that we have the combination raises the probability of success from .77 to .89."

"Says the computer?"

"Yes. You see, the question is one of timing. We can check the rooms leisurely all day, but the safe is the pot, and we have to hit it at just the right time. At 12:48, I enter the manager's office and go to the safe. That will be precisely the moment that all the lights go off. It will also be four minutes after a fire breaks out in the nightclub."

"You didn't say anything about a fire," Miguel protested.

"I'm getting to it. The fire will be caused by this." He tossed it onto the bed, where it landed with a heavy thump. Miguel picked it up.

"Get rid of your cigarette first," Jencks said.

Miguel stubbed it out and examined the pack of Chesterfields carefully. "Napalm?" he asked.

Jencks nodded. "They used these things during the war, disguising them as fountain pens and other small objects. They were a saboteur's dream."

"Yeah," Miguel said, "but they used an acid fuse. You won't get much timing with that kind of fuse."

"This one has a clockwork mechanism, accurate to three seconds. We'll set it for 12:44. Bryan will leave it in the nightclub, behind some draperies." He hefted the package. "When this much jellied gasoline catches fire, there'll be a hell of a mess."

"And it will certainly draw the manager out of his office."

"On the run." Jencks laughed. "That will allow me to enter the office, open the safe, and remove the contents. At the outside, allow one minute fifteen seconds for the whole operation, though I expect to finish between forty and fifty-two seconds."

"What if the combination has been changed?"

"My information is that it hasn't, but it's always possible. If the safe does not open the first time, I will try once again. That is why I have given myself a margin of an extra half-minute or so—in case I must run through it twice. If I don't open it the second time around, I will leave and we will proceed with the final stages of the operation. There isn't really much choice."

Miguel grunted, and Bryan shifted in his chair. They were acting, Jencks thought, the way he felt—it was an unpleasant thought. They had to consider the possibility that the safe might be beyond their reach.

"Successful or not, I will emerge from the manager's office around 12:50. I will walk quickly to the lobby and meet Bryan. By that time, Bryan will have already picked up your take, Miguel. All our 'earnings' will be neatly stored inside watertight rubber bags, like these." He held up three rubber sacs, which looked like small hot water bottles.

"Not very large," Miguel said.

"They don't have to be, that's the point. We're not stealing candlesticks, we're stealing money and jewels. They don't take up much room." He adjusted the drawstring on one of the bags. "Notice how they are made—by slipping this string over your shoulder, you can sling the bag under your armpit, like a shoulder holster. If you wear a jacket, nobody is the wiser."

Miguel nodded. He was overwhelmed with the plan, with its brilliance and preparation.

"I will meet Bryan in the lobby and go alone, with all three bags locked in my briefcase, outside, past the pools to the dock. A motorboat will be there, a particularly fast motorboat with an engine which has been muffled to my specifications."

Bryan listened to this with no surprise. Jencks could decide how to muffle an engine as well as he could do practically anything else.

ODDS ON

"I will hand over the briefcase sometime between 12:50 and 12:51. Nobody will see me, and nobody will hear the motorboat as it pulls away. Because every damned person in this hotel will be concerned about the bridge, which has just been blown. I will walk casually back into the hotel, joining the chaos caused by no lights, a fire, and no bridge. The job will be done." He sat back in his chair.

"One thing," Miguel said. "The house fuzz."

"What about them? There are three, in rooms 104, 244, and 273."

"Don't they have to be taken care of?"

"No. You miss the point—this is a robbery that nobody will know is happening. The detectives won't have any idea what's going on, any more than the guests will. They're principally alerted to watch for con men snowing little old ladies, or cat burglars slinking around at four in the morning. Nothing in broad daylight. And certainly not a major robbery of the hotel."

Miguel thought about this and let his mind run over the entire plan, in all its complexity. He was comforted by the fact that it was not simple; this was not a simple job, and a simple solution would be an unsatisfactory or deceptively dangerous solution. "It can't miss," he announced, finally.

Bryan, who had been brooding, chin on his chest, looked up. "What does the computer say?"

"The computer says that, within reason, it can't miss."

———

Jenny Cameron sat up in her bed, her back cushioned by two pillows, and thumbed through a copy of *Time* magazine. "Go away," she said to Peter, without looking at him.

Peter was sitting in a chair across the room, smoking and

trying to appear suavely in control of a situation which he knew was beyond him. "Come on," he urged. "Let's go to the night-club." He watched her, sitting there with the sheet tucked up under her arms. Her shoulders were bare, and he guessed she was wearing nothing beneath the sheet.

"I've already told you I'm tired, Peter. I've told you several times. I simply want to read my magazine and then go to sleep. Why can't you understand that?"

"Just one drink? Come on."

Jenny sighed. He was impossible. She would never have let him in the room in the first place, but she had left the door un-locked, as she always did. She never locked the door, even in the bathroom. It was a thing with her, locked doors. But Peter had come in without knocking. Swaggering, too, though the swag-ger had vanished when he saw her in bed. She had thrown her clothes across a chair before retiring; her bra was draped over her skirt and blouse. Peter had stared at that bra as if it were a living thing. Peter was such a bore.

"Go away," she repeated.

"You said you'd go to the nightclub tonight," he pouted.

"I said perhaps I would. That was at dinner. After dinner, I was tired, so I got into bed. I am still tired, and you're making me more tired."

He sat there, silent, and she could almost feel his frustration. Normally, she would have found that frustration interesting, even exciting. But he was such a whiner. If he wanted her, why didn't he just come over and take her? She needed a man, not a sick-faced puppy.

At last, he stood up and stubbed out his cigarette. "All right," he said, "But give me a kiss."

She frowned, marveling that she had ever agreed to meet him in Europe. The whole business was a fiasco. Peter had been fine for football games and cocktail parties in Cambridge, but that was all he was good for.

He came over and bent to kiss her lips. She turned her face away and received a wet smack on the cheek.

"Good night," he said mournfully.

"Oh, for Christ's sake, Peter. Good night." She reached up quickly and drew his head down to her, giving him a soft, lingering kiss. She was being too hard on the boy. She didn't like to be a bitch; it was just that he infuriated her so.

His hand darted down in a swiftly furtive gesture, caressing the bare breast beneath the sheet. Gently, but firmly, she pushed him away.

"Good night," she said.

Nodding to himself, he left. At the door he paused, and for a moment she felt that he was going to return and take her. The prospect filled her with a strange mixture of anger and excitement. But in the next instant he was gone, the door shut behind him.

She looked blankly at the door, then began to read the magazine. Under "Modern Living," there was an article on Balenciaga. She read with interest, then flicked off the light and rolled over on her side, but sleep did not come. Her body burned, and she considered going to Peter's room. But that was no good; it would be an admission of defeat, and he would never let her forget it.

She shifted restlessly in bed, as if suffering from physical pain—a bad sunburn perhaps. The thought reminded her of the pool. She would go to the pool tomorrow and see who was there. Somewhere, in all the rooms of this hotel, there must be a real man.

ODDS ON

Steven Jencks lifted the thick computer output in his hand. "This is it," he said. "This is what the computer had to say." He watched as Miguel and Bryan puffed uneasily at their cigarettes. They were instantly wary of the green-and-white striped sheets of typed numbers. Mathematics was so forbidding, he thought. Why? To Jencks, it was simple and elegant, like a fine poem. Only the language of the poem was different—but languages could be translated. Particularly this language.

The top line of the first sheet of the print-out read as follows:

CRIPA, MAXIMUM PATH ANALYSIS BEGINNING WITH RAW SCORES

After this came the date, the name of the person who had coded the program, and a basic statement of the program in matrix algebra. This was followed by a notation that subroutines VARIMIN, RSPACE, and PARA were required. Finally came the instructions to the machine.

DIMENSION FMT (36), FMR (36), X (50), SX (50), SS (50,50)

```
DO 1      I=1,M
XL(1)     =ABSF(1)
DO 2      I=1,M
DO 2      J=1, M
B(I,J)    =X(I,J) * XL(J)
```

These instructions continued down the page, until the instructions finally noted END. On the second page of the printout was a listing of storage locations for variables that would have to be called out, and on the third page were columns listing

ODDS ON

entry points to subroutines requested from the library. Finally came notations of TOTAL WRITES, TOTAL READS, NOISE RECORDS, TOTAL REDUNDANCIES, POSITIONING ERRORS. There were long columns of zeros here.

And finally, the last word:

EXECUTION

"This is FORTRAN," Jencks explained. "FORTRAN is a language the computer understands, just as a Frenchman understands French. You give the computer a certain program, or set of directions, in FORTRAN. These are very explicit directions. You can't tell a computer to average five numbers—you must say first add all the numbers, then divide by five, then write out the answer. You must tell the computer exactly what you want it to do. It assumes nothing; if you don't ask it to print out the answer, it won't. You see?"

They nodded, cautious and uncertain. Jencks could almost see Miguel thinking, "It's not that simple." But it was.

"A computer program is a set of directions which can be used for any number of jobs. It's like adding. Once you teach a child how to add, he can add anything—apples, airplanes, bust measurements. The computer is the same way. For this project, I used a certain program called CRIPA. It stands for Critical Path Analysis.

"Like most computer programs, CRIPA was developed for a single, special task, and then applied to others that were similar, but not precisely the same. Originally, CRIPA was used to find out the most efficient way to build a Polaris missile. It was a complex piece of equipment, requiring thousands of separate parts. If any of the parts were held up, or not assembled in the right order, the entire project was delayed. The analysis asked, what is the best order in which to assemble the parts? That is the critical path."

ODDS ON

"I don't see what this has to do with the hotel," Bryan said.

"Nothing, directly. But the situations of building a missile and robbing a hotel are analogous. Each requires timing, and each requires a succession of known events. In each case, we want to know the best order of events, the best arrangement of steps, to reach our goal. To take a simple example, should we blow the bridge and *then* rob the rooms, or the other way around? The computer decides."

"On the basis of what?" Bryan asked.

"On the basis of information it is given. If we were building a missile, we would tell the computer that the last time we ordered a guidance assembly, it arrived two weeks late, and so forth. The computer would decide that the guidance components must be called for extra early, so that they will be on time and not delay the project. In the case of the hotel, I fed in what I thought were average times for examining each room, the total number of rooms, information on how commonly the pool, bar, and tennis courts are used—things like that."

"I see," Bryan said.

"The computer fed back a certain optimum order of events to me. It advised, for instance, that the fire in the nightclub should occur first, then the lights go out, then the bridge blown. It gave best time intervals between each event. I have followed the computer's advice."

"Why didn't you just figure it out yourself?" Miguel said.

"I couldn't possibly. At various times, the computer was handling twelve thousand facts at once, evaluating them all together. No human being could match that."

Miguel nodded. Jencks noted with satisfaction that they were slowly overcoming their fear of the output, and were looking with new confidence at the sheets of paper.

"Not only did the computer figure the best order, it figured

ODDS ON

the chances of success for all possible combinations of events. It wrote them out here." He flipped past pages of scaled vectors and correlation matrices, saying, "You can ignore all this. Consider it the machine's scratch pad, where the scribblings are written down. Here is the result we want."

CRIPA OPTIMUM PROBABILITY ALL COMBS

J, K, L, M	.89
J, K, M, L	.83
J, L, K, M	.77
J, M, K, L	.76

"And so on, down through the twenty-four possible combinations of the four steps, each represented by a letter. Naturally, I chose the order with the highest probability, .89. Since complete certainty of success is represented by 1.00, you can see that our chances are very good indeed. I have determined that the average criminal venture has a chance of success of only .68, with a great many projects having less than a fighting, 50-50 chance."

Miguel lit another cigarette without taking his eyes off the output.

"These figures include certain assumptions. One is that the safe will open with the combination I have. Otherwise, our chances of success would fall considerably, as I said before. Another assumption is that nothing basically unrelated to the project—such as a heart attack for one of us—will occur. Another is that, through meeting the guests, we will be able to eliminate 20 percent of the rooms before Saturday. If we can eliminate 25 percent, our chances of success increase to over .90, and if we eliminate 30 percent, they go all the way up to .94. In other words, the robbery would succeed 94 times out of 100."

"I'll take those odds," Miguel said.

"Several other tests were run," Jencks said. "I won't bother with some of them, like the tests of significance. I wanted to know, for instance, if it made any difference if we used order J, K, L, M or order J, K, M, L."

"Sure it does," Miguel said. "One is .89 and one is .83."

"That's true, but statistically, it may be unimportant. Suppose you flipped a penny twenty times, and got heads fifteen of the twenty times. Does that mean you'll get heads more often than tails if you keep flipping?"

"No, it was just luck."

"That's right. And the same is true for these probability numbers. Some represent real differences and some don't. You can perform mathematical tests to find out, but they're complicated, and I won't go into them.

"One test that is important is a second check I performed. You already have our chances of success. The chances of failure can be deduced from them. But I wanted to know more than that. I wanted to know our chances of *getting caught.*"

Bryan and Miguel sat bolt upright. "The computer can do that?" Bryan asked, incredulous.

"Not well. I had to feed it all sorts of uncertain data, but I thought you'd be interested in the result. It is .006. That means, if we robbed the hotel a thousand times, we'd get caught six times."

"Is it significant?" Miguel asked. Jencks smiled. The little guy caught on fast.

"No, it's not. Those six times in a thousand are chance, random figures. There is no reason to believe that, successful or not, we will be caught."

"Hot damn," Miguel said.

Bryan smiled.

"One or two other things," Jencks said, glancing at his

ODDS ON

watch, "and then we can break up. I used the computer for several simulations of the robbery. By that I mean that I recreated the robbery on paper a number of times—twelve, to be exact—and each time I added a different factor. Some kind of unexpected error. One time, somebody decided to report to the desk that his checks had been stolen. Another, the incendiary in the nightclub failed to ignite. Another time, one of us was caught red-handed in somebody's room. I did this for twelve different circumstances and combinations of circumstances. In each case, I wanted to know what we should do.

"I was using a system of alternatives which was developed for defense strategists. Briefly, the way it works is this: in any difficulty, what is called an 'uncontrolled situation,' you have a number of things you can do. I used three general approaches, and you can look at any of them in a betting framework. The bet is placed, so you react by following a maximin path—which is to go for broke—or a minimax path—to cut your losses. Or, finally, you can hedge the bet, using what is called the 'criterion of regret.' What I discovered was surprising.

"The computer indicates that few situations are serious enough for us to worry about, and in any of them we should follow the maximin path. We should go for broke, and carry out the operation. The single important exception is if one of us is caught red-handed in the act of stealing. That kills the project immediately." Jencks looked at them steadily. "Let's not get caught."

He sighed and stood up. The explanation, the continuous attempt to find the simple example, the clear case, had wearied him. Perhaps he would allow himself one more dry vermouth before going to bed.

As he got up, Miguel said as casually as he could, "What's the cut going to be?"

"Five-three-two," Jencks replied crisply. "Myself, Bryan,

ODDS ON

and you. I'm paying all incidental expenses, as well as the cost of the cabby and boatman, from my half. Fair?"

"Fair."

The three shook hands briefly, arranged the next meeting, and Miguel left the room. Bryan waited thirty seconds, and was about to go when Jencks said, "I have a small problem."

Bryan sat down, lit another cigarette, and said, "Yes?"

"I had some trouble on the plane. A man stole my passport for a while, and had me tailed in Barcelona. A big hefty American who told me his name was Alan Brady. But he registered in his hotel as a Frenchman, called Bernet."

Bryan frowned. "Doesn't ring a bell. Any clue about what's going on?"

"No. I certainly didn't do anything unusual, except for that one night. I shook the tail, but I did it naturally—nothing obvious."

"Law?"

"I doubt it. I don't know why, but he just didn't strike me that way."

"Have to watch our step in any case," Bryan said. "I'll keep it in mind. Should I tell Miguel?"

"No," Jencks said. "I'd rather not."

Bryan shrugged. "Okay." He got up to go, then said, "By the way, I've made contact with a member of the staff, as you suggested."

"Good." That wasn't in the program, but Jencks had mentioned it to Bryan in London. It would help if they had a clear idea of the staff routine. "Who is it?"

"Assistant manager."

"What kind of fellow is he?"

"It's a she," Bryan said, grinning. "The girl at the desk."

"Reddish hair?" Jencks's eyebrows went up.

ODDS ON

"That's right. She's very nice, actually."

"Enjoy yourself," Jencks said.

Bryan left, and Jencks was at last alone. He picked the charts and photographs from the bed, and carefully replaced them in his briefcase. Then he called down for room service and ordered his drink.

The next few days would be busy. They would have to eliminate 20 percent of the rooms, hopefully more, and that added up to a great many casual acquaintances. But perhaps Bryan would get useful information from the girl—shortcuts would be invaluable. She might be able to save them all a great deal of work, eliminating the bad prospects among the guests.

He got up, and walked to the window. Outside, the sky was black and moonless over the dark ocean. The stars were clear and very bright.

They were on their way.

WEDNESDAY, JUNE EIGHTEENTH

VALENCIA, SPAIN

They passed endless orchards of orange and lemon trees under a hot, cloudless sky. The Continental was running smoothly, its air-conditioning system maintaining the inside temperature at a cool 68.

Jean-Paul felt good. He was making money again, easy money, and his hip flask was filled with Cutty Sark. Though he was smoking a cigarette, he allowed himself to whistle through his teeth.

From the back seat, Miss Shaw looked up from her book, a second-hand copy of *On the Beach* which she had purchased in Rabat. She liked books in which everybody was killed off, she had confided in Jean-Paul. For that reason *Fail-Safe* had been unsatisfactory—only two cities had been destroyed in that one.

"Jean-Paul," she said, wrinkling her nose. "Must you?"

"If you wish, I will whistle 'Waltzing Matilda,' for the background." As was his custom, Jean-Paul had not read the book, but he had seen the movie. He thought Ava Gardner was a piece of ass.

"That will not be necessary," Miss Shaw announced,

readjusting her position on the back seat like a pillow fluffing itself out. "Just see that we don't run over any chickens. And *do* take that dangling cigarette out of your mouth. It makes you look like a Frenchman."

"But I am a Frenchman."

"There," she said. "You see?" And with that, she returned to her reading.

The scenery glided by, monotonous in its uniformity. The land was hot and pale gray, bleached by the sun. It reminded him of parts of Greece around Nauplia. Greece was a good country, one of Jean-Paul's favorites; he particularly liked one little house in Piraeus, where Madame Pappas dressed the girls in the most incredible costumes. And she selected her stock well—they were all fine girls, with good bodies and expert, if somewhat exotic, techniques.

Actually, he thought, Miss Shaw looked something like Madame Pappas. Both of them were short, heavy, dumpy little toads of women. Both had bright eyes set in wrinkled faces, and both had acidly sharp tongues. Some people weren't softened by age.

He remembered the last time he had seen Madame Pappas. It was '63 or '64, in the spring, just after he had escaped from that dreadful business with the Countess Morelli and her lunatic husband. He had met the countess on Hydra, and she had taken a liking to him. She was a young girl, barely twenty-five, and strikingly beautiful. It was not his fault the count had come bursting in on them; she should have known he was coming back from Rome.

And what an aftermath! Jean-Paul had spent three weeks running for his life with two ugly thugs hot after him. Brutal fellows, they had nearly caught him when he was hiding on Mykonos. And then in Corinth, one had actually grabbed hold of him, but Jean-Paul had kicked him rather hard where it mattered. Finally, tired and desperate, he had slipped into the Athens Hilton and caught the count by surprise. For half an hour he had explained the situation while holding a knife at the man's throat.

The count had listened to reason; his jealousy disappeared. People were so agreeable when they had a knife at their throats, Jean-Paul thought.

He sighed.

Traffic was light, and he was making good time. The speedometer needle stayed steady at 85 miles an hour. How fast was that? He tried converting it in his head—about 130 kilometers an hour, something like that. Well, that was one thing you had to say about Miss Shaw; she kept the car in fine condition and didn't mind having it driven fast. Some of the older ones squealed like pigs if he went over 80 kilometers. That was terrible. Jean-Paul hated to move slowly.

"Lunch in Barcelona," he said. "A late lunch."

Miss Shaw gave an unladylike grunt. "It is the custom of the local barbarians," she said. "How late?"

"Three."

"We will be very fashionable and very hungry. Do you want a banana?" She waved one at him. "No? As you will. I adore bananas. A natural food, if ever there was one. And of great historical importance. Look how many of our apish brethren enjoy them." She munched on one with unconcealed relish.

"Sometimes I think I'm atavistic," she said. "Sure you won't try one? I'm about to have another."

Jean-Paul smiled. She could eat as many as she wanted and still not make a dent in their supply. For piled up next to Miss Shaw, forming a heap almost as large as she was, was a vast load of bananas.

ODDS ON

But Jean-Paul's smile was indulgent and understanding, not mocking. He was a man who believed that everyone ought to be allowed their idiosyncrasies and little vices.

"By the by," Miss Shaw said, "where is the stuff?"

He nodded toward the glove compartment. "In there."

"Locked?"

"Yes." He hesitated. "What are you going to do with it?"

"Are you *quite* certain you won't have a banana?"

"Please. I would like one very much."

"Good, good." She peeled one rapidly and handed it to him. "Actually, I have great plans for that little package. I think it will be highly amusing, don't you?"

He had no idea what she was talking about. "Yes."

"Some of it is for my niece," Miss Shaw explained. "You'll like her."

Jean-Paul nodded politely.

"Believe me," Miss Shaw said. "You will."

HOTEL REINA, SPAIN

Peter watched Jenny with distaste. He was sitting on a deck chair, and she was several yards away by the side of the pool. She was quite obviously posing. It was working, that was the trouble— the other men were staring. Peter hated them. They could find women of their own. Didn't they realize this one was taken?

Taken. The word stuck in his mind, irritating him.

Jenny stood and languidly walked over to him. She was rolling her hips, conscious of every movement and its effect. She dropped into a chair next to him.

"Why don't you cut it out?"

"Cut what out?" Her voice was tired, lazy; her eyes closed to the sun.

ODDS ON

"You've been strutting like a beauty queen."

"Don't be ridiculous, Peter."

"I'm not being ridiculous. And I'm not a fool. I saw you looking at that man."

"What man? What are you talking about?"

"The one in the corner, with the gray hair and the book he was reading until you showed up. The handsome one."

"I didn't notice him," Jenny said, sitting up. She squinted in the sun. "Where is he? Point him out."

"Oh, never mind." He lit a cigarette angrily. "Just cut it out, will you?"

She looked over at him, her face suddenly serious, no longer teasing him. "Peter," she said, "I'll do anything I want, any time I want."

He felt a pain in the pit of his stomach at her words. Her body was so magnificent: she was deeply tanned now, and had a tawny, athletic, lush look.

"And you can do anything you want," she added.

Jenny watched the uncertainty form in his face, the half-conceived resolution. It quickly disappeared. She sighed and leaned back in her chair. Hopeless, she thought.

She thought of the gray-haired man at the far end of the pool. He was handsome, all right, and well-built for his age—there was no flabbiness, no deterioration. He had the kind of clean, cruel good looks that appealed to her. His face was sharp, rather aristocratic, and she guessed he would be marvelous in bed. Perhaps she would meet him in the bar that night. If she did, events could damned well follow whatever course was natural. It was time Peter got the shock that was coming to him.

She sighed again. There were messy scenes ahead, in the next few days. Their semi-official engagement would have to be broken; he would whimper endlessly.

ODDS ON

"Aren't you going to talk to me?" Peter asked.

She did not open her eyes. "I'm enjoying the sun. What do you want to talk about?"

"Oh, the hell with it," he said. She heard his chair scrape against the concrete; he was standing up. His shadow fell across her. She still did not open her eyes.

"I'm going to get a drink," he said.

"It's early."

"I need it." He hesitated. "Are you coming?"

"I don't think so."

"All right, then."

———

Bryan Stack, at the opposite end of the pool, watched the pimple-faced boy stomp off, leaving the girl alone. Almost immediately, she sat up and looked around, looked at him. Stack looked down at his book and lit a cigarette; he was not going to get involved in this.

He knew, without even hearing the conversation, what was going on between them.

The girl lay back on her deck chair and closed her eyes. He got up and went into the hotel. Time to go back to work.

She was behind the desk, wearing a black, sleeveless jersey and a navy-blue skirt. Her head was bent as she filled out forms; her hair fell over her face.

"Good morning," he said.

She looked up. "Good morning. I've been thinking about your offer last night."

She hesitated, looking directly at him. He thought for a minute she was going to call it off, but she said, "How is four o'clock?"

"I'll have to consult my calendar," he grinned, "but it sounds good. Where?"

"That's a bit of a problem. It's bad form to be seen socially with the guests, so I'm afraid the bar or the pool is out."

"My room," he suggested.

She considered that, then nodded. "But do me one favor, would you? Order the drinks from room service before I arrive. The staff of this hotel is small, and gossip can be unpleasant."

"Of course," he said, smiling inwardly at her Swiss discretion. "What are you having?"

"Do you drink weak or strong?"

"Strong, usually."

"Stronger than a vodka gimlet?"

"God, I hope not."

"Good. Four o'clock, then." She smiled, a gentle and slightly hopeful smile. He didn't know what to make of it.

"Four o'clock."

He returned to the pool. As he went out, he passed Jencks. The two men did not even glance at each other.

———

Miguel awoke, and surveyed the morning sunlight benignly. It was too early for the light to reach into his room, but it splashed over the balcony. He looked up at the sky, confirmed his feeling that it would be a good day, and went to the bathroom to shave.

It was 11:45 when he began to dress. In less than an hour, he would meet Cynthia, and they would consider possible activities for the rest of the day. He had a few suggestions, he thought, as he slipped into a pair of slacks, a sport shirt, and loafers. He was hungry, but it was too late for breakfast unless he had it sent up to the room. It didn't matter; he would have an early

ODDS ON

lunch with Cynthia. Lunch before or after? He'd wait and see. He smiled at the prospect and lit a cigarette. His eyes no longer saw the women at the poolside below. His mind was elsewhere.

———

Cynthia was on the balcony, sunbathing. She lay on her stomach on the bearskin rug which she always carried with her wherever she went. She enjoyed the feeling of the fur as she stretched on it, nude.

A soft, warm breeze blew in from the sea, caressing her bare buttocks. She yawned and reached over for her watch to check the time. It was twelve. Soon that Miguel fellow would arrive. She considered dressing before he came, but decided not to.

There was a knock at the door.

"Come in," she called. She could not see the door, but she heard it click open. "Who is it?"

"Miguel."

"You're early."

"Couldn't stay away. Where are you?"

"Out on the terrace."

"Nice day, isn't it?" Miguel said lightly, coming through the room.

She heard him suck in his breath as he saw her. She glanced forward and saw his feet, then raised her head to look up at his face.

"You're amazing," he said.

She laughed. "Just in time. I need more suntan lotion. Would you take care of it?"

He picked up the tube and sat down alongside her. His hands began to rub the lotion over her shoulders.

"How was your dinner date?" she asked.

"What? Fine, just fine."

"Good." She rested her head on a forearm and looked out at the ocean, feeling his hands work down her back. His touch was firm, yet impersonal. He was trying hard. When he reached the base of her spine, he stopped, shifted his position, and began to rub her ankles, working up toward her knees. Her legs tensed as his hands reached her thighs. He paused once again.

"All over?"

"Ummmm," she replied dreamily. His hands went to her bare buttocks, rubbing gently at first and then with increasing strength, until he was kneading them fiercely. She felt her loins grow warm.

"That's very nice," she said. She wanted to savor this feeling, to make it last. "Why don't you sunbathe, too?"

"I didn't bring a suit," Miguel replied automatically, and then caught himself. He stood, and she heard him slipping out of his clothes. In a few moments, he was lying alongside her, his face looking into hers. His features were strained with desire.

"In a little while," she said. "Rub me again."

He reached over and ran his hand down her spine, from her neck to her hips. His fingers lingered there, caressing slowly. The warmth became heat.

"I haven't ordered lunch yet," she said. "Should I do it now?"

"No," he whispered, "not now."

She rolled over on her back and silently handed him the tube of lotion. He raised himself and bent over her. His hands ran over her high cheekbones, her forehead, her chin. Down to her neck. Her heat was building fast now.

Miguel looked into her face beneath him. The eyes were languid and her mouth was half open, showing her white teeth. Her long, glossy black hair streamed out, framing her face. Her breath came quickly, and he saw the muscles in her neck tense.

He moved his hands down to her shoulders, running his fingers over her collarbone and down to her breasts.

"You're beautiful," he said. The nipples grew firm against his palms. The lotion coating her body glistened in the sun. He continued down to her stomach, massaging it gently, and slipped his hands inside her thighs. The skin was smooth as satin. He went to her pubis, cleanly shaven, smooth and soft. The touch excited him immensely.

Cynthia groaned as his hand reached her very essence. It seemed to her that she was burning, that her fire had to be quenched. She pressed herself up against him.

"I want you. I want you now . . ."

———

Exhausted, Miguel lay next to Cynthia. She was a wonder, he thought to himself, a genuine wonder. He also suspected that she was obsessed with sex, but that didn't matter to him. Women with excessive sexual desires had their place in this world, and Miguel always enjoyed them when he found them.

They had made love three times in as many hours—and they had managed to have lunch sometime during that period. At lunch, he had questioned her obliquely but thoroughly, and had decided that her room was worth a check. But he had been a little disturbed by the fact that she had questioned him as well. Questions always made him uncomfortable; they required lies on his part, and lies were tricky. You could never tell when you would be confronted with a lie which you had forgotten. Miguel preferred to lie as seldom as possible, but sometimes it couldn't be helped.

She was a funny girl, he thought, looking around the room. It was bare, uncluttered by the usual lotions, curlers, and bottles of female paraphernalia. And there was that Polaroid. It lay on the dresser, next to the developed photograph of the interior of her room. He had asked about it, and she had said she always took pictures of rooms she stayed in. She said she traveled a great deal. Actually, he didn't buy that—but he could imagine the sort of pictures she *did* take with the Polaroid. That was the nice thing about it; you didn't have to send the pictures out to be developed.

Funny girl.

She was sleeping soundly, her breasts rising and falling gently. Her legs, just a short time before so strong and grasping, now lay relaxed on the bed. He was tired too, he realized. He rolled over on his stomach and in a few moments was fast asleep.

———

Jencks turned to face the man with the thinning white hair and the neatly clipped moustache. He wore a white linen suit and a Balliol tie. He was an old man, sitting straight as a ramrod next to a wrinkled old wife.

"Excuse me," Jencks said politely. "I'm very sorry, but I couldn't help overhearing your conversation about Africa. I was wondering if you knew my father."

"Was he in the Eighth Army?" the old man asked, moustache quivering. He was thinking to himself, "This fellow doesn't sound English. Perhaps half English."

"Yes, sir. Major Jencks, Seventh Armored Division. Does it strike a bell?"

The old man considered gravely and shook his head. "Sorry, no, but I was only there a short time. Not that it wasn't enough, you understand." He guffawed. "Bloody well enough for any man, unless he was a scorpion lover or a devotee of sand. To this day, I can't abide sandy beaches. Your father was British?"

ODDS ON

"Yes," Jencks said. "My mother was, too. They met at Oxford."

"But surely you're not English?"

"No longer. I'm the black sheep that left the fold. Six years ago I accepted an offer to join the Ford Motor Company in Detroit."

The old man nodded. Perhaps this fellow's father had worked for Nuffield after Oxford. Automobile people tended to keep it in the family. "Your father wasn't a career officer, then?"

Just like the English, Jencks thought. Pin it down, to the last ancestor and the final drop of social status. Get everything right. "No, he worked for ICA until the war. He died at El Alamein."

"Dreadfully sorry," the old man said.

"Doesn't matter. I hardly knew him." Jencks maintained the right note of cheerfulness and quiet poignancy.

"Yes, quite."

"What brings you to the Costa Brava?" Jencks asked, as if he wanted to change the subject—which in fact, he did.

"We're on our way to Africa," the woman said. It was the first time she had spoken, and her voice was remarkably strong for her age. Jencks didn't even want to guess how old she was— sixty or ninety, it was impossible to say. "We're visiting Alfred's old haunts."

Alfred laughed. "Yes, you know, Shepheard's and all that. Although, of course, Shepheard's has been rebuilt. But it was quite the place in the old days." He smiled, and patted his wife's hand reassuringly, as if to tell her that he was not going to explain how racy it had once been—at least, not in her presence.

"I've never been to Africa myself," Jencks lied. "I understand it's quite exciting."

"Oh, marvelous," the old man said. "Simply marvelous."

The discussion rambled on. Jencks managed to discover that

the old man could easily afford the trip; he was retired, but went around the world every second year, though getting clothes for each journey was such a bore. Simpson's simply wasn't as efficient as it used to be. That was in the days of George VI, ha-ha. But Alfred was looking forward to this trip; he had a new Leica which he wanted to try out. Jencks also noted that the old man wore a Rolex watch.

He asked if they had a nice room and was told that they did. Only on the second floor, but it faced out on the sea. Look, you could see the room from here—it was the one with the striped towel over the balcony railing. They had set it out to dry. Wonderful the way things dried in this climate.

Jencks looked up and made a quick mental calculation. It was room 148. It would be included on Saturday.

Conversation turned back to Africa and Montgomery. Jencks, who had read Montgomery's autobiography, threw himself into the discussion, recalling in particular one comment which had impressed him greatly, "In battle, the art of command lies in understanding that no two situations are ever the same; each must be tackled as a wholly new problem to which there will be a wholly new answer."

After an hour, he excused himself, pleading hunger.

"Nice enough chap," Alfred said to his wife, as Jencks left. "Bloody nice for an American."

"Don't forget, dear. British parents. It softens the coarseness of the New World."

"Quite, quite," Alfred said, stroking his moustache.

BARCELONA, SPAIN

They stopped for lunch at a roadside restaurant just east of the city. It was a distressing region, Miss Shaw thought unhappily,

ODDS ON

as she sipped her gazpacho. An area of cheap, middle-class resorts at the southern end of the Costa Brava.

Miss Shaw disliked anything cheap, and everything middle class. From her birth in Hampstead through her life in Brighton, she had been raised in an elegant and expensive fashion. When her family fortune, heavily invested abroad, was lost in the war, she had done her best to continue a life becoming a gentlewoman. And thus far, she had succeeded. It was a struggle, of course, and she could not call it pleasant. But success had its own satisfactions.

She looked out at the road, and at the Continental parked in front of the restaurant. It was a bit too much, that car. Oversized, overpowered, too flashy. As a purchase, it could not be justified on the grounds of taste. It was a luxury, an indulgence, and she regarded it in that manner. She liked big cars, despite their essential vulgarity. Someday, perhaps, she would buy a Ferrari. That would be nice.

She looked over at Jean-Paul, who had already finished his soup. "You must learn to eat slowly," she said. "You are in too much of a rush. Moderation in all things."

Jean-Paul smiled wanly and took a pull at his flask.

"Not in public, please," she said. "It is bad enough that I allow you to eat your meals with me—after all, you are my chauffeur. Do not abuse my democratic instincts. I have very few."

He returned the flask to his hip pocket. He really wasn't a bad boy, she thought—good natured and agreeable, despite his appalling habits. He would be useful to her.

"You know," he said, "I really am becoming curious about you." Could this little lady be a dope peddler?

"Patience," Miss Shaw said sweetly.

The waiter came, bringing the second course, *pollo con ajillo,*

107

chicken with garlic. They would both stink frightfully when they were through, Miss Shaw thought; she would have to remember to buy some mints. Mints were the answer, as they were in so many of life's situations—a little judicious sweetening, to mask the unpleasantness.

Bananas, she thought, did the same thing. Perhaps a banana after lunch instead of a mint.

———

Later, they took the coast road through Mataro, Blanes, and Tessa del Mar. The landscape grew more rugged, the road narrower, until finally it was a thin strip cut into the wooded hills which plunged into the sea. It was tortuous; Jean-Paul had all he could do to maneuver the big car around the hairpin turns. They passed one small resort after another— the hotels newly constructed, cheap and white, built for the tourist boom which had come to the Costa Brava in the last three years. Signs in foreign languages, mostly German, advertised plots of land, housing developments, apartments for sale. The air was clear and salty, the earth red, the sea a clear blue.

"Not *precisely* unpleasant," Miss Shaw said, looking at the view. Jean-Paul noticed that she sniffed whenever they passed a German.

He swerved the Lincoln around to pass a little Hillman sedan. A man was driving, heavyset, with a thick red neck. He looked hot and uncomfortable.

"Gracious!" Miss Shaw said. She looked back at the man as they passed. Her view was cut off as they took the next curve.

"Someone you know?" Jean-Paul asked, braking gently.

ODDS ON

She peered back silently for several moments. The car was in sight again, then blocked once more. She turned back.

"No," she said. "Nobody at all. Drive on."

———

Bryan Stack opened the door, and Annette stepped into the room.

"Hello," she said, smiling. She had a nice smile, he thought. He smiled back.

On the writing table was a large silver tray, with a bottle of vodka, a bottle of lime juice, a pitcher of ice and two glasses. She looked at it.

"You seem to be planning a party."

"I was hoping you might stay for more than one. It wouldn't do to run dry."

She laughed and sat down on the bed. He wondered if that was significant; after all, she might have chosen a chair.

"Are you a good bartender?"

"Why," he said, "are you looking for one?"

"As a matter of fact, yes. We've hired three since the hotel opened, and none have been satisfactory. The dry martini that all the American and English clients ask for is just beyond their understanding."

"Watch," he said. "Two vodka gimlets coming up, dry as the Sahara." He paused, looking discomfited. "I forgot the lime peel. Is that all right?"

"Probably."

"I see you're not a purist."

"Not where drinks are concerned."

"A man lives as he drinks."

"A woman doesn't, necessarily."

He went to the tray, added ten shots of vodka to the pitcher

ODDS ON

and a few drops of lime juice, and stirred the mixture. He poured it over ice and gave one drink to her. She sipped it and puckered her lips.

"Dry enough for you?"

"You're hired."

"What's the pay?"

"Not enough, I'm afraid."

He sat down across from her and suddenly found himself with nothing to say. It was odd; they had certainly begun well, and he should have had no trouble nudging the conversation toward her work and the life of the hotel. He looked into her blue eyes and just didn't feel like it. Getting soft, he thought. He smiled.

"What's so funny?"

"Nothing." He took out his cigarettes, offered one to her. "I was just thinking you're very pretty."

Come now, he thought. You can do better than that. Put your heart into it. It's a million dollars, after all. Certainly a worthy price for a little deception.

She got up and walked to the balcony and stared out. "What do you do?" she asked.

"Import-export. Mostly fruit."

"Do you travel a lot?" She was looking at his battered suitcase.

"Almost constantly," he said. "How about you? Do you have much chance to get away?"

"Yes. Odd weeks, here and there."

"Where do you go?" He could not shake the feeling that he was stiff, stultified, too obviously acting.

"Majorca, places like that. You'd think I'd go north, to get away from the sun, but I don't. I like it."

He looked at her skin, a light honey color. "You don't have much of a tan."

ODDS ON

"I work indoors most of the time."

"At the desk?"

"Ummmm." She looked back at him, a very direct, slightly puzzled stare. She held her drink in slim fingers, the nails carefully lacquered. She was standing very straight.

"Something wrong?"

"No. But it's a very good drink. May I have another?"

He took her empty glass and refilled it. As he did so, he was aware of her eyes on him, and he had the distinct feeling that he was doing something quite wrong, something she did not understand.

"What brings you to the Hotel Reina?"

"I'm on holiday, the same as everyone else, I expect."

"Married?"

Now that, he thought, is getting right to the point. No pleasantries, just straight home. What had become of that Swiss discretion? "No, as a matter of fact. Does it matter?"

"No," she said, a little uncertainly.

Bryan got up and walked over to her. Go on, he thought, get started right now. Kiss her and press her up against the glass and get started. It's always easier to talk in bed.

He stood looking out at the tennis courts and said, "It must be a pleasant place to work."

She shrugged. "Yes and no."

"Why did you ask if I was married?"

"I don't know," she said. "I really don't." She thought, I've never asked anyone else before.

He laughed and finished his drink. "Let's have another."

"I shouldn't. I have to work this afternoon."

"You work every afternoon?" He hated himself, as he poured another drink.

"Yes. Four to seven."

ODDS ON

"At the desk?"

"Yes. I have an office, near Mr. Bonnard's—he's the manager—but I hardly ever use it."

"And after seven?"

"Officially, I'm free. But there are usually odds and ends that I—"

"Free for dinner?"

She shook her head. "Not usually. But—"

"Yes?"

"Tomorrow I have the entire day free."

"What a coincidence. So do I."

She smiled.

"Would you care to be spirited away from here for a day?"

"I'd love it."

He raised his glass in a toast. "Consider yourself spirited away."

———

Jencks stopped by later, after she had gone. He glanced over at the drinks, the half-empty bottle of vodka and the melted pitcher of ice. Bryan was sitting in a corner chair, smoking a cigarette and staring at nothing.

"How'd it go?"

"Fine," Bryan said. "It went fine."

"You don't seem very pleased about it."

"I'm just tired. I'll be all right in the morning. We're going away tomorrow, for the day."

"Just the two of you?"

"Right."

"Good," Jencks said. "See you later."

He shut the door, and Bryan was left alone, still hating

himself. Why do they always have to be so damned nice, he thought. Why couldn't she be a real bitch?

———

"Son of a bitch," Dr. Baker said. "I tell you I'm terrified. I've never been so scared in my life. Because it's a worldwide trend, no doubt about it."

"None at all," Jencks agreed, trying to think of a way to end the conversation. Dr. Geoffrey Baker was an ass, conceited, narrow-minded, and priggish. His wife was the same, but fortunately she had already left to dress for dinner. Now Baker was giving it to him, man-to-man.

"Take France. It's typical of the state of European medicine in many ways—suppositories for everything, even sore throats. Now doesn't that strike you as ass backwards?" He laughed heartily, then broke off to light a cigar.

He waved it in the air. "The leadership is uncooperative, that's what I mean. Absolutely uncooperative and unsympathetic. DeGaulle. That's what I mean. Do you remember what he said when the doctors were considering a strike for better pay?"

"Not clearly."

"Well, that son of a bitch said the doctors could damned well go on saving patients at their current pay, because after all 'he saved France on a colonel's pay.' Now, that's typical. No wonder there's no progress, no advancement, no decent treatment. Initiative is stifled, standards fall, everything goes to the dogs. And who suffers? The patients, that's who!"

"I couldn't agree more." Jencks said. Jesus, would this fellow never shut up? Long ago, he had discovered what he wanted to know. Dr. and Mrs. Baker were returning from a three-week

ODDS ON

visit to the French Riviera, where they had bought a great deal of art and had spent a great deal of money. In a moment of chummy indiscretion, Dr. Baker had confided that it was a good thing they had paid their room charges at the Reina in advance, because otherwise they wouldn't have the money to get home. They'd spent it all. Of course, they might hock some of Emily's jewels (Baker chortled) but she hadn't brought any this trip. Nasty thing had happened to a fellow doctor and his wife in Cannes—burgled during the film festival in May. So Emily had decided to leave her jewels home this trip.

It was all Jencks wanted to hear, all he needed to know. Yet Dr. Baker rambled on.

"Now, take England. God damn it, you haven't got the same kind of medical facilities there that you had before National Health. You may not be aware of it, but standards have fallen, I tell you, fallen dangerously. Doctors don't care anymore—how can they? Their offices are filled with cranks and hypochondriacs. And when I think that my own office in Grand Rapids soon will be in the same shape, I tell you I'm just plain terrified. No other word for it. Terrified."

"I can see your point," Jencks said, rubbing his eyes and sighing.

———

The sun was setting as the big Lincoln Continental rumbled across the bridge and drew up in the traffic circle. Jean-Paul leaped out and opened the door briskly, before the doorman could. Miss Shaw stepped out slowly, and breathed deeply.

"*Marvelous!*" she said.

Jean-Paul was amazed. Her whole manner, her expression and bearing had changed. She was now an absent-minded,

ODDS ON

soft-headed, puffy old lady; the gleam of shrewd intelligence was gone from her eye, replaced by a stupidly happy look.

"Do park the car, Jean-Paul," she said. Jean-Paul bowed stiffly. She went inside.

"Good evening, my dear," Miss Shaw said, smiling sweetly at the girl behind the reception desk, "My name is Shaw."

She stood quietly, head back, looking down her nose while Annette checked through the register. "Of course, Mrs. Shaw."

"Miss." A slight, prim, stiffening of the body.

"Of course. I'm sorry. Two singles, I believe."

"Quite so, quite so. I'm pleased to see we have *that* straight."

"Yes," Annette said, taking out the forms. "May I have your passport, please?"

"I dearly love this country," Miss Shaw said. "Such marvelous fruit. Do you know, I don't believe I've ever been here before. Is this a new hotel?"

"It opened last year," Annette said, filling in the form.

"That's before my time," Miss Shaw said vaguely. "But I must say it looks *splendid.*"

"Thank you."

"Splendid," Miss Shaw repeated, still looking around.

"Yes," Annette said. She hesitated. "The second room . . ."

"For my chauffeur, of course."

"I see. If you prefer, we could arrange for him to stay in the servants' quarters, on the mainland. They are quite nice, and it is more the rule . . ."

Miss Shaw held up her hand, closed her eyes, and shook her head, making little tutting noises. "Never, my dear, never. Though I must say you're very sweet. Frankly, I do not believe in treating servants like dogs. A bit out of fashion, you know, although it had its advantages in the old days. Nowadays," she said, "nobody knows his place."

115

ODDS ON

Annette was unsure whether the old lady was angry with her. She said nothing as she pushed the second set of registration forms across the desk.

"I'll just sign for Jean-Paul," Miss Shaw said. She scribbled busily. "I'm sure we'll have a simply glorious time here. But there is one small matter I should like to clear up first."

"Certainly. What is it?"

"This hotel is rather isolated . . ."

"We have a doctor, and complete services of all kinds."

"Oh, I'm sure of that, but . . . do you have a good supply of bananas?"

"I beg your pardon?"

"Bananas. Do you have a good supply on hand?"

Annette struggled to keep her face blank. "I believe so, I'll check for you, if you like."

"Ah, there's a good girl," Miss Shaw said, pressing a 100 peseta note into her hand. "I *adore* bananas," she said, in a low conspiratorial tone.

The bellboy came up, and took Miss Shaw's key. "Dinner at eight," Annette said.

"You're so kind," Miss Shaw replied, and followed the boy to the elevator.

Funny little woman, Annette thought. The way she talks about bananas, you'd think they were heroin.

———

The minute Jencks saw her, he wanted her. She was in the bar, sitting on a bar stool, wearing a scoop-neck, emerald-green dress with a flounce on the skirt. Her knees were crossed, hiking the hem above her knees. She wore no stockings, but her legs were deeply tanned. Above the dress, the tops of her lavish breasts

ODDS ON

bulged enticingly. Her face, framed by short, honey-blond hair, was almost childish and sweet; the eyes were a gentle blue beneath long lashes and the dimples that creased each cheek were endearing.

She was a big girl, tall and full-bodied, and she was surrounded by five or six panting men, including one sick-looking, pimply college kid who seemed to be her escort. Jencks felt abstract sympathy for the kid; this girl was obviously too much for him to handle.

One of the men said something, and she laughed, throwing back her head and opening her mouth to show even, brilliantly white teeth. It was a calculated gesture, and the men responded, their eyes widening, their breath quick. She uncrossed her legs, and stretched one foot, clad in a slingback high heel, to the floor. The movement bared a slim, firm young leg to mid-thigh. The men squirmed. The kid looked sicker than ever.

Jencks watched the entire proceedings with growing interest. His logical mind told him that he had several alternatives, and he briefly reviewed each. In the end, it was the sight of that outstretched leg which convinced him—this was a direct, brazen girl. He walked right up to the group and took her hand in his.

She had been sipping her drink and looked at him, startled.

"Alice," he said, in a breathless voice. "Thank God! I've been looking all over for you."

For a long moment, she hesitated on the brink of action. Her eyes ran over his face, coolly surveying him, judging his motives. She knows, he thought. She knows exactly.

"Henry," she said. "I'm so glad you arrived. Please take me away from these frightful bores."

The men looked green. The kid stood up, clenching his fists.

"Of course, darling," Jencks said. "Come with me."

He gave the men a polite nod, and threw the kid a warning

ODDS ON

glance. The fists unclenched, and the kid sat down again. Well-trained little thing, he thought.

Jencks steered her to a corner table, aware of the way she was swinging her hips, aware of the stares of the men at the bar. They sat down, and he ordered two Scotches. Jencks did not drink Scotch, but he would see that she drank his as well. She looked at him, then over to the group of astonished males she had just left, then back to him.

"Steven Jencks," he said. "Very glad to meet you."

"Jenny Cameron. Where do you get off?" She was trying to seem angry, but it wasn't very effective.

"Nowhere. I just came along for the ride."

She was staring at his face, which he knew was hardly hand-some. His eyes held her. She was caught. Now he would slowly reel her in. Jencks, though not a conceited man, was self-assured, and he knew his abilities. He would have this girl.

"Cocky bastard, aren't you?" she said.

"You're not speaking from experience."

"I'm not sure I want to." She picked up her purse and made small motions indicating that she intended to leave the table. She did it absurdly slowly, making sure he had plenty of time to react. He did not react. She faltered and finally opened her purse, withdrawing a cigarette.

"Do you have a light?"

"No, I don't smoke."

For a moment, she looked puzzled, then she shrugged, and lit her cigarette with her own lighter.

"What do you do?" she asked.

"Various things. What do you do?"

"I'm a student. Wellesley."

"Is he a Wellesley student, too?"

"Peter? Almost." She laughed bitterly.

ODDS ON

"Are you friends, or just acquaintances?"

"What does it look like?"

A real bitch, he thought. A perfect, incredible bitch. He felt the beginnings of desire stir him. "It looks," he said, "as if you are barely acquaintances."

"Good enough," she said, blowing a plume of cigarette smoke toward the ceiling. She held the cigarette archly. "Why did you pick me up?"

"I didn't pick you up. I merely gave you the opportunity to escape from a dull situation. You took advantage of it."

Don't give her an out, he thought. Keep the burden of action and initiative on her. And slowly, ever so slowly, reel her in.

"That's your opinion," she announced.

The drinks came, and she downed hers with a quick swallow. Showing off, he thought, but in such an obvious way. He realized then that she was young and wondered if he had made a mistake. She might simply be a little girl trying to act grown up.

"How old are you?" he asked.

"Old enough to know what I'm doing."

"That's not an answer."

"Twenty. Why do you ask?"

"Curiosity."

"How old are you?"

"Eighty-seven," Jencks said.

"Very well preserved," she said.

"I fight alligators with my bare hands."

"It sounds like interesting work."

"I've learned to handle thrashing creatures," he said.

"Is that a challenge?"

"That's a statement of fact."

"I'm not sure I believe you," she said. "You don't look like the believable type."

ODDS ON

"Very sensible of you."

She paused, now completely confused. It was the moment he had been waiting for. He pushed his untouched drink across to her.

"You don't want it?"

"I don't drink."

"You don't smoke, and you don't drink. It seems that there are a great many things you don't do."

Jencks sighed, as if exasperated. "I do what interests me."

"What interests you, Mr. Jencks?" Her eyes were wide, mocking him.

"High-energy quantum physics."

"Oh." She paused. "Are you very good at it?"

"Unusually."

"And are you normally obnoxious, or is this a special occasion?"

"I try to tell my patients what I think they want to hear."

"You're a doctor?"

"Psychiatrist."

"How fascinating. I had a psychiatrist once, a bald, funny-looking man with a crooked nose—like yours—who always used to ask me about my sex life. Are you going to ask me about my sex life, too?"

"No. I'm not interested in your sex life."

That hurt. She leaned across the table, giving him a generous view of the smooth mounds of her breasts. "Why not?"

"Because I imagine it's very dull."

"You're wrong."

"That," he said, "is perfectly possible, but I doubt it. Particularly if you've had anything to do with Wellesley over there."

"He's very rich."

"Money doesn't buy a stiff prick."

ODDS ON

She gulped the drink. "Listen, if you think I'm going to sit here and let you insult me, you're—"

"Dinner?" he asked, mildly.

She hesitated, then smiled a sweet angelic false smile. "I'd love it. Then I can tell you more about my psychiatrist. He had a queer little chin, just like yours. In fact, there's a remarkable resemblance between the two of you."

"How interesting," Jencks said, standing.

She looked up at him. "Are we going to dinner now?"

"Yes," he said.

He did not touch her as they left the bar and went in to the dining room.

———

At 10:30, Miguel, sitting in the lobby reading a newspaper, looked up and saw the last arriving guest of the evening. He nearly choked on the spot.

The new guest was a big man, heavy, florid, in a wrinkled suit. Shortish, with balding head and a leering grin, but very nimble hands. The fingers quivered slightly as he held his hands at his sides, and checked in.

Big Brad Allen.

What the hell was he doing here?

Allen looked around the lobby, and Miguel ducked behind his newspaper. A moment later he peered around. There was no doubt about it. Brad Allen. When had he last seen him? It must have been Nassau, when Big Brad was up on charges of running a phony real estate office which sold land on islands that didn't exist. He'd gotten off that one; he got off anything. He was the greasiest, slickest operator Miguel knew.

The buffoon was Allen's natural role; nature and temperament had suited him to it. Physically sloppy, extroverted, and dim-witted in manner, he could fool anyone into thinking he was a fool. It was his stock in trade, his one great talent, and in a reasonable way, it had made him rich.

What was he doing here?

Again Miguel returned to the question. Several answers occurred to him, none of them reassuring. He would have to speak to Jencks about this first thing in the morning.

———

It was almost midnight when they came out of the nightclub. Jencks was pleased; it had been a satisfactory evening. She had thrown everything at him during dinner, and he had parried each move. By the time they went to the nightclub, her initial anger had deepened into frustration, but still he gave her no opening, no opportunity. Slowly, she had become more docile, more yielding—but he knew that she wasn't finished. It was only the temporary effect of exhaustion and too much alcohol. In the morning, she would have something new planned.

Jenny said, "Where do we go from here?"

"To bed," Jencks said.

"You think you own the world," she pouted. She slurred her words in an exaggerated southern drawl. She was quite drunk.

"No," he replied, "but I own my own bed. Good night." He smiled at her. "Can you find your way to your room?"

Her eyes were wide with disbelief and confusion. "What? You're just leaving me here?"

"Well, I'll take you to your room if you prefer, but you're a big girl now."

"I am," she agreed, grinning lasciviously.

ODDS ON

"Good. Then you won't have any trouble by yourself. Good night."

He left her, noticing that she had been about to say something more, but had stopped herself.

He was almost to the end of the corridor when she said again, "You think you own the world!"

THURSDAY, JUNE NINETEENTH

Jencks was awakened in the morning by the ring of the telephone. He rolled over and groped for the receiver. "Hello?"

"Steve, honey."

Instantly he was awake. "Good morning, Miss Cameron."

"Call me Jenny." Her voice was a soft, insinuating purr.

"Whatever you wish."

She paused. "I'd like to see you today."

I'll bet you would, he thought. The losing gambler wants to recoup her losses in another round. Well, good luck to her.

"Wonderful," he said.

He heard her inhale on a cigarette. "Do you have a car?"

"Of course."

"Has it got any gas in it?" Before he could answer, she seemed to reconsider this remark, and said quickly, "I thought we might take a ride."

"That sounds fine. Any place in particular?"

"No, I just want to be taken for a ride. Can you arrange it?" Her voice was now frankly seductive. He could imagine her sitting by the phone, smoking and thinking out each line before she said it. He had to give her credit; she was doing a good job.

"I think so. Name the time."

"Is ten minutes too soon?" She seemed apologetic and eager at the same time.

Damn you, he thought. "Not at all," he said, already looking across to the closet, deciding what to wear. He would miss breakfast, but that couldn't be helped. The hard hours that teachers work, he thought. But he was determined to be well paid for his efforts.

"I'll meet you in front," she said. "See you then, Steve."

Her voice lingered invitingly, and the line clicked dead. Jencks got out of bed, and dressed swiftly in a pair of slacks and light sweater. He finished by running an electric razor across his face. As he stared in the mirror, he considered what Jenny might have planned. His habit of anticipating events carried over into his affairs with women, and he found it valuable. He had little patience with men who claimed that they would never understand women. Jencks always understood women.

He finished shaving, left the room, and took the elevator to the lobby. Jenny was waiting for him outside, wearing a sleeveless white blouse and a powder-blue skirt which matched her eyes. She looked golden and healthy and very sexy—tawny was the word, he thought. The blouse was thin, and through it he could see her large breasts, restrained by a lacy half-bra. He was careful not to stare.

"You're looking good this morning," he said.

"I'm feeling good this morning." she said, in a low voice. Her eyes lowered demurely, and she rubbed one thigh through the skirt.

She wasn't wasting any time.

ODDS ON

The attendant brought the car from the garage; it was a Caravelle convertible, white. They rolled the top back.

"Pretty car," Jenny said, "but feminine and underpowered."

"I don't really mind," Jencks replied, "and besides, it's rented."

He shrugged, climbed in behind the wheel, and they started off across the bridge and onto the twisting mainland road that hugged the rocky coast. It was a beautiful day, hot but clear, and the air was redolent of pine. Jenny kicked off her sandals and threw her head back, letting the wind catch her hair. She looked proud, sensual, and stunning, and for a moment he wondered if he would be able to wait until her cure treatment had been finished.

"Sleep well?" she asked, smiling slightly. Her cheeks dimpled.

He knew he could wait.

The road curved in long, twisting hairpins, giving them magnificent views of clear blue water meeting the reddish cliffs of the coast. A gentle wind blew in from the sea, producing small whitecaps. Offshore, a pleasure boat moved south toward Tossa del Mar and Barcelona.

"Where shall we go?" he asked.

"You're driving. I don't really care. I wouldn't have accepted your invitation, except that I had to get away from that idiot Peter." She paused, remembering her conversation of the morning. "I mean, I—"

"That's all right," Jencks said. "I understand your position." He did, too. She wanted to be seductive, but was unable to keep to her line.

Jenny puffed on her cigarette in silence. The car came around a bend, and a deserted cove lay visible below—a short stretch of white beach, nestled between rocky walls.

"I feel like a swim," Jenny said. "Why don't we go down there?"

126

Jencks knew that she had not brought a suit. "Actually," he said, "I don't really feel up to it. But I'll be glad to stop while you take a dip." He pulled the car over to the side of the road.

Jenny hesitated, then said, "Never mind. I'll wait until we get back to the pool."

Without commenting, he slipped the car into gear and continued down the road. She tossed her cigarette into the wind and shifted restlessly. Out of the corner of his eye, he saw her unbutton one button of her blouse. The material sprang open, revealing the tops of her breasts. She shifted again, raising her legs and placing her bare feet on the dashboard. Her skirt slid down around her full, brown thighs.

"It's very warm today," she said.

"You should dress in lighter clothing."

She took a deep breath, and her blouse opened further. She reached inside and rubbed one breast, slowly.

"Do I have a good body?"

"Very nice."

"You haven't even looked at it."

"Of course I have. I've been looking at it ever since I met you."

"And what do you think of it?" The skirt slipped still further back, baring the edges of blue lace panties.

"Very nice."

"Doesn't it interest you?"

"It would interest any male up to the age of ninety or so. Maybe older."

She was pushing very hard, he thought. Unbecomingly hard, though it was a good sign. She would crack soon.

"And how old are you?" Her hand ran absently over the firm flesh of her thigh.

"Thirty-eight."

Go on, he thought. Giggle and say you are, too. But Jencks

ODDS ON

was surprised. Her approach was different; her voice remained cool.

"Not nearly ninety, are you?"

"I'm wise beyond my years."

She thought for a moment, then asked innocently, "Are you a queer?"

For shame, he thought. "Would you like to find out?"

"Maybe. Maybe not."

He reached over and patted her shoulder paternally. "I'll wait until you've made up your mind."

She fumed silently.

He decided to take the pressure off. "Are you free for dinner?" He asked the question directly, but his tone indicated that she could refuse if she wished. He knew that he could have been much rougher, could have simply informed her that she was dining with him. By relaxing with her now, he was allowing her to become bitchy again if she wished; he had given her an opening which she might take advantage of. He waited for her answer with interest.

"Yes," she said. "I am. What time?"

"Nine?" Again, a question, not a statement.

"All right," she said. Then, grudgingly, "Thank you."

He nodded, still keeping his eyes on the road. She was more subdued, but some extra sense told him the battle was far from over.

———

Bryan met Annette by the saltwater pool. She was wearing a white cotton pullover and pink capri slacks, and she looked very fresh and desirable.

"Hello," Annette said. He noticed that she carried a neatly

rolled towel under one arm, and he was glad he had had the foresight to bring along his swimming trunks.

"Where are we off to?"

"Do you mind walking a bit?" He shook his head. "Good. I've been here a year, and I know the coast very well. There's a wonderful little place we can go to, if you don't mind fighting some brambles."

"I'm game."

They walked around to the front of the hotel, across the bridge, and abruptly turned off into the hills. He noticed that they were following a path, narrow and indistinct, but a path nonetheless. It climbed one sandy, red hill, then followed down the other side. The hotel, high as it was, disappeared from view. Birds in the nearby, scrubby pines chirped and twitted; the breeze was gentle and soft. As they continued on, the path disappeared, and soon Annette struck out to the right, toward the sea. Thorny bushes clung to his legs; he could understand why she had worn slacks.

They descended, fighting for balance in the loose earth, and came at last to a small beach, completely hidden from sight from above.

"We're just around the corner from the hotel," Annette said. "I don't think anybody knows about this place except me—and now, you." Her voice had a hint of conspiracy, like one child showing another his secret tree-fort.

"I won't breathe a word," he promised. The water lapped at the pebble beach, and it was very quiet. He had a strong sense of being alone with her, and of being responsible for her in an odd way. She stood next to him, waiting for his reaction. He kissed her, almost unwillingly, very gently.

"How do you like this place?"

"It's marvelous." To his surprise, he felt a slight irritation that she was not more moved by his kiss. The whole damned business was annoying and he was filled with conflicting emotions.

She spread her towel on the beach, and anchored it with rocks at the corners. She tossed a green print bikini down on the towel, straightened, and looked at him. Her hand went to the zipper of her slacks. "Would you admire the view?"

"With pleasure."

She pointed to the ocean. Obediently, he turned his back to her. He heard the sound of her zipper, and the ruffling sound of her pants dropping to the ground. There was a brief silence, then a snapping sound—her bra—followed by another silence. He felt nothing at all, certainly none of the intense eroticism he might have expected. Instead, he felt as if he were far off, looking down on this little beach from a great distance, seeing a man staring at the sea, and a girl undressing behind him. It was a weird vision, lonely and surrealistic.

He shrugged and lit a cigarette.

She came around and faced him, momentarily striking a comic, pinup pose.

"You pass inspection," he said lightly. "Shall we take a swim?"

"I'll wait for you in the water." She ran down the beach and plunged in. He slipped into his trunks, trying to assess his feelings, and got nowhere. With a sense of relief, he threw himself into the water, and swam out toward her.

Later, they lay in the sun, feeling the salt dry on their skin. He was on his side, head propped on his hand, looking at her as she lay on her back, facing the sun. As he watched her, he had a sudden image of Jane, lying in bed as the rain pounded on the window. He had a sudden twinge of feeling, which might have been conscience, but could as well have been regret.

They talked for an hour, and it was productive; Bryan picked up a good deal of useful information, particularly about Mr.

ODDS ON

Bonnard's routine, and about the night staff. He discovered that nobody kept watch over the pier and pools at night, and that was of critical importance. Most of the servants lived on the mainland, another important point—Jencks had been unsure how many spent the night on the island. He found out a little about which guests were particularly wealthy.

When they finally decided to go to Gerona for the rest of the day, a certain detached part of him was pleased. Another was depressed, for he had discovered what he had feared all along, that he was growing very fond of her.

———

By the pool, Miguel pushed aside the leaves of the potted palm and watched Big Brad Allen lumber across the concrete deck. He headed directly for the little lady with the bananas and drew up a chair at her table. He didn't lack nerve, that was for sure. The two talked quietly for several minutes; then the old lady put down her book and listened with full attention.

Miguel was disturbed. He had awakened late and had found that both Jencks and Bryan were gone when he phoned. Not knowing what to do, he had followed Allen during the morning and had watched him travel unctuously from one group of guests to another, talking, laughing, buying drinks. It looked, from a distance, like a con game, but you could never tell.

Allen finished talking with the old lady and stood to leave. He pointed to her half-empty glass, and she shook her head. He bowed politely and walked off. Soon he was talking with a lanky man in a broad straw hat. Apparently, he seemed intent on meeting everyone at the hotel.

Miguel got up and walked inside to the lobby. As he passed

ODDS ON

the elevator, he considered visiting Cynthia, but decided against it. He was not in the mood.

He found the manager behind the desk.

"I'm sorry," he said, "but I have something terrible to ask."

Mr. Bonnard looked sorry, too.

"A man checked into the hotel yesterday evening, a big man with a red face. He's out at the pool now. I'm sure I know him, a business associate from somewhere, but I can't place him. Can you tell me his name?"

"I think so." Mr. Bonnard shuffled through the registration forms, found one he wanted, and put it down on the desk. Casually, Miguel looked at it. "Mr. Brady is the man, Alan Brady."

Miguel frowned, and scratched his head. "Brady, Alan Brady." Suddenly he snapped his fingers. "Of course—Al Brady!"

Mr. Bonnard smiled.

Miguel smiled.

He left the desk, still smiling, and returned to the pool. He had read the card, and had the room number—51.

Back at the pool, he found Brady talking to a girl in a blue-and-white checked bikini. She did not seem very interested, and neither did he. Miguel took up his seat by the potted palm and watched. He noticed that none of the guests who had already met Brady paid him any attention; they were oblivious to his wanderings. In a way, that was a sign of great skill on Mr. Brady's part.

———

"Oh really?" Jencks said.

"Why yes," the lady replied. They were sitting in the bar, drinking lemonade. She was American, tall, bony, and aristocratic in a plain way. "I have always taken champagne baths. Not

ODDS ON

pure champagne, of course—just a bottle or two in the water. If you use dry champagne, it's simply marvelous. I even induced my friend Gertrude to try it, and she's so stodgy; if she can do it, anyone can do it, I always say. Gertrude must be the stodgiest person I know. Even her bridge game reflects it. Stodgy."

Jencks nodded wisely. Mrs. Cleeves continued her discussion of stodginess in the human species, liberally sprinkling it with examples from her acquaintance. She was a middle-aged, wealthy Connecticut bore, but he listened patiently. His occasional questions were sufficient to steer her monologue in the direction he wanted, and she had the fortunate habit of following any thought to its most detailed conclusion. When finally she got around to it, she mentioned that she was traveling alone—separated from Eric, her dreadful second husband—to meet her nephew, who was working for A.I.D. in Afghanistan, a miserable job but you know the pioneering spirit of the young. Still, travel was so strenuous, and she had to worry constantly about her "things." She didn't know why she had brought them; jewels certainly wouldn't be any use in Afghanistan. Force of habit, she supposed. Jencks nodded in agreement. Half an hour later, she mentioned her room number. Fifteen minutes after that, Jencks was desperately looking for a way to break away.

He saw Miguel at the entrance to the bar. Miguel beckoned.

"You must excuse me," Jencks said. "I have to see this fellow. It's been very pleasant."

He left before she could protest.

"Anything wrong?"

"Yes. There's a crook in the hotel."

Jencks's eyebrows went up. Somehow, he knew what was coming.

"A big fat guy," Miguel said, "named Brad Allen. He's registered as—"

"Alan Brady," Jencks said.

"You know him?"

"He borrowed my passport on the plane from Madrid to Barcelona. Looked at it, slipped it back to me. He had me tailed in Barcelona. Is there a skinny runt with him?"

"No," Miguel said.

"What's his game?"

"Straight con, as far as I know. Very good."

"I can imagine."

Miguel lit a cigarette. "He's staying in room 51. Should I search it?"

"No," Jencks said. "Not yet. I want to think about this for a while."

He wandered off, deep in thought. All his earlier misgivings returned to him; this could not be coincidence, could not be mere chance. The odds against this chain of events were incredibly high. Brady must be following him, must be after something, or afraid of something.

He considered every possibility and drew the same blank he had drawn before. Unless Bryan had talked—and that was very doubtful—Brady could not know what Jencks intended. Therefore, he must be here for another reason. That was the only logical conclusion.

He didn't like it. His brain accepted that, but his instincts rebelled. There was only one thing he could do. He went out to the pool to make arrangements with Miguel.

———

"You're out of your goddamned mind," Peter said.

"Shut up, and don't make a scene," Jenny replied. She jumped off the pier into the water, and slipped into the skis.

ODDS ON

A short distance away, the boat was idling, its motor putting softly.

"I wanted to talk to you, not water-ski."

"You can talk to me, but you're not going to spoil my fun. Are you coming? I can't wait all day."

Furious, he dropped into the water, and struggled with the rubber foothold in the skis. He was not a strong swimmer, and he had trouble staying afloat. For that matter, he was not a good water-skier, though he had tried it once or twice. He regarded it as a dangerous sport, like mountain climbing or skin diving in shark-infested waters. You could break a leg—or your neck—water-skiing. It was ridiculous.

"Having trouble?" Jenny laughed.

"No. I'll be ready in a minute." He swallowed some water as he spoke and broke out coughing. It was embarrassing.

"Maybe you'd be happier with a life jacket," Jenny said, observing his difficulties.

"I told you, I'll be ready in a minute."

"All right, all right."

The man in the boat threw them two ropes. Jenny took hers and handed the other to Peter. Their hands touched briefly, but it was cold and impersonal.

"Listen," Peter said. "I want to talk to you about our engagement. I have to tell you that you are acting in a manner—"

"Ready?" the man in the boat called.

Jenny waved to indicate that they were, then turned to Peter. "You were saying?"

At that moment the boat started, and they were both drawn forward, slowly at first, and then lifted up. Peter felt the wind on his dripping body; it was cold. They began to go faster. He shivered, tensed, and fought for his balance.

"Yes?" Jenny called to him, laughing.

ODDS ON

They were drifting apart, he to the left of the wake, she to the right. "I don't know what kind of a game you're playing," he shouted, "but I won't stand for it. Do you understand?"

"I can't hear a word you're saying." she shouted. He heard her distinctly.

She began to come toward him, and he ducked. Her rope passed over his head. He crossed the wake, bouncing and fearful, and their positions were reversed.

"Whee!" Jenny shouted.

"You're being insulting!"

"Whee!"

"Childish!"

She laughed. "Isn't this fun?"

"No!" he screamed.

She shook her head pityingly.

"Don't give me that shit! I want an explanation."

"Can't hear you. Sorry."

"Then listen!"

"What did you say?" She was cocking her head toward him, an amused smile on her lips. Then she was coming toward him again; again, he ducked, and they changed sides. As she passed him, she said, "Scared, sweetie?"

"Damn you!"

They were moving out from the coast into rougher water. The wind was picking up, and he was bouncing. It was difficult to maintain his balance. Jenny didn't seem to be having trouble. Where had she learned to water-ski, anyway?

She made a signal to the man in the boat. They picked up speed. She was trying to dump him, waiting for him to fall. She had planned it from the start, with the intention of humiliating him.

"Who do you think you are?" he shouted, but he could

ODDS ON

hardly hear his own voice in the wind, now, and he knew that she was not fooling when she shook her head.

And then, quite suddenly, his left leg twisted out and up, and he felt himself lifted up, spun sideways, and flung into the water with a hard slap. The cold water enveloped him. When he broke surface, he saw the motorboat circling around, coming back. It passed him, then slowed, and Jenny sank gracefully into the water beside him.

"Did you hurt yourself?"

"No, dammit."

"Don't be angry, Peter. You should have said you didn't know how to water-ski in the first place. I wouldn't have made you go with me, if I'd known."

"You didn't make me go with you, and I do know how to water-ski."

"I must admit, you did well for a beginner."

"Now you listen to me," he said. "I can take only so much. I'll give you another day to come around, and if you don't, you'll have to suffer . . . suffer the consequences."

She nodded politely.

"Better grab your rope," She said, "I think we're about to be taken in."

"Did you hear what I said?" he demanded, his voice taut with anger.

"Yes, Peter," she said soothingly. "I heard."

———

Jean-Paul knocked on the door and waited. The package, wrapped in a newspaper, was under his arm. He looked up and down the hall nervously, but there was nobody in sight.

ODDS ON

Anyway, he had nothing to worry about. Who would know? Who would even suspect?

The door opened, and he found himself staring into the eyes of a dark and beautiful girl. She wore a bulky, shapeless sweater that came just below her hips, but her long, slim legs were bare. She wore no slippers.

"Yes?"

"I am Miss Shaw's chauffeur."

"Oh." Cynthia smiled radiantly. He liked her slanting eyes, her dark skin, her full lips. He particularly liked the long black hair that flowed over her shoulders. "Please come in."

He entered the room and shut the door behind him. She walked to the dresser, picked up a drink, and sipped it. She seemed perfectly at ease and surveyed him coolly. "Not bad," she said. "But Aunt Elizabeth always did have good taste in men, considering her age."

"Aunt Elizabeth?"

"Yes. She's not really my aunt. It's just an affectionate term. We met in London a while ago. Where did she pick you up?"

"Tangier."

Cynthia nodded thoughtfully, then waited. "Well?"

"Oh," Jean-Paul said, remembering the newspaper. He had been daydreaming, staring at her firm legs, with their smooth muscles. He wondered if she was wearing anything beneath the sweater and guessed she wasn't.

He handed the newspaper to her, and Cynthia took it eagerly. She set it down on the dresser, opened it, and took out the gray package. He wandered around the room and noticed the Polaroid camera.

"You have one, too?" he asked, picking it up.

"Yes," she said.

"You mean, you're . . ."

138

ODDS ON

"Yes. I've gotten quite good with it."

"So have I," Jean-Paul said.

He saw that she had opened the gray package, displaying a heap of packed, green, grainy material. With her fingers, she felt the texture, then smiled. "It's good stuff. Nice and pure. Ever tried it before?" Her eyes were on him; he could feel them gauging him.

"Of course," he said.

She smiled. "Why don't you stay a while, and share a couple of cigarettes with me?"

"All right," he said, trying not to think of her legs.

She sat down on a chair and crossed her legs, then raised one and pointed it forward. The skin was smooth and taut, dark brown, and lightly oiled. "My name is Cynthia," she said, relaxing the leg.

"Jean-Paul."

"You look strong, Jean-Paul."

He shrugged.

"Don't be embarrassed. I like strong men. Why don't you make some sticks while I change clothes?"

He nodded numbly, disappointed to see her enter the bathroom. Reaching into his pocket, he withdrew a packet of Marlboros and began squeezing one of the cigarettes, rolling it in his fingers. The tobacco fell out in long strands. He continued to work it in his hand until it was an empty paper tube.

"You want it straight, or mixed with tobacco?" he called to her.

She opened the door and looked out. "Straight."

He put the cigarette between his lips and bent over the pile of green marijuana. Inhaling, he sucked the substance into the tube, pausing occasionally to tamp it down with a matchstick.

139

Soon, the cigarette was completely refilled; he twisted the end closed, and prepared a second.

Cynthia came out of the bathroom wearing very tight black slacks and a tight black sweater. Her feet were still bare, and her long hair hung loose. She picked up one cigarette and pinched it gently. "You pack them like an expert," she said. She looked at him and frowned. "What's the matter? You seem unhappy. Don't you like the way I look?"

"You were better before," Jean-Paul said.

"You mean I was barer before," she laughed. "But I wasn't very bare, was I?"

Her laugh was open and earthy. It reminded Jean-Paul of something, but he couldn't remember what exactly.

"Make up two more," she said. "I'll get some water. *Kef* always makes me thirsty."

She disappeared again into the bathroom, and he squeezed out another pair of cigarettes, filling them quickly. When she returned, he handed her one and took one himself, lighting both. Cynthia sat down on the bed, and he sat in a chair across from her. They puffed in silence, staring at each other.

"We'll have to do something interesting," Cynthia said. "It would be a shame to waste it."

Jean-Paul smiled slightly. The room filled with acrid, sweet smoke, which reminded him of cinnamon burning, though that was foolish—he had never smelled cinnamon burning. Cynthia smiled her earthy smile once again, and he remembered where he had seen it. It was in a little village outside Madrid. As the marijuana began to take effect, he saw the scene again vividly.

He had stopped for coffee at a roadside cafe, which faced out on a dusty square with a stone fountain where the townspeople came to draw water and wash clothes. As he drank his coffee, a girl came to the fountain, young but full bodied, wearing a faded light blue dress. She had dirty, tangled hair but an open, smiling face and eyes which promised the richness of her body. It was the eternal peasant, earthy and wonderful, and he had desired her for the few moments he had passed over his coffee. Then he had gone on to Madrid and forgotten her.

Jean-Paul began to feel slightly dizzy and cold around his ankles even before he had finished his first cigarette. The stuff was damned strong, he thought. Cynthia was now lying on her back on the bed, gently massaging her stomach.

He had not noticed her lie down. It was taking hold; the stuff was beginning to work through his lungs to his brain. He could almost feel it coursing through his bloodstream, up to his ears.

"Nice," Cynthia said, to nobody in particular.

Jean-Paul closed his eyes and saw the world drift gently. He was in a warm, damp jungle surrounded by green ferns. The scene faded to one of a blizzard and a gray sky over the prairie, and then a forest, very chilly and still, and then a desert, where the sand blew endlessly. The visions passed, and he looked across at Cynthia.

"*Bonjour,*" she said. "All the French I know."

"I know you," he said, feeling very high indeed.

"You want to watch me undress," she replied, in a slow, heavy voice. She spoke interminably slowly, the words stretched and twisted like taffy in the air. Why taffy? He was off in his dream world again, tumbling like a yo-yo falling down the stair-well, spinning end over end, side over side . . .

Cynthia got off the bed and stood before him. It was all slow motion. "You can undress me," she said.

"All right," he agreed, thinking he was speaking so slowly, like a tape at half speed.

"And I can undress you."

ODDS ON

"All right." It was a stupid answer, sluggish and uninterested, but he could not help it. He was concerned with himself, feeling his body drift and spin, slowly, pleasantly.

She stood before him, guiding his hands to her buttons and snaps. The slacks burst open, slowly like a flower opening, and he pulled them down her legs; her groin was right before his eyes, and he could sense the heat and desire radiating from it. She turned around, and he reached up to unzip her sweater. It was so far to reach, it took hours for his hand to get up there.

Cynthia stepped back and allowed him to look at her. She was lovely, beckoning, tensing the muscles in her thighs as she stood, hands on hips, smiling.

For many hours, he did not say anything.

"You're incredible," he said finally. He felt his eyes, running and feeling like hands, look down her body, to the clean collarbone, to the firm, small, tense-nippled breasts, to the neat waist with the large navel, to the narrow hips, to the quivering thighs.

He stood up, slowly, dreamily.

She moved close to undo the buttons on his shirt. She slipped it off his shoulders and ran her hands slowly across his chest, while her almond eyes, wide and bright, pierced his face. He could smell her perfume, now; her whole body glowed with desire. Her fingers were at his belt, then his pants and zipper, and they dropped to the floor. Her hands moved to his shorts, caressing him lightly before pulling them down.

She lay back on the bed and watched him standing before her. He did not move for a long time. "This will be perfect," she said. "I can look at you, and you can look at me." She gave a throaty laugh. "Because I want to look at you. I want to do a lot more than look."

ODDS ON

"You can look later," Jean-Paul said, and stretched out beside her. His hands ran over her breasts and stomach; her body glowed like coals, a blazing fire fanned. She drew him over to kiss him.

He slid on top of her and felt her heart thump against his chest. He let himself into her with soft gentleness, savoring each exquisite instant of penetration. Her legs were wide for him, quivering and open. He pressed himself home to the hilt, and felt her thrust up her pelvis to meet him.

"That's good," she said, kissing him and locking her arms around his neck. Below she felt him in her, plunging and withdrawing.

"Slower, darling," she whispered. Her voice dragged. It took days to finish the sentence. "Keep it beautifully slow. Like a long, slow pendulum. Very long, swinging . . . swinging."

Jean-Paul heard her as if from a distance. She was speaking from the end of a dark tunnel, but some corner of his mind told him that she was high. Her voice told it all, even from a great distance.

He slowed his stroke and felt her sex ripple and clutch at him. She had muscles in there, and she knew how to use them. It was a delicious, tightening, sensual feeling. Like a boa constrictor, like squeezing a rubber ball, like flexing a bicep. Her legs came around his, and she pressed her heels inside his knees, getting better leverage for her hips, which moved in slow sure time with him.

Her breasts strained against his chest. Her legs tensed against his. "Oh, it's going to be so good . . . so good. Yes, that's it, very slow, oh yes that's it."

In himself, he felt the coiling; the snake was preparing to strike, the spring was growing tense, until it would burst the mechanism.

ODDS ON

"That's it, lovely. It's lovely, yes."

So slow, so slow.

Endless.

Continuing.

And then she was pressing herself to him tightly, straining as he pierced her. And soon Jean-Paul felt himself carried on a wave, then it was a tram railway up a mountainside, then a rocket, up and up, and she screamed slightly and pressed forward like a thirsty mouth to water, like a sucking clam.

Time passed.

She got up and walked around the bed, surveying him from all sides. Around and around she walked, his eyes following. He smiled.

"That," she said, in a drawn-out whisper, very hoarse, "that was the slow one. Are you ready for the fast one?"

He did not understand, until she grinned wickedly and floated down beside him. She stroked him, lingering, gentle.

"Surprise," she said. "You seem ready to rise to the challenge again. Or is it just my exciting body and not your sense of manhood?"

It seemed to Jean-Paul that they had been in this room for years. Years and years, just the two of them, together.

She was in front of him now, running her hands up her sides, finally reaching her breasts. Her hands rotated them, and then she took her hands away. The nipples were tensed and firm.

Cynthia's face was calm, almost peaceful. Her hands were running up and down her thighs now, caressing her pubis. Her body was leaning slightly back, so that her loins were forward. He could smell her heat, the body smell of desire. He felt himself stiffen.

For Cynthia, the world was a calm boat, rocking on a placid sea beneath milky clouds. She was moored solidly, but still rocking, lulled but happy, anticipating with pleasure the darkening of the clouds, and the final deluge of the storm. The air was warm and moist with the coming thunderbolt; it was still, fetid, waiting.

Dimly, she saw Jean-Paul, lying naked on the bed watching her. His eyes were bright, and in a few moments his member began to rise. She watched with unabashed interest; it was always such a marvelous thing to see, this strengthening which would bring her appeasement. She wanted to reach forward and touch him, to feel his hardness. Her own body was ready to receive it. Her thighs were already flexing rhythmically, as she would if he were already there.

She put her hands to her breasts once again, and stretched. Then she felt Jean-Paul's hands reaching for her. She was aware of every sensation, each individual fingertip. She began to see colors, passing one after another . . . indigo blue . . . fire red . . . a blazing orange . . . a hot yellow . . .

Her boat was rocking hard now, and the sky was the color of smudged chalk. The first white-hot bolt of lightning cracked across the heavens. Soft drops of rain pelted her face, soaking her hair. It was still a warm rain. Lightning cracked again, and the sky split in a jagged crease, then folded shut. It was like a clam shell which had been pried open for a brief glimpse before clamping down. Clam clamping. Clamped down on a clam. Clammy hands and feet.

Alternate waves of heat and cold blew across her. Jean-Paul was driving her, pushing her, splitting her with loud smacks. Exquisite pain began, a nugget at first, then suddenly exploding like a single kernel of popcorn. She saw white light, and her boat was lifted on a tidal wave. She was being carried toward the shore, where she would be dashed to pieces against jagged rocks, white in this lightning glare. She was coming down now, off the wave, up to the shore.

With a small scream, her storm broke, and she was safe.

———

"You look bored, dear fellow," Miss Shaw said.

"I am," Georges Dumas said. "Very." He was here at the hotel alone, having been deserted by his mistress a week ago for—he shuddered at the thought—a circus tumbler. And while it was true that Louisa had cabled she was coming down from Paris to meet him here, he put no faith in her. Louisa was always cabling something. He sighed. Very, very bored.

"You need something to cheer you up."

"You are right." A horrible thought occurred to him. Was this desiccated old thing offering her services?

"Something unusual," Miss Shaw continued. "Unconventional. Out of the ordinary."

"Yes," he said slowly.

"Daring."

He nodded.

"Exciting."

Georges Dumas looked at her. "What do you have in mind?"

"A draught of pleasure," Miss Shaw said airily, waving her pale white hand. "A potion of dreams."

"You have this?"

She smiled slightly, and sat back in her chair. "Are you interested?"

"LSD?" He had tried it once, in Stockholm. Marvelous stuff—heady, but exhausting. He remembered the experience with pleasure.

ODDS ON

"I'm sorry," Miss Shaw said. "I did have some, but I'm out at the moment. How about some nice marijuana?"

He stopped and looked at her quizzically. Was it possible that this sweet powdery old thing was selling *kef*? "Well," he said, "as a friend I would be happy to relieve you of—"

"I'm most *dreadfully* sorry," Miss Shaw said, "but I do have an overhead to look after, that sort of thing. It is painful to be a businesswoman at my age, but one must try, mustn't one?"

"How much?" Georges Dumas said, his mouth tightening.

"Well, I look upon myself as a sort of doctor," Miss Shaw said. "I take care of people, relieve their depressions. Naturally, my fees are scaled."

"How much?"

"Oh, you men can be so nasty about business." She patted his hand reassuringly. "Six thousand pesetas."

Six thousand pesetas was five hundred francs, one hundred dollars. "I do not want much," he protested.

"I assume so."

"All right," he said, "I'll give you a check."

"As a superstitious old lady, I must tell you that I've never put much faith in anything but plain money. You understand, of course. The whims of a senile mind."

"As you wish."

He got up to leave.

"I'll stop by your room later," Miss Shaw said. "Around six?"

"Fine."

"A pleasure, Mr. Dumas. By the way, are you any relation to the author?"

"None," Georges Dumas said. "None at all."

As he left, he heard her giggling softly.

ODDS ON

Jencks walked into the bar shortly before six. Brady was there, hunched over his drink. Jencks sat down next to him.

"Well, hello there," Jencks said. "Fancy meeting you here."

Brady looked up. For a brief moment, there was surprise, almost shock on his features. It quickly disappeared, replaced by mindless cheer.

"Damnation!" he said, slamming his palm down on Jencks's knee. "If it isn't my Detroit friend. How's Spain treating you?"

"Can't kick. Buy you a drink?"

"You twisted my arm," Brady said, laughing. "What brings you to the Reina?"

"Curiosity," Jencks said. "I heard it was a spectacular place."

"And isn't it? I think it's downright fabulous. Have a good time in Barcelona?"

"Very fine."

"Meet your girl okay?"

Jencks allowed himself to appear uncomfortable. "I didn't, actually. She was supposed to fly over from Munich, but—"

"Little German number, eh?"

"That's right, and—"

"Little *heine*, as we say." He roared with laughter.

"Yes," Jencks said, looking still more uncomfortable. "But you see, she found out—"

"Hmmm?" Brady stopped laughing.

"I'm married."

"Say no more," Brady said, raising a beefy hand as if taking an oath. "Say no more. I understand just how the hell you feel. Goddamned shame—all these modern communications back-firing. Problem of the modern age."

Their drinks came. Brady lit a cigarette, and raised his glass in a toast. "Well, here's to better hunting."

ODDS ON

They drank. Jencks was drinking vermouth, Brady, bourbon. He finished quickly, and they had another round, then another. Jencks played a troubled man, Brady the fountain of bubbling encouragement and cheer. After half an hour, the liquor was beginning to show. His hand lingered when he slapped Jencks's knee or shoulder. His words slurred slightly. His eyes had a wandering, mildly vacant look. It could be an act, of course—he was a big man—but Jencks decided to take a chance.

"You know, Al," he said, "I have a small confession to make. You see, when I was coming over on the plane, I didn't want word to get back to my wife, so—"

"I know," Brady said, in a tut-tut voice. "I know just how it is."

"So I made up this little story."

"Sure, baby. I know just how you feel."

"About being an automobile designer, and all."

"Of course," Brady said sympathetically.

"And actually I'm not. I'm in industrial counterespionage."

"A cop?" Brady did not seem surprised, though he pretended it.

"Yes," Jencks said sadly. "A cop."

"Detroit?"

"Yes. I have to make sure nobody steals design drawings, all that sort of thing. It's security."

Brady nodded slowly, sluggishly. He seemed to be thinking this over. Finally he sat straighter, and said, "This calls for another round."

"Really? Why?"

Brady motioned for the bartender. "Because we're in the same business."

"Is that right?" Jencks said, astonished.

"Damn straight. I have to tell you, I *thought* you might be

149

a cop, when I met you on the plane. I had that little feeling, you know?"

"Yeah."

"Well, you're pretty good, Steve boy, but you can't fool an old pro like me. How long you been doing this work?"

"Five years. I began low down, cleaning out the locking wastebaskets, doing night duty. Now I'm running security at the test track."

"Which one?" Brady asked, casually.

"Near Flagstaff, Arizona. We have five, you know. Different climates."

"Then you must be used to this weather," Brady said.

Another round arrived. They pushed their empty glasses aside.

"I'll tell you," Brady said, "a little confession of my own. On the plane, I did something kind of bad."

"What's that?"

"I fingered your passport and had a look at it."

"You did?"

"Ummm. Sorry, really. I had to do it, though. I also had you followed in Barcelona."

"Followed?" Jencks hesitated here. An industrial security man wouldn't have much experience with tails. On the other hand, he wouldn't want to admit it. "Oh sure—you mean that tall guy with the moustache."

"That's the one," Brady said, not batting an eye. "I can see you're a sharp operator."

"Well now, tell me," Jencks said, sipping his drink. "What's your game?"

Brady looked furtively around the room, then leaned over and whispered, "CIA."

"*CIA?*" Jencks said, very loud.

ODDS ON

"Shhh."

"Oh, sorry." Now Jencks looked around. "I hope I didn't get you into any trouble."

"I think I can handle anything that comes along," Brady said, breathing deeply. "I had quite a rough posting in Shanghai, a few years back."

"Pretty exciting."

"Damned tooting. Lots of snatch too, baby." He slammed Jencks's back and roared.

"This is terrific," Jencks said. "Both in the same business. How long are you here for?"

"Just a couple of days. I leave Saturday morning."

"Listen," Jencks said. "You can tell me. Are you here on vacation, or is it . . . business?"

Brady looked reluctant. "I'd rather not say."

"Sure, sure. I understand. I don't want to compromise you."

"Speaking of compromises," Brady said, "will you look at *that*."

Jenny had just walked into the room, looking very cool and tanned in a white evening dress.

"All mine, I'm afraid," Jencks said getting up unsteadily from the bar.

Brady clutched his sleeve. "You shitting me?"

"Nope. I'm going to dinner."

"Je-sus Christ," Brady said. "Would I like that. What's her name?"

Jencks winked. "I'd rather not say."

He went over to Jenny, took her hand, and walked out of the room with her.

"You're drunk," she said.

"I'm not." He straightened, and smiled. The sappy look was gone from his face, the slouching, tentative walk replaced by a firm, direct step. "Just a minute," he said. "I forgot to pay the bar bill."

He left her and returned to the table. Brady was looking at the bill, one hand in his pocket. He seemed very unhappy.

"Thought I was going to stick you with that?" Jencks said. He took the bill and signed it. "Not a chance. Listen, I need something from you."

"Anything," Brady said, smiling expansively.

"You got a room facing the ocean?"

"Yes."

"If you're leaving Saturday, could I take it? My room isn't so good."

"Sure thing. I'll speak to the desk about it."

"Don't bother," Jencks said, "I'll do it." He rubbed his fingers together in the universal sign. "I doubt that speaking alone will do the job."

"Haw," Brady said, and punched Jencks in the arm. "You old devil." He laughed, and Jencks went out to Jenny, and took her to dinner.

———

Jencks sat alone in his room, thinking. He did not know what to make of Brady or their conversation. In all, he thought that it had gone rather well; he had stopped at the desk after dinner and asked if he could have Mr. Brady's room when he checked out; Brady was indeed scheduled to leave on Saturday. It all seemed to be on the up-and-up. Of course, the business about the CIA was garbage, but that didn't matter. Men in bars always lied, whether their motives were sinister or merely ego-boosting.

The telephone rang. "Room 205," he said.

"Can't make it tonight." Bryan's voice.

ODDS ON

"Sorry to hear that," Jencks said. It was necessary to conduct a normal conversation, since the switchboard might be listening in, but he managed to convey his strong disapproval. "Where are you now?"

"Gerona."

"Having a nice time?"

"Very nice."

"What's the problem?"

"A bird. I can't get out of it without looking funny."

So he was busy with the receptionist. Well, that was excusable. "Can I see you tomorrow?"

"I'll stop by at noon."

Spending the night with her. "Fine."

"I can tell you what I've got. Ten offs, and half a dozen Qs. Okay?"

"Have a nice time," Jencks said.

He sat back in his chair and sipped the dry vermouth which had been delivered to his room a few minutes before. His thoughts wandered from Bryan and the receptionist to Jenny. She was beginning to get under his skin. He recalled their conversation at dinner; at one point, he had asked, "Is your hair naturally that color, or is it dyed?"

"Natural," Jenny had replied. "Why?"

"Curious."

"There are more interesting ways," she had said, "of finding out than asking."

"Really? You'll have to explain."

On the surface, he had come off well, as usual. But she had somehow cut deeply into his growing desire. She was a bitch, all right, but such an attractive one. It was irritating.

A knock on the door, and Miguel entered.

"What did you find?"

ODDS ON

"His room's pretty clean. Nothing obnoxious, like a gun. Just a straightforward tourist—who happens to have three passports. American, name of Alan Brady; French, name of Alain Bernet; Italian, name of Marco Bernino." Miguel shrugged. "Other than that, nothing. Clothes from every capital of the world, but that's hardly a crime."

He sat down.

"Listen," he said, "I've been thinking. We want to get him out of the way, right? If I pushed him down some steps, just easy and inconspicuous, we'd have him in the hospital for the next week. Nothing to it. What do you say?"

"He's leaving Saturday," Jencks said.

"Does he say that?"

"Yes. But I checked at the desk. It's true."

Miguel lit a cigarette. "Then it's no sweat."

"That's what I think. We leave him alone."

"I still wish I knew why he's here."

"So do I," Jencks said, "but I can't worry about it now. Did you bring the list?"

Miguel produced it, and Jencks ran his eye down the two columns of numbers, one for rooms which could definitely be skipped, and one for possibilities—or Qs, as Bryan had called them. Each of the three men had prepared such a list.

"Where's Bryan?"

"Busy. I'm getting his information in the morning."

Jencks ignored Miguel's lewd, knowing look, and placed the list alongside his own. He ticked off all the certainties on a master sheet, and noted the question marks. Then he burned the small lists in the ashtray.

"How many?" Miguel asked.

Jencks tallied quickly. "Twenty-one to pass over, nine to check again. Bryan says he has ten checks and six questionables,

154

which raises our total—assuming no duplication—to thirty-one and fifteen. That's not very good." Jencks rapped the desktop with his pen. "We need more rooms. Unless we come up with at least sixty by Saturday morning, we may have a little trouble. The program calls for a 20 percent write-off."

Miguel nodded, and stepped to the door. "Do my best," he said. "See you."

"Good luck."

The meeting was over. Jencks looked at his watch. It had taken two minutes and five seconds. That was better than he had expected, though, of course, Bryan was absent. He glanced down the master sheet, frowning. They really were behind schedule; he had hoped to cross off more than forty rooms at this meeting, and they hadn't come close. Supposing they only came up with fifty rooms by Saturday? In his mind, he reviewed the computer printout. He looked down the memorized page of numbers.

Chances of success fell from .87 to .77. That meant that they'd have to choose a number of rooms at random to skip, in order to get the full 20 percent required to keep the probabilities up. It would be easy enough, but it might cut into the total profit. That prospect was unappealing.

———

Bryan Stack came out of the phone booth. She was waiting in the car.

"Did you get through all right?"

"Yes, fine."

He started the car and drove in silence. They had spent a pleasant day in Gerona, the peaceful inland capitol of the Costa Brava, wandering through the hilly, narrow cobbled streets. Gerona had a good cathedral and an excellent Romanesque

ODDS ON

cloister; like a pair of goggle-eyed tourists, they had seen each sight with a kind of innocent wonder. He had enjoyed himself, enjoyed being with her, and had relaxed—though a part of his mind still prodded her, directing the conversation.

There had been just one bad moment, when they had plunged into the cool, arched interior of the old Moorish baths. Bryan had tossed a coin into the large, mossy fountain and had made a wish. She had teased him, trying to discover what he had hoped for, and that depressed him. He had hoped that this would be the last time, that he would never do anything like this again.

They had eaten dinner in a small restaurant off the main square, a hectic place which served wonderful *paella* and produced, after a little coaxing, an excellent bottle of local white wine. Stuffed and happy, they had walked along the river, watching people take in the day's laundry from their balconies. The sun had set, turning the river molten gold. Then Bryan had made his call. Now they were going back.

As he drove, he tried to conjure up an image of Jane and failed. That disturbed him. Annette reached over and took his hand, she brushed it lightly with her lips.

"Are you happy?"

"Yes," he said.

He wanted to let it go at this, to take her back and send her to bed alone. It was enough; he had found out enough; he had intruded enough into her life. It was not necessary to go further—except that, perhaps, she expected it. He sighed.

"Something the matter?" She curled up in the seat and put her head on his shoulder.

"No, just tired."

"I feel very safe with you," she said, kissing his shoulder. "You must think I'm very foolish."

ODDS ON

"I don't," he said.

They drove on, through the sleepy little town of Cassa de la Selva. The road was deserted.

"Are you going to try and interest me in a nightcap?" she asked.

"I was just about to suggest it," he lied.

"Thank you. I accept."

Hell. He tried again to think of Jane, and again he failed. He decided he wanted a cigarette, and at that moment Annette sat up, lit one with the dashboard lighter, and placed it between his lips. Her fingers were cool. She stroked his cheek.

"How did you know?" he asked.

"I didn't," she said. "Just lucky, I guess." She curled up against him. In a few minutes she was peacefully asleep.

FRIDAY, JUNE TWENTIETH

One day to go. Steven Jencks awoke in a philosophical mood. He was still slightly depressed by the fact that their work had fallen behind schedule, but somehow everything looked better in the morning.

He allowed his mind to wander over the scheme, and its basis, the marvelous mathematic concept of probability, of chance.

To the layman, chance meant risk, uncertainty, weakness. Jencks had a more sophisticated understanding, the kind of understanding a physicist has when he talks about diffraction through a double slit. It was, basically, an awareness that chance governs—not in an individual case, but in many cases. He could accept that paradox and all it implied. You could not predict what would happen in a single instance, a single throw of the dice, a single pitch in the seventh inning, a single toss of the coin. But you could predict three out of five, four out of ten, seven out of sixteen, and to that extent chance governed everyone, all the time.

Just as surely as two equals two.

ODDS ON

He got out of bed, and went into the bathroom to shave. For some reason, quotations came into his head.

Henri Poincaré: "Chance is only the measure of our ignorance."

Laplace: "Probability is relative, in part to our ignorance, in part to our knowledge."

And one quotation which occurred to him, for no particular reason, and amused him as he ran the razor over his chin. C.S. Peirce: "To be logical men should not be selfish."

Well, he was embarked upon a venture of chance, and it was a most logical and selfish venture. He was not afraid; he welcomed this opportunity to test his mind against the vagaries and uncertainties of life among three hundred souls temporarily inhabiting the Hotel Reina. In fact, it was the element of chance, of carefully calculated—no, computed—risk, which made the project so interesting.

Jencks was not a man given to broad generalizations, but he fervently believed that mathematics was the foremost source of power in the modern world. Its potentialities, for both good and evil, far outstripped atomic energy. Because mathematics was a source of discovery, a tool of inquiry. It was mathematics, after all, which made atomic energy possible in the first place. One little white-haired German refugee working with chalk and a blackboard. He shook his head, half-amused, half-wonderingly. It was really quite incredible.

And in his own modest way, Steven Jencks was making a contribution to knowledge. He was using mathematics, and using the computer, to carry out the first genuinely scientific crime in the history of mankind.

He had to admit he was eager to begin.

Annette opened her eyes slowly and stared across the room. She saw her dress and stockings placed carefully across a chair, her shoes on the floor. She looked outside; the sun was shining, but she could not see the ground—this room was on a higher floor than her own. She had a brief moment of panic until she remembered where she was.

"Hello," Bryan said. He was sitting up in bed, smoking.

"Hi," she said, stretching. The movement exposed one breast above the edge of the sheet, but she did not hurry to cover it. She had spent the night lying naked next to him; she was not afraid and not falsely modest.

She thought back over the evening before and discovered that she could remember nothing after the drive in the car.

"Listen," she said, "this may sound ridiculous, but I don't remember what happened."

"Not surprised," Bryan said. "You were dead to the world. I just brought you back and popped you into bed."

Happy and still sleepy, she pressed up against his warm body. He ran his fingers through her hair, holding the soft dark strands gently. "Did we . . ."

"No," he said. "You kept mumbling something about it, but you were too tired."

He did not sound annoyed, just accepting. She sat up and kissed his cheek, feeling the stubble of beard.

"Want a cigarette?" She shook her head. "I've ordered coffee for eight o'clock. It'll be here in ten minutes."

Suddenly she was wide awake. "My God," she said, "I have to be at work at eight. It's Mr. Bonnard's day off."

Bryan remained calm. "Coffee first. Why don't you go take a shower? It'll be here when you get out."

She got up and walked to the bathroom, feeling no embarrassment although she knew he was watching her. That was

ODDS ON

unusual; other times, when she began an affair, she had been acutely self-conscious under a man's eyes. She wondered why Bryan should be different, and realized that it was because he was not embarrassed. He seemed to accept her.

She came back feeling fresh and clean, a towel around her. She sat down on the bed and he handed her a cup of coffee; she sipped it, feeling it warm her throat, making her feel instantly awake. The towel fell down around her waist. She leaned over and kissed him on the lips. Her breasts brushed against his chest.

"You're handsome," she said.

"You're beautiful, and neither of us is saying anything new."

She laughed, and watched as he balanced his cigarette, coffee cup, and saucer with the deft aplomb which only an Englishman could acquire, the accumulated training of endless tea and sherry parties.

"I used your toothbrush," she said. "I hope you don't mind."

He smiled. "Will I see you tonight?"

"I can't," she said. "I have to work late. Tomorrow?"

It would be difficult, he thought. "I can't plan that far ahead."

She finished her coffee and stood up. "I really have to get to work now," she said. She kissed him again. He took her hand firmly.

"No."

"No?"

"You're going to be a little late today," he said, and drew her down against him.

———

"I see," Miguel said, listening with every appearance of attention to the pimple-faced kid. No, it was more than attention. It was an interest and fascination that bordered on adulation. The kid was lapping it up, poor bastard.

ODDS ON

"Yes," Peter replied. "I've always had that ability. Not with all women, of course—but with many of them. I find that the right amount of pressure and cajolery, in the right combination, works wonders. The only problem is finding the combination, though I've been lucky there, most of the time. And I find women so interesting, particularly older women. That's the trouble—the young ones have the bodies, but the older ones know how to use them."

"I agree," Miguel said. He did not allow his eyes to leave Peter's face. Basking in the luxury of attention, Peter was growing more excited and voluble; his words poured forth in confusion, and Miguel was certain that he was lying fabulously.

"Now an exception," Peter said, leaning over confidentially, "an exception happens to be the chambermaids in this hotel. Have you tried them?"

"As a matter of fact, no. I haven't gotten around to it. You see, I've been busy with other . . . matters."

Peter chuckled, man-to-man. Miguel detested him at that instant, and purposely looked away, across the empty bar. It was empty with good reason; only people with real problems frequented the bars at nine in the morning. He had seen Peter here the day before and today had found it easy to strike up a conversation. The kid wanted desperately to talk, to impress someone. "Who's the lucky number?" Peter asked, smiling lecherously.

"That's her, now," Miguel said, waving to Cynthia, who was passing by on her way to the pool. She appeared hungover, but with her sultry features, it looked good. He beckoned her over and introduced Peter.

"Pleased to meet you," Peter said, nodding slightly at Miguel's wink. His attention was focused on Cynthia's bikini, which was not as brief as it might be—though certainly brief enough.

ODDS ON

"So glad," Cynthia said, extending her hand and half-yawning. Miguel gave her a warning glance. It was the least he could do for her, he felt.

"I must be running along now," he said, finishing his drink. Peter's eyes widened in gratitude as Miguel walked out; poor bastard, Miguel thought. But Miguel had been looking for a way to break up the conversation for the last fifteen minutes, ever since Peter had told him all he wanted to know.

Cynthia regarded Peter with less distaste than disinterest. She had been pleasantly but thoroughly exhausted by Jean-Paul the day before, and this morning she had no stomach for men. Miguel had unloaded this panting kid on her, and she resented it—though only mildly. She felt everything mildly today; she lacked the strength for strong emotions.

"Would you like a drink?" Peter asked. His eyes were shining. Cynthia thought he looked as if he wanted to scratch his crotch.

"Jesus, no," she said. The very idea of drink was horrible.

"Perhaps some lemonade? Coffee?"

What was the matter with this boy, anyway? Did he think he had to pour liquid down her or she would walk away?

"Come join me at the pool," she said wearily. He leaped up, and together they walked outside to the pool. Peter brought the rest of his double bourbon with him. They found two chairs on the grass, some distance from some squealing, splashing brats who had temporarily monopolized the pool. Cynthia noticed idly that a four-year-old boy was trying to strangle his little sister. Good for him, she thought.

She flopped down in a chair, shut her eyes, and turned her face up to the sun. Peter sat beside her, making fidgeting, restless sounds.

"Cigarette?" he asked.

163

ODDS ON

She smelled tobacco near her nose. She was very sensitive to smells this morning. "No thanks."

His lighter clicked; he was lighting one of his own. "Sure I can't get you anything?"

"No, no." A far, conscientious corner of her mind told her to talk to him, but she simply wasn't up to it. Not this morning. Besides, he was so crashingly, nervously dull. Like a pregnant hummingbird, she thought, suspended above a pink carnation.

My God, she thought, am I still high?

The sun warmed her face and shoulders, and she relaxed. Peter was talking to her in his scratchy, tense voice; she ignored him. She began to feel beautifully warm. In a few moments, she was asleep.

——

Jencks was sitting at a table on the fourth-floor terrace, drinking his morning coffee. The wrinkled old woman was talking to him as she sipped tea and peeled one banana after another.

"It's so very pleasant here," she was saying. "Don't you agree? I have always felt that spending time in a hotel such as this is rather like returning to the womb, in a manner of speaking. You understand my point, I'm sure; you seem an intelligent young man. What did you say you did?"

"I'm an industrial programmer," Jencks said.

"Is that television?"

He smiled. "No, computers."

"How fascinating!" Her face darkened as she popped a large chunk of banana into her wrinkled mouth.

"Gone bad?" he asked.

"No, it's just fine. Lovely fruit in Spain, you know. It's just . . . did you mention this computer business to me before?"

164

ODDS ON

She seemed very concerned. "I am afraid my memory isn't all that it used to be. Age hath its compensations, but a good memory isn't one of them."

"I can't remember," Jencks said, knowing perfectly well that she had not asked his occupation earlier. "Just woke up. I'm always half-asleep for the first two hours of the day."

"Like a zombie," Miss Shaw said, cackling. Her jowls quivered, and little flakes of talcum powder and rouge were shaken free.

"I wouldn't put it quite like that," he said.

"No, of course not. Excuse me, I keep forgetting you Americans are so literal. You must learn to take yourselves less seriously. It's the result of the atom bomb, I expect," she said. "Do you enjoy your computers?"

"Yes, actually. They can do incredible things."

"So I've heard, so I've heard. I confess it's quite beyond me. *Although*," she said, "I understand that shipping companies now use computers to tell them when to send boats to pick up the banana harvest. Now that's progress, and don't think I'm unappreciative. I adore bananas."

"Delicious," Jencks said. "Are you staying here long?"

"Not long. Just through the weekend. I'm on my way back to Brighton to visit my maiden sister. I'm maiden, too, but I don't let it bother me. Not at my age. How long are you staying?"

"About a week," Jencks said. "I'm not sure."

"And then you return to the United States? I've never been, myself."

"No, then I'm going to Rome. Consultation with some Italian industrial firms. Computers are just getting a foot in the door there."

"Yes, but they're getting a foot in the door everywhere. Soon

ODDS ON

we shall all be a series of little holes on somebody's file card. I find that prospect depressing, frankly. Are you married?"

"No," Jencks said. He displayed just the right amount of embarrassment about the subject. Normally, people would notice his discomfiture and drop the subject immediately.

"You should be," Miss Shaw said. "A bright young man like you needs a wife. You must have a very good job, in a field with a future." She looked at him over her tea, awaiting confirmation.

"I just haven't gotten around to it, I guess."

Miss Shaw shook her head, as if to say it was quite beyond normal comprehension.

"How did you come here?" Jencks asked. It seemed unlikely that she would drive herself.

"My chauffeur," Miss Shaw said. "Marvelous chap, simply gorgeous, though a bit messy as a person. French, you know. That may account for it. But he drives well."

"Unusual in a Frenchman. What kind of car is it?"

"Oh, one of those American Continentals. The houseboats. I detest it, of course, but it is *so* comfortable. Simply divine, the seats. And I've had it fitted out with a portable teapot, so I'm quite at home."

Clearly, Jencks thought, this was a woman to investigate further. He considered how to maneuver discussion to the subject of rooms.

"Do you have a nice room?" Miss Shaw asked.

"Fine, thanks, though it doesn't face the sea."

"What a pity. Although if you're high up, you have a nice view over the wooded hills. When I was here the last time, they put me on the third floor, and it was very pleasant indeed." Again, she looked at him for confirmation.

"I'm on the second floor," Jencks said. "Where are you?"

"Second floor as well. Fancy that. What number are you?"

ODDS ON

"205."

"Ah, well, we're hardly neighbors, Mr. Jencks. I'm 257."

They laughed. Miss Shaw had a twinkle in her eye.

"Do you know—if you'll excuse me—I think that you are a little bored and restless. Is that true?"

"Well," Jencks said, "yes."

"What you need is something to pep you up, get your blood moving. A different experience. A little excitement."

"True," Jencks said, thinking of Jenny. Then of the robbery.

"Something new and daring."

"I agree."

"Something unusual, out of the way."

"What do you have in mind?"

"Well," said Miss Shaw, leaning close. "I'll tell you."

———

Annette was happy. The world seemed to her pleasant and optimistic; her work was fascinating; her clothes looked well on her; the staff was not loafing as much as usual; the guests were relatively quiet and uncomplaining. Though she arrived an hour late for work, she had breezed through the usual morning paperwork, humming to herself. The doorman gave her a knowing look, which she returned with a wide and genuine smile. She was happy—unreasonably, incredibly happy.

But it was a surprise to see Mr. Bonnard waddle up to the desk shortly before noon. He had never appealed to her—she found him physically unattractive and intellectually uninteresting, which made for a good business relationship between them. She did not know much about his private life, except that his wife had died during the war, and that he had been married to hotels ever since. On his days off, he drove south toward

Barcelona, returning late at night. Nobody knew what he did, and Annette had never inquired.

"Miss Dumarche," he said, rather stiffly, "I will not be taking the day off."

She had never known him to do such a thing before. "Is it anything to do with the hotel?"

"No." He reconsidered that. "Well, not exactly. To be completely honest, I awoke this morning with a—a premonition. Something is going to happen, I'm sure of it."

"I see." What could she say? It was hard enough to keep from laughing. At times, he really was an absurd little man.

Mr. Bonnard rubbed his fingers. He seemed genuinely distressed. "I do not normally have such feelings, but this one was unusually compelling. I feel that I should not leave today; nor, in fact, for the rest of the weekend. So," he said, breathing deeply and standing as straight as he could, "I will be in my office as usual. By the way, what have you heard recently about the guests?"

Annette shrugged. In truth, she had heard nothing, and she had thought little about the hotel in the last few days. She was pleasantly distracted. "Nothing much."

"Any news about 313?"

"She seems to be a very warm young woman."

"You mean she is sleeping around?"

"Apparently."

"Professional?"

"I don't know. She is checking out on Monday."

"And what about all the single men?"

Annette smiled. "They seem to like her."

"This is no time for levity," he said, scratching his thinning hair. "I am most concerned, Miss Dumarche. Most concerned. I feel something terrible is about to happen. We must prevent it."

"Of course," Annette said, feeling ridiculous.

ODDS ON

"Be sure you notify me if anything happens," he said vaguely, and walked off toward his office.

Annette was frankly puzzled.

"What's got into him?" the switchboard girl asked, as Bonnard left.

"I don't know. He's worried about something." She rapped her desk with a pencil. It was strange, completely unlike him. Mr. Bonnard was not a worrier; he prided himself on his efficiency, on his control of the situation.

"Did he receive any calls this morning?"

"As a matter of fact, yes," the switchboard girl said. "One came at 7 a.m. I put it through to his room. It was long distance from Barcelona."

"And?"

The switchboard girl looked hurt. "And what?"

"You listened in, didn't you?"

"Please," the girl said, in a shocked voice.

Annette snorted impatiently.

"I was too busy," the girl finally said. "Three other calls came in right afterward. I had to put them through."

"So you have no idea what the topic of conversation was?"

"No," the girl said, "I don't."

"Was it a long call?"

"Fifteen minutes."

It must have been quite a call, Annette thought, if Mr. Bonnard had canceled his day off.

———

Jean-Paul groaned, and rolled over in bed toward the phone. He picked up the receiver, dropped it, picked it up again. He was having trouble seeing. "Hello?"

ODDS ON

"Clumsy," Miss Shaw snapped.

"Sorry."

"Do you expect to lie in bed all morning?"

Even over the phone, her voice was sharp. He looked down at himself, and saw he had fallen asleep with all his clothes on. He was a mess.

"Sorry."

"Don't be sorry. Earn your salary."

The phone was dead. He winced as he discovered a pounding headache and stumbled into the bathroom to find his aspirin.

———

Sitting in an armchair in his room, Jencks looked up. An envelope was being slipped under his door. He opened it and found Bryan's list. He wondered briefly why he hadn't come in, but Bryan would have a good reason, whatever it was.

Probably that girl, he thought, smiling to himself. A thorough researcher, Bryan. He took the new list and ticked the rooms off against the master sheet. There were no duplications. That was encouraging.

———

Mr. Bonnard looked up from his desk at Annette, who had just stepped into his office. "A Mr. Jencks to see you," she said in Spanish. "A guest."

Mr. Bonnard raised his eyebrows, asking silently if it concerned a complaint; he seemed nervous, on edge. She shook her head and stepped back, allowing an enormous American to walk into the office. He was not really so tall, just big, heavyset and broad-shouldered, with the bunched muscles of an athlete.

His face had the coarseness which Mr. Bonnard associated with athletes—gross ones, like weightlifters and boxers.

Mr. Bonnard stood and extended his hand. "How do you do?" Bonnard expected a bone-crushing grip, but received none. "Please sit down," he said, gesturing to a padded, tan leather chair. His office was small, and so he had made certain that it was furnished in light colors, to make it appear larger. He did it not out of vanity, but simply to be comfortable. He spent a good deal of time in his office.

Jencks sat down and beamed a broad, slightly foolish smile. "I just wanted to tell you," he said, "that I think you're running a damned fine little hotel here."

Mr. Bonnard was startled, and his face must have shown it.

"You do understand English, don't you?" Jencks asked.

"Yes, yes, of course. Thank you for your compliment, Mr. Jencks."

Jencks relaxed in his chair and smiled again. "Not at all. I don't mind telling you, I can appreciate the kind of job you people are doing here. From a professional standpoint, I mean. I'm an insurance salesman. It is easy for me to see how well you're handling your possible risks at the Reina. I'm very pleased to see it. I believe in telling people what I think, and not just when I have a complaint. I complain about bad service and sloppy management, but fair's fair. I wanted you to know that in my book, you're doing a damned fine job. Damned fine."

He seemed suddenly embarrassed, as if he had run out of words. Filling the silence, Mr. Bonnard said quickly, "You're kind to take the trouble to say so. And I hope you will not hesitate to inform us of any lapses in the treatment you receive here. It has always been my personal belief that a customer does a hotel a disservice if he does not report any irregularity."

Jencks nodded, and stood. It was an inane conversation, but

ODDS ON

necessary for his purposes. He did not understand why Bonnard was so nervous, but perhaps he was always nervous.

"I'll certainly do that," Jencks said. "And I'll certainly recommend this hotel to all my friends." He held out his hand and said, "Oh, one thing. Can you handle large parties—banquets, things like that?"

Behind him, the door opened.

"There's your answer, Mr. Jencks," Bonnard said.

Jencks turned to face a policeman, swarthy and grim looking.

AFTERNOON, JUNE TWENTIETH

Jencks felt a sick, twisting feeling in the pit of his stomach. It was impossible; they couldn't know, couldn't have discovered. This couldn't be happening to him.

He clenched his teeth and faced Bonnard. "What is the meaning of this?"

Bonnard looked puzzled. "I don't understand."

"Outside," the policeman said, nodding over his shoulder to the door.

"What did he say?" Jencks asked Bonnard, although he understood perfectly well.

"He wants you to leave. He and I have some business to discuss. You see, an important government official is giving a party tomorrow—his daughter's wedding reception, to be exact—and I have—"

"Outside," the policeman said again, placing a firm hand on Jencks's shoulder. Jencks shrugged it off, still pretending fury though relief was flooding through him.

"How can you sit still for this? It is an outrage. It is—"

ODDS ON

"Mr. Jencks," Bonnard said wearily, "you are in Spain. In certain cases, we must make allowances. I will be most happy to speak further with you, but now . . ." He gestured toward the door.

"All right," Jencks said, pushing past the cop and slamming the door behind him. He went directly to the bar, ordered a vermouth, and took it to a side table. It was only then that he allowed himself to react to the situation. He shivered violently for several seconds, then knocked back his drink. That was a close call. He had very nearly given himself away in a moment of shock.

The drink calmed him, and he began to think more rationally, his mind returning to calmness. Official reception or not, their project could proceed as planned; his visit to Bonnard's office had accomplished what he had hoped. He had seen the interior of the office and satisfied himself that nothing had been rearranged, no furniture had been shifted. He would easily find his way through that office in the dark on Saturday night.

Bryan came in, looking just as desperate as Jencks had some minutes before. He got a drink from the bar and brought it over to Jencks's table.

"You shouldn't be doing this," Jencks said. "We don't know each other, remember?"

"Cops," Bryan said. "Cops all over the place. In the halls, all over the lobby, behind the desk checking the guest register. What the hell is it?"

Jencks explained what he knew, but Bryan did not seem satisfied.

"I don't like it," he said. "I don't like it one bit."

"We have nothing to worry about. They'll be checking the guest list for politicals. We're not in that category." Jencks paused. "Are we?"

ODDS ON

"Not me," Bryan said. "Not Miguel, either. But I don't like it anyway."

"Finish your drink."

Jencks sat for some minutes in silence, thinking. At last, he said, "Later this afternoon, stop by the desk and say you've heard a rumor about an official reception. Find out when it's being held, and anything else you can about it."

"I'm meeting her for drinks this afternoon," Bryan said.

"Good," Jencks said. "That will be perfect."

———

What the hell, Miguel thought. Cops all over the place. What kind of a deal was this? He looked down the second floor hallway. He had just stopped by Jencks's room in the hope of catching him in—he wanted to know about all these cops. Cops made him nervous.

But Jencks wasn't in. Shrugging, Miguel continued down the hall. He'd discuss it at the meeting tonight. As he reached the elevator, the door opened and the blond stepped out, the one that was spending so much time with Jencks.

"Good afternoon," he said.

She gave him an icy nod and walked quickly away. She wore high heels and a steel-blue dress of light wool, rather tight and thin. He could see her rear end move enticingly through the cloth; the twin hemispheres of her buttocks were clearly defined, with none of the blurred smoothness that comes from a girdle. She was wearing nothing under that dress.

"Down, sir?" the elevator boy asked.

Miguel looked over, startled by the interruption of his thoughts. Usually the hotel didn't bother with elevator boys. It wasn't really necessary, since the elevators were all automatic.

175

ODDS ON

He stared at the operator, a short dark boy of perhaps twelve or thirteen. He had an impertinent, obnoxious look on his face.

"Down," Miguel said, stepping in. The motor came softly to life, and they began to drop. He looked at his watch. It was almost 3 p.m. Time was running out.

What were they going to do about these cops?

———

Jencks had walked upstairs, looking down through the well at the black-and-white checked floor of the lobby below. He was still thinking, still revising his plans, still considering possibilities.

He had forgotten Jenny until he came to his door and found her standing outside, impatiently tapping her foot on the floor. They had arranged to meet at three, he remembered now. Seeing her, he felt the tension of the last half-hour rise in him, and he knew that he needed something to take his mind off the project.

"Sorry," he said, unlocking the door.

"Your humble servant," she said. "On schedule as ordered."

"I merely asked you if you would like to come up this afternoon," he said. "And as I remember, you considered refusing for a very long time."

"Don't be impossible," she said, entering the room and throwing a copy of *Elle* on the bed. She flopped down next to it. "Is there anything to drink?"

"Water," Jencks said.

"Fine," she replied, to his surprise. He went into the bathroom and ran her a glass from the tap. When he came back,

ODDS ON

he found her sitting with an opened half-pint bottle which she had apparently brought in her purse. She took the glass, drank half the water, grimaced, and replenished it with clear liquid.

"Vodka?" he asked.

She nodded. "I take my pleasure strong," she said, sipping the drink and kicking off her sling-back heels. She scratched one bare foot. Jencks watched each move carefully, judging her mood.

Today was the day, all right. He had promised himself that if conditions were right, he would conclude the treatment. The business with the police had reinforced that conviction, and so far, everything seemed excellent. Jenny was acting contrarily, but was strangely relaxed. She was reacting out of habit, now. She no longer felt such a strong sense of frustration. She was beginning to see that he was indomitable.

"Why did you ask me here today?" she said.

"To make love to you."

Jenny said nothing, but gulped back her drink and set the glass on the floor beside her. "Don't I have a say in this?"

"Of course you do."

"Well, I say no. Not on your life. You've got the chance of a snowball in hell."

"We'll see," Jencks said. "Would you like more water?"

"Trying to get me drunk, huh?"

"Don't be foolish. I can have you without getting you drunk."

"Talk is cheap."

"Are you asking me to prove it?"

She looked at him carefully, trying to understand what he was doing. She lit a cigarette, then said, "No, I don't want you

177

ODDS ON

to prove it. You're the last man in the world that I would want to go to bed with. Peter is infinitely preferable."

"How interesting. You never gave that impression before."

"Oh, shut up and get me some more water. No, never mind. I'll take it straight."

He moved quickly across the room and snatched the bottle from her fingers. "Sorry. I think you've had enough."

"Listen," she said, "who the hell do you think you are, anyway? You don't own me. You don't control me."

"Yes I do."

"Well then, you can control me from a distance, because I'm leaving."

She got up, collected her purse and magazine and started for the door.

"Don't bother," Jencks said, wearily.

Her hand hesitated. She did not reach for the knob. "You've locked us in here. You're a real bastard."

She returned to the bed and sat down.

"The door isn't locked," he said.

"Like hell. It's just the sort of sneaky thing you'd pull."

Jencks shrugged. "If you don't believe me, why don't you check?"

"I don't have to check. I know it's locked—it's justlike you."

"You're very trusting."

"Go to hell. I hate you. You're detestable. You're scum. You're nothing but a rotten, stinking—"

"That's the way I like my women—fiery."

She stopped. "Go to hell," she said again.

"Of course," Jencks said, "if you don't want to leave—"

"And maybe I don't. What of it?"

"Nothing. I just wish you'd say what you mean."

She lit another cigarette, puffed twice on it, and stubbed it

ODDS ON

out angrily. She looked at her watch, adjusted the hem of her skirt, scratched her elbow. Her breathing was harsh; Jencks knew that it was time to end these little games.

He stood, went to the door, and opened it. A cool breeze blew in from the hallway.

"Last chance," he said.

She shook her head. He shut the door. It was very quiet in the room.

"Come here," he said.

She walked over to him, excited and slightly afraid. She stood inches from him, not touching him, her soft blue eyes looking into his.

"Please don't hurt me," she said.

He kissed her. He could feel a ripple of pleasure pass through her. Reaching to her back, he unfastened the snap at her neckline and drew down the zipper that ran along her spine. He slipped one hand into the dress, feeling for the bra, but encountered only flesh.

"No bra?" he asked.

She shook her head. Her eyes were wide and bright. She looked steadily at him as he slid the dress off her shoulders. It bunched around her hips. He admired her breasts. They were very large, beautifully shaped, and extremely firm for their size. The nipples were pink buds.

He reached forward and pulled the dress down over her hips.

"No pants, either," she said, a little unnecessarily. She kicked the dress away and stepped back from him, slightly defiant but still afraid. It must be a new experience for her, he thought, to lack confidence in the power of her body.

"Do you like me?" she asked.

He did not reply but scooped her up in his arms. He lifted

her effortlessly, as if she were a child. She seemed to enjoy it and wrapped her arms around him and kissed him, her mouth open, her tongue probing. Her kiss was wet, cushiony, and full.

He carried her to the bed and set her gently down. She lay on her back, one leg stretched out, one knee bent, and watched while he undressed. Neither said anything. When finally he was through, she appraised his body. "You're a big man," she said. There was no mockery in her voice, only wonder and desire. He lay down beside her.

"You're a big girl," he said. He kissed her and ran a finger along her jaw, up to her ear. He kissed her ear, then the soft spot at the base of her neck. She shivered with delight.

"Steve," she said. "I have to tell you something. I have a hard time. I mean, I don't make it easily. Do you—"

He put his hand over her mouth, and kissed her nose. "You won't have any trouble," he said,

Her fingers ran across his chest, then down to his member. She held it lightly, feeling it. "I think you're right," she said.

He put his lips to her breasts and licked her nipples with his tongue. They stiffened immediately, and she sighed. His fingers ran along her side, down to her loins, and then to her legs. She had beautiful legs, soft but strong. He caressed her knees, then the tops of her thighs. Her hands were in his hair, drawing his head to her, but still he continued to stroke her legs. Finally he slipped his hand between her thighs, and her legs parted slightly. His forefinger reached between her lips and found her moist and ready. At the touch of his finger, she moaned again.

"Don't wait too long," she said breathlessly. "I want to feel you in me."

ODDS ON

Her legs opened wider, then wider still. He came over her, and entered her with one long, powerful stroke. He felt himself reach her depths, and her legs came up and locked around him. He placed his hands beneath her, holding her clenched buttocks.

"Take me," she whispered, "take me hard."

He increased his rhythm until he was pounding into her, slapping against her. She offered no resistance, only willing help in the penetration which occurred again and again. She bit his tongue, and he felt her body tense beneath him, slightly at first, and then with increasing force until her back was arched and her hips thrust forward to receive him. Her breath came in short gasps, then little flutters, and suddenly she clutched him in a spasm of desire, and he felt her muscles grip him, relax, and grip again.

For a long time, they lay spent together, catching their breath. Then he got up and lit her a cigarette. She took it with a shy smile.

"You're right," he said. "You take your pleasure strong."

"Just the way you give it," she said, and smiled. "It's never been so easy for me. You're ruining me for other men. I won't be able to marry a man unless he can do this to me, and I don't think there are many in the world."

"Maybe you've never allowed another man to do it," he said, and instinctively she realized it was true. To surrender like this, to place yourself in the hands of another person and release your consciousness into his care for any period of time, no matter how brief, was a fearsome thing. Steve had forced her to submit. Nobody else had been able to. But there was such a thing as submitting of your own free will.

"I understand," she said.

"Had enough?"

ODDS ON

"I'm sure of it. Have you?"

He nodded, and she kissed him. The fire inside her was turning pleasantly cool. She felt happy, and relaxed, and satisfied.

———

"I'm ready for that drink," Annette said, stepping into Bryan's room. "What a day!"

"As a matter of fact, they're already made up," he said, pouring one from the pitcher. "Try that for size."

She sipped it and sat down. "Very good. Where were you all day? I didn't see you."

"I was water-skiing," he said.

"You missed quite a commotion. Just before two o'clock, a half-dozen motorcycles pulled up in the circle and the *policía* stomped into the lobby. They took over the place. One went off to see Mr. Bonnard, another started checking the register, and the rest snooped around, frightening the guests. And I had to calm the guests down afterward. They were so excited, you'd think they were all crooks."

"What was going on?"

"It seems the deputy mayor of Lerida is holding his daughter's wedding reception here Saturday. He's a distant cousin of you-know-who, so he rates all sorts of fanfare and protection."

"One day's notice? Isn't that rather irregular?"

"Spain," she said, "has its own rules for everything. You should have seen those policemen stomp in with their big boots and uniforms. The staff was terrified, of course; oh, it was dreadful. And to top it off, they left black streaks all over the lobby floor. Those boots." She frowned.

Bryan understood. Once, in Malaga, he had attended a very

ODDS ON

good *corrida;* El Cordobes was the third toreador, and the tickets were selling at a scalper's dream—twenty dollars apiece. At one point during the bullfight, a fight had broken out in the stands, in the sunny section, the cheap section. Two policemen came in to break it up, and suddenly 20,000 people began to hiss. The sound, magnified by the circular arena, was so loud it was almost a roar. It came from nowhere, from no one; the faces of the spectators were impassive, but the sound was there. It did not cease until the police left.

That was Spain. It was a police state and an oppressive dictatorship. The people did not like it, and they vented their resentment whenever they could, which was seldom. The anonymity of a hiss in a bullring was one of their few opportunities.

"What finally happened?"

"They roared off in their motorcycles, apparently satisfied that nobody was out to get the deputy mayor or his daughter. I was furious. It was like—"

"Germany," Bryan said.

"Yes." She finished her drink, and he gave her another. "When I finally leave Spain," she said, "I won't have many regrets."

"I know," he said. He also knew that she was saying something else, something to do with them. Did she want him to take her with him? Impossible.

"Well," he said. "Tell me all about this official reception. It sounds terribly interesting."

———

It was 9 p.m. when Bryan entered the room. "Hello, Steve," he said. "You get into a scrape? You look done in."

183

ODDS ON

Jencks made an irritable grunting noise, and said, "You're not exactly fresh yourself, Romeo. I could store walnuts in those bags under your eyes."

"Women," Bryan sighed, dropping into a chair. "Devastating creatures, in every sense of the word. Was it the blond?"

Jencks nodded.

"Well, it's one way to stay fit, I suppose. She looked like a vigorous sparring partner."

"Are we going to exchange reminiscences?" Jencks asked.

"No," Bryan replied. "I got the information about the cops, and—"

Miguel burst into the room. He was dressed in bathing trunks and a baggy terry cloth bathrobe. His trunks were still wet. A rolled towel was under his arm. "Ah," he said, "the pleasures of a quick dip before bed." He tossed the towel on the bed, and it unrolled to reveal five sticks of dynamite. From his pockets, he withdrew the timers and blasting caps, which he treated more respectfully, setting them down gently on the writing table. "All there, ready to go. I brought along an extra cap, just in case." He glanced over at Bryan and Jencks. "Well, you two are certainly dead-looking. Steamroller, or dames?"

"Dames," Jencks said wearily. "Sit down. Just watching your energy is tiring."

Miguel produced his list of rooms, handed it to Jencks, and sat on the bed.

"Not on the bed. You're dripping wet." Miguel clucked good-naturedly, as if amused by some private thought, and moved to a chair. He looked at Jencks, who had collected Bryan's list and was checking the two lists against the master sheet. The room was quiet. The others waited tensely while Jencks made the final tabulation.

ODDS ON

"Sixty-three rooms," Jencks said, his voice triumphant. "Good, solid odds."

The tension in the room eased. Bryan and Miguel lit cigarettes.

"About the police," Bryan said.

"I found out about them," Miguel said. "There's a bigwig party here tomorrow."

"What time?" Jencks asked. This was crucial. If it were to be held at night, they would have to postpone the operation. It wouldn't do to be stranded on an island with a small police force.

"Afternoon," Bryan said. "Three to seven. Then they all move off to Barcelona or Tossa or someplace."

"It's being held in the small dining room," Miguel said.

"All right," Jencks said. "Then we proceed as planned." He went to his closet, bringing out the pack of Chesterfields. He handed them to Bryan. "You want to review the priming technique again?"

"No. I've got it."

"Okay. Then there's nothing left to do but give you the keys." He dug in his pocket and produced two bunches. He handed one bunch to each man, then returned to the desk and made out two lists. "These are the rooms you can skip as you make your rounds," Jencks said. "Memorize the lists tonight, and then burn them. They're on a special paper that leaves practically no ash."

They took the lists. Jencks examined the dynamite and blasting caps. He held one up, a small plastic tube with a metal tip and two fine wires leading out. "How are these rated?"

"Fifteen grains of fulminating powder," Miguel said. "They'll set off anything."

"And the sticks are fresh?"

185

ODDS ON

"Yes."

"All right." He looked at them both. "Any final questions?"

"I'd like to go over the canceling procedure again," Miguel said.

"Three steps," Jencks said, holding up his fingers. "I am the only person who can cancel the project. If something goes wrong, I'll telephone Bryan on the hotel phone and say I can't meet him for dinner, but would he be agreeable to drinks in the bar. If I mention the word 'bar,' it means the operation is off, and we are to meet in my room immediately. If I say anything else, it means the operation is off and stay the hell away from me. Got it?"

"Yes," Miguel said.

"When Bryan gets the call, he will telephone you and say something that will sound logical to the switchboard operator who may be listening in. Again, the key word will be 'bar.' If it is mentioned, get to my room as fast as you can. If it isn't mentioned, dump anything you've collected in a trash can in the hall and play stupid for the next day or so."

Miguel nodded.

"Just remember, no calls means no cancellations. And you can rest assured that I am very unlikely to call it off. This thing is sure-fire, wedding reception or not. We can't slip, we can't lose, we can't miss."

He handed them the rubber sacs and two pairs of nylon gloves. Miguel left the room. Bryan checked his watch, waiting out the thirty seconds before he, too, would leave.

"Get some sleep, Bryan," Jencks said.

"You said that before," Bryan said, smiling. "Better take your own advice. Big day tomorrow, and you're in a position to lose some fingers."

Jencks smiled too, remembering how busy his fingers

ODDS ON

had been that afternoon. Bryan left the room, and Jencks was alone with his thoughts. Jenny had been difficult when he had told her she couldn't spend the night with him; she had been more difficult when he had been vague about meeting her the next day. But it couldn't be helped. He shook his head. He was very tired. And Bryan was right. Tomorrow would be a big day.

SATURDAY MORNING, JUNE TWENTY-FIRST

Jencks rolled over and looked at his watch. It was 7 a.m. He could still get another hour of sleep if he wanted it, but he wasn't sleepy. Nor, he reflected, was he tired. His excitement was fresh, without any hint of nervous tension. That was good. He climbed out of bed and went over to the timers—a pair of small aluminum boxes, each the size of a paperback book. He picked up one and slid back the cover, exposing the workings—two dials, and banks of button-shaped mercury batteries. One dial was a miniature galvanometer, which recorded the battery charge; the other was the face of an Omega wristwatch chronometer, extremely accurate, which provided the clockwork mechanism for the timers.

He wound the watch ahead by hand until contact was made. The galvanometer needle jumped. The device was in perfect working order. Rapidly, he ran through the same procedure with the second timer; again, the galvanometer indicated a satisfactory flow of current. But then, he thought it should. These timers were of his own design, made up by a little machine shop in Reno which specialized in odd jobs for hobbyists and amateur inventors. The owners of the shop hadn't batted an eye when Jencks had presented them with his plans. He had explained that they were for his home toaster and coffeemaker—he wanted them to turn on automatically in the morning. The owners had praised the ingenuity of his designs and questioned the advisability of making a unit so small and accurate, since it raised the cost, but that was all.

Toast and coffee sounded good to him now. He dressed quickly, and went downstairs for breakfast.

———

Characteristically, Miguel arose and shaved without once considering the job he was going to begin. He had the ability to live entirely in the present, with no thought for the future, no fears and no imaginings. Besides, he had a miserable hangover which puffed his eyes and pounded his head. He had gotten quite drunk the night before, after the meeting broke up.

He cut himself shaving and swore loudly, releasing a torrent of profanity. It made him feel a little better; his head seemed to clear slightly. Encouraged, he lit his first cigarette of the day and stared at the bleary-eyed face in the mirror. A degenerate bastard, he thought, but not deteriorating yet. There were a few good years left. He dabbed at his cheek with the styptic pencil and swore again as the stinging began.

———

Bryan shifted uneasily in his bed. He was passing trucks on a highway, weaving in and out among them in a little green sports car. Each time he passed one, he sighed with relief, and felt happy that at last he had the road to himself. And as he came over each hill, there was another truck to be dealt with. His was the only car on the road; otherwise there were only trucks moving in both directions. As time went on, he grew exasperated with the tiresome routine of slowing down, peeping around the rear wheels of the truck, gauging the road ahead, and pulling out just as the truck changed gears and discharged a great stinking cloud of exhaust.

His exasperation led him to take chances. He began to pass on hills and curves. He began to cut things very fine, often just avoiding being crushed between an oncoming truck and the one he was passing. His safety margin decreased each time. Every new maneuver was more risky than the last; he wanted to stop, but he was compelled by his frustration at sitting behind the creeping trucks, breathing their black exhaust. And so he continued to pass, knowing that sooner or later there would be an accident. There always was.

He woke up sweating. It was the same dream he had had, off and on, for months now. It was the same each time he dreamed it, horrible and realistic. Shivering, he got up and went into the bathroom. He took a hot, soothing shower. By breakfast, he had forgotten all about the dream.

———

Miss Elizabeth Shaw hopped out of bed and walked briskly to the window. She stared up at the clouds and frowned. It really did not look like a good day. Not at all. Nasty dark clouds were forming to the east, and the sun seemed weak-willed and fluctuating. Undoubtedly, it would rain; the only question was when. She hoped the weather would hold until evening. All these people cooped up inside a hotel could be ghastly, and they would make a terrible racket. Rain never seemed to dampen anyone's enthusiasm for making noise in hotel rooms. She sighed as she thought of the din the brats next door would raise. There were three of them, little French devils with cherubic faces and nimble, noise-making hands. And the walls of these new hotels were paper thin. Not like the good old days, when people made a building to last and to give a little privacy.

Still sighing, she began peeling a banana. Her supply was running low. She would have to see that charming girl about it.

———

"Jenny!"

Slowly, she opened her eyes.

"Where were you yesterday afternoon?"

"Oh, it's you, Peter." She burrowed under the pillow. Why couldn't he leave her alone? He knew she hated to lock her door. He was taking advantage of her. Besides, she had had to leave it unlocked last night, in case Steve came to her in the middle of the night.

"I'm serious, Jenny. Come out of there. I want to talk to you."

"Go away," she said, her voice muffled by the pillow.

"You keep saying that. Pretty soon," he said, lowering his voice ominously, "I'll do it. Where will you be then? In the arms of that gross disgusting boxer. I really don't know what you see in him. He's repulsive."

Jenny brought her head out and looked at him. Her eyes were relaxed, almost bored. "Peter," she said, yawning, "you are a jackass."

He recoiled, as if slapped. "Well, if that's the way you feel about it, I'll leave. That's all, just leave. Here and now. Goodbye."

He stepped to the door. She watched him impassively. He was aware of a change in her, a new disturbing lack of interest in him. He didn't seem to exist, for her. He stopped, his hand on the door. "Are you really serious?"

"Yes." She stretched happily, acting as if he were already gone.

"How can you go for somebody like that? Somebody that coarse, and rough, and . . . and—"

"Peter," she said, "he's a man."

He threw out his chest. "And I'm not?"

"No. Sorry."

"Well then, the hell with you."

He left, slamming the door behind him, but he still heard her laughter in his ears.

———

Smoking a fat cigar and trying not to gag on the smoke, Steven Jencks nodded politely to the girl at the desk, and stepped outside for his morning constitutional. By now, he knew, the staff of the hotel was accustomed to him; each morning he strode briskly out of the lobby and headed across the bridge, puffing on a particularly expensive and foul-smelling cigar. He would cause no comment today.

He crossed the bridge, hearing his feet make hollow sounds on the road. Thirty feet below, the water lapped and sucked at the jagged rocks. He glanced anxiously at the sky. Clouds hung low in the east, and the air had a damp, foreboding quality. Storms blew up quickly on the Costa Brava, even in summer, and he had taken that into account when doing his computer work. Using meteorological records for the past five years, he had determined that the chances were one in seven that the day of the robbery would be overcast; one in nine that it would be overcast and below seventy degrees; one in eleven that it would rain part of the day; one in fourteen that it would rain hard and continuously. Those were chances that you had to take.

Jencks had checked weather reports for the day, and they predicted rain beginning early Sunday morning. That would be all right. In fact, it would be ideal.

He left the bridge and continued along the road, walking with a jaunty stride. As soon as he was out of sight of the hotel, he tossed aside his cigar with a grimace. They really were disgusting things. His eyes followed the telephone and electric lines which ran along the road. Two days earlier, he had spotted the perfect pole for his job. It was a good fifteen minutes from the hotel, set into the ground at the base of a wooded hill. Trees partially screened it from the road, and that was useful; it would not do for anyone to drive by and notice a tourist fiddling with the wires at the top of a telephone pole.

He reached the place and unbuckled his belt. It was an unusual belt, with holes for the buckle near the center, as well as at the tip. When he was wearing it, nobody would notice that it was actually twice as large as it should be. Using its full length, he passed it around the pole, and rebuckled the belt at the tip. Then he began to climb, getting a sufficient grip on the wood with his heavy crepe-soled shoes. The pole was rough hewn, like most in Spain, and not smooth like American telephone poles. That was to his advantage. He had packed a pair of light track shoes—field shoes, actually, with longer spikes—just in case, but his preliminary inspection on Tuesday had indicated that they would not be necessary.

It took only a few moments to shinny to the top. There were two cables, one for the seven telephone lines the hotel maintained, and the other for all the electric needs of the Reina. Both were held away from the wood by crude, heavy, ceramic insulators. He taped one charge around the two insulators, delicately fixed the blasting cap, and set the timer for 12:48. Then he taped the timer to the pole and attached it by the two wires to the blasting cap. After a final check to make sure that all the components were firmly in place, he slid down to the ground, freed his belt, and readjusted it around his waist.

He checked his watch. Nine minutes for the operation from start to finish. He had estimated eleven; it was nice to see that he had been overcautious. It was not twenty-five minutes since he had walked out of the hotel lobby. On previous days, he had been gone an average of fifty-five minutes. Plenty of time. He walked slowly back down the road.

A casual observer, watching from the hotel, would have seen Mr. Jencks returning with a happy smile on his face. He was obviously a man who liked the outdoors, who enjoyed "taking the air." But he was also passionately interested in flowers; the doorman, for instance, had once engaged in quite a long conversation with Mr. Jencks on the varieties of wildflowers and when they blossomed. Mr. Jencks seemed quite knowledgeable, and there was no denying that he was observant. Always stopping to sniff a flower here and there, always noticing little things.

And so, it would not have surprised the doorman to see Mr. Jencks pause as he reached the bridge and look down toward the water with great interest. A few moments later, Mr. Jencks was scrambling down to the water; when he returned, he was carrying a bunch of blood-red poppies which he seemed very pleased with. The maid knew, if anyone cared to ask her, that Mr. Jencks always kept fresh flowers in his room. He was that kind of man.

Actually, Jencks had left a reddish-brown, earth-colored package from one of the inner pockets of his raincoat beneath the bridge. That had been his purpose in going down; he had picked the flowers as an afterthought.

He brandished them cheerfully before the doorman as he went inside. He found Alan Brady at the reception desk, checking out.

"Hi, baby," Brady said. "How's the boy?"

"Fine. Do I get your room now?"

"You know it. She's all yours, and I hope you use it in good health. Hell of a bed," he added.

Brady paid his bill, and walked with Jencks back out to the traffic circle. He noticed the flowers.

"What're you doing with them?"

"Giving them to a girl."

"That's not all you're giving her, I hope." He laughed coarsely. Jencks was relieved to see he slapped his own knee this time, not Jencks's.

A car, a little Hillman convertible, pulled up in front of the door. The skinny man from Barcelona was driving. Jencks talked with Brady while the porter loaded the bags into the trunk. Then he stuck out his hand.

"Have a good trip," Jencks said.

"Thanks, thanks. Enjoy the rest of your vacation, baby. And remember to eat regular—keeps your strength up for flower picking."

With a final laugh, he got in the car, and the little man put it in gear. A last wave of a heavy red hand, and they were gone, across the bridge, out of sight.

Jencks went back inside to the desk, and noticed that the receptionist was looking unusually radiant. He'd have to mention that to Bryan.

"I would like to rent an aqualung," he said.

"Yes, of course. Would you like it now?"

"After lunch, I think. Say about two, when I've given my food a fighting chance. Can that be managed?"

"It will be ready at the sea-bathing pier."

"Where the sign is?"

"That's right. You want the regulator as well as the tank?"

"The whole works." He watched her record his name and the time on a slip of paper, and drop it onto a pile of outgoing messages. "Thanks very much."

"Don't mention it."

Still carrying his poppies, he stepped into the elevator and went to his room. Once there, he threw out yesterday's flowers and put the new bunch into the glass which he used as a vase. They added a pleasant touch of color to the light gray neutrality of the room, he thought, as he stepped back to survey them. Jencks felt extra little touches were important.

———

Peter looked up and saw Jencks enter the dining room and sit at a table at the far end of the room.

"I just don't see it," he said under his breath. She was a bitch, he thought. She had never intended to sleep with him; she just enjoyed tormenting him. That was why she had chosen the ugliest man in the hotel to go to bed with. It was a deliberate, carefully planned insult.

ODDS ON

The hell with her.

He watched as Jencks gave his order and then got up to go to the buffet table of *hors d'oeuvres*. He moved like a jock, Peter thought, a hulking insensitive chunk of meat. Three jocks lived in his entry at Eliot House—big loutish football jocks, all of them practically on probation, who drank beer every night and fingered adoring girls and took gut courses in Social Relations. Everyone knew that Social Relations was the jock field; the courses were geared to their brains.

And the girls. The way those girls would scream and giggle at the parties, the way they would throw themselves at a guy just because he trotted around with a big number on his back. Peter just didn't see it, himself.

It was hero worship, that's all, a quirk of the culture, that made brutes more attractive. The more beat-up, the more cuts on their faces and cleat marks on their shins, the better the girls liked it. It was unnatural.

Jencks returned to his table with a plate of appetizers, and Peter's attention shifted to the spic who had entered the dining room. What was his name? Mickey, or something like that.

Peter couldn't be sure he was a spic, but he certainly looked it, with his slightly oily dark skin and dark hair. And there was something Latin about his features, too.

He recalled the girl that the spic had introduced him to, the one who had fallen asleep while he was explaining the thesis he planned to write on mysticism in George Eliot. She looked like a spic, too, though he had to admit she excited him. He would have willingly planked her, if she hadn't fallen asleep. That had been too much. Every man had his pride, Peter thought, pouring himself another glass of wine.

He decided, quite suddenly, that he would leave Jenny.

He would leave tomorrow, in the morning, and not even call her before he went. If she wanted to find him, she could get herself to Barcelona and look him up there. And maybe he'd be nice to her when she arrived. Maybe.

In his mind, he created a poignant, slightly sadistic and very satisfactory reunion scene. When he was finished with her, she was dissolved in tears.

AFTERNOON, JUNE TWENTY-FIRST

Jencks grunted as he slipped the heavy cold tank on his back. The crew-cut, blond American who acted as lifeguard, beach-boy, and propman looked concerned. "Too tight around the shoulders?"

"I think so," Jencks said.

"Tilt your head back. Can you feel the regulator? Yes, you touch it. I'll set the tank lower." He adjusted the straps so that the pressurized cylinder rested farther down on Jencks's spine. Again, Jencks leaned his head back, but this time did not feel the metal of the regulator against the base of his skull.

"You're okay now," the American said. He flipped the hoses over Jencks's shoulders, so the mouthpiece rested on his chest. Then he pointed to the remaining canvas straps hanging down from the tank harness. "That goes around your waist, and hooks to the third strap which passes under your crotch. Make it as tight as is comfortable. I'll get you a weight belt." He looked at Jencks critically. "You float easily?"

"I sink like a stone."

The American nodded. Jencks's big frame was all muscle,

no fat. "I'll just get you enough to overcome the buoyancy of the tank. What's your shoe size?"

"Eleven."

He returned with a belt, a mask, and a pair of flippers. "Dip your feet in the water and try these." Jencks did; they fit. He took the mask, rinsed it in the water, then spit into it and rubbed the saliva over the inside surface of the glass. That prevented condensation and fogging. He rinsed the mask again and pulled it over his eyes and nose. The rubber strap tugged against his hair.

He placed the mouthpiece between his teeth and tasted hot rubber. The American reached behind Jencks and turned on the air. There was a momentary hiss as the regulator adjusted; then Jencks took a few experimental breaths. The air was cool, clean, and dry.

"Okay?"

Jencks nodded and stepped carefully to the edge of the concrete pier. He felt top-heavy and clumsy from the extra weight and the flippers on his feet. The American helped him down the steps to the water's edge.

"You've got an hour at one atmosphere," he said. "That's any depth up to thirty-three feet. If you go deeper, there's less time."

Jencks listened politely. He knew all this; though he had never dived with a lung, he had read every book he could find on the subject, including the authoritative manual of the U.S. Navy. He knew that the pressure doubled by one atmosphere of pressure—14.7 pounds per square inch—every thirty-three feet, so that at sixty-six feet, the tank would have only a half-hour supply, and at ninety-nine feet, just fifteen minutes of air. He knew the decompression tables, though decompression was unnecessary with a single tank. He knew about the dangers, the air embolisms and the attacks of nitrogen narcosis. None of it

ODDS ON

was particularly relevant to what he was doing, but he preferred to have the information anyway.

"Go in backward," the American advised. "Squat down and fall in on your back. The tank will break surface for you, and the water's deep enough. Bend your neck forward, and hold the mask tight against your face with your hand—otherwise it'll tear free."

Jencks squatted at the edge of the pier with his back to the water. He balanced himself, then rocked back on his heels, and fell into the cold sea. Silver bubbles gurgled around him. Twenty feet below was the rocky bottom, strewn with large boulders. Seaweed waved back and forth in the gentle current, and he heard the minute clicking of crabs as they ate. Otherwise, it was quiet. He began to breathe.

The noise of the regulator, and his exhaled air fluttering to the surface, seemed terribly loud at first. It made a rhythmic, rasping sound as he kicked gently downward. He followed the underwater outline of the island—the island on which the Reina was built—to the bottom, and there paused to clear his ears. He swallowed hard, and felt the pain ease. He swam through a school of fish, small ones with blue fluorescent spines. The fish did not seem to mind him; in fact, they were curious about his bubbles. He kicked lazily, his arms at his sides. He passed crabs, brilliant red starfish, and sea anemones clinging to the rock. He continued on, close to the bottom, feeling the sea grass tickle his chest, feeling the wet canvas straps which held the tank to his back.

He noticed an octopus several yards out to sea. It was large, at least 15 pounds, and a dull gray. It moved over the rocks quickly, its bulbous head looking like a ball of slime as the tentacles stretched forward, then contracted. It was incredibly, repulsively ugly, especially in contrast to the fish which swam with such smooth coordination around it.

201

The water grew shallower as he came around the island, and soon up ahead he saw the first of the concrete supports for the bridge. He was surprised by its delicacy—but then, it was not a very large bridge, perhaps fifty or sixty feet long.

A few rays of light played across the bottom. Jencks paused at the first stanchion and looked toward the surface, twenty feet above. The concrete ran straight up and disappeared in a ring of bubbles where it broke the surface. He looked across the bottom, and saw three other pillars. It took only a moment to orient himself; he swam to another pylon, kicked up, and broke into the early afternoon sunlight. A few yards away, on the mainland shore, he spotted his package.

He looked around for an easy way to get out of the water and finally found it. Even so, he spent a good minute grunting and slipping on the rocks before he was able to stand up and release the harness of the tank. He eased it off his shoulders and shut the air valve. It felt good to have the weight off his back, he thought, as he sat down and pulled the flippers from his feet. He leaned back for a moment, and allowed the sun to dry him. It wouldn't do to drip all over the explosives.

It was quiet down there alongside the bridge; he heard the sound of a band playing, and people cheering and clapping. The reception was in full swing. Although he was hidden from the view of anyone at the hotel, Jencks knew that there were two policeman flanking the doorman, and that at any time, one of them might decide to stroll out toward the bridge. That would be disastrous; he would probably be shot on the spot.

He pushed the thought from his mind, straightened, and rubbed his hands in dirt, to make sure his fingers were dry. When he was satisfied, he turned to the package wrapped in brown paper which he had left during his walk that morning. Opening it, he took out four sticks of dynamite, the caps, the

ODDS ON

timer, and several coils of wire. He stepped into the shadow of the bridge and looked for the points.

There were seven points, each a critical construction junction necessary for the support of the structure. From his examination of the blueprints, he knew which two to hit. He took two sticks and clambered up the hillside to the place where the bridge met the mainland. He placed the dynamite and the caps in a few moments, then returned to the package.

Now came the hard part. He climbed back up to the roadway, and, holding on to the understructure of the bridge, swung out over the water. He held the explosives and timer in a small sack between his teeth. It reminded him of his childhood, when he played on the monkey bars in the school playground. His muscles strained, and he was glad it was no more than a few yards to the point where one pylon met the road. He clamped his legs around a diagonal strut and proceeded to wire the sticks to the bridge.

Above his head, a car rumbled across the roadway. The noise and vibration startled him; it all seemed terribly near.

The car stopped. Jencks caught his breath.

The roadway was made of slatted planks, with a half-inch gap between them. Anyone who was interested or suspicious could look right down and see him. He waited, tense.

A woman's voice, harshly unattractive, said in French, "What's the problem?"

A door opened, then slammed shut. Jencks heard footsteps walking around the car. "Did you remember to pack my razor?" Another sound—the trunk opening.

"Yes, Henri, I am sure I did."

"I'll just check." Two sharp clicks as the latches of a suitcase came open.

"Henri, let's go on. I'm quite certain I packed it."

ODDS ON

"I'll just make sure."

"You're being impossible."

"And who left that nightgown in Granada? The one I gave you for our anniversary?"

"That was a mistake. One mistake. Anyone's entitled to a mistake."

"We had to go back for it. Two hundred kilometers, each way."

"Henri, *sois gentil!*"

Two more clicks. The trunk closed with a muffled thud.

"There," said the woman, "what did I tell you?"

The car door opened, then closed. "I just wanted to check."

"Henri, why don't you have any confidence—"

The rest was lost as the car rumbled across the bridge and up the mainland road. Jencks sighed and returned to his work. He set the timer, taped it to the pylon itself, and added the wires from the dynamite. Then he attached two more wires, which would run from the timer to the other explosives at the edge of the road. Swinging back was hard; he had to pause twice and hang by one arm while he wrapped the wires around the understructure with his free hand. Fortunately, he was naturally strong, and his strength had been built up by patient exercises over the past five weeks. When he finally reached the mainland and made the final connections, he was hardly panting.

For a moment, he surveyed the job. It was good; the wires didn't show, and no casual eye would spot the two bundles of charges. Now, at last, everything was ready.

He returned to the aqualung and shrugged into it. The straps were wet, making it more difficult, but he was soon back in the water. He held the wrapping paper, now a soggy mass, clenched in one fist. He took it down forty feet and set it beneath a small rock. Eventually, it would find its way to the surface, but only as unrecognizable shreds of pulp.

He felt a certain tingle of excitement at the knowledge that the project would now proceed irrevocably to conclusion. Technically, of course, that was a disadvantage; he had at one time considered detonating the charges by radio control, since this would allow him to cancel the firings at the last minute. It fitted better the model of the "criterion of regret." But in the end, he had chosen the timers, which had the virtue of greater simplicity, and which eliminated the fear that some ham radio operator would accidentally set off the explosives in the middle of the day.

He moved out to deeper water and headed for the bottom. The colors blended into a dark green, then turned grayer. He was quite deep now. He swam slowly, waiting for his oxygen to run out. It was only a matter of minutes before his breathing became labored; he reached back and pulled the rod of the reserve air supply, and, drawing steadily on the air, kicked toward the surface.

———

Bryan looked up and down the corridor, then stepped into the room. This was where the pimple-faced kid was staying; he looked with distaste at the disordered mess of collegiate paraphernalia—a gray sweatshirt, with "Harvard" stenciled in red; a nylon windbreaker, lying rumpled on the bed next to a paperback copy of *Live and Let Die*, the button-down shirts with dirty collars, and the faded dungarees. He paused for a moment, fixing the position of each object in his mind. He flexed his hands, feeling the gloves taut against his fingers. Then, quickly and thoroughly, he began his search.

———

ODDS ON

"Steve!"

He stopped. Jenny ran over to him from her chair by the pool. She looked bright and happy.

"I haven't seen you all day."

"I've been around," he said. "Just took a dive with an aqualung. Ever tried it?" She shook her head. "They're terrific."

"I know something better," she said.

She waited patiently, and he knew what she wanted. This was ticklish; he had been evasive the day before, but now he would be forced to spend some time with her. Any unwillingness on his part might seem strange to her the next day, when everyone in the hotel would be thinking back over the people they had met since their arrival.

"How about a drink and dinner?" he asked.

"I was hoping you'd ask. But isn't it a little early for a cocktail?"

"We might think of some way to fill the time," he said.

She grinned. She was wearing a bikini today, and her white stomach had turned a light pink. But she looked stunning, lush and full, straining the cloth around her breasts and hips.

"Come up to my room."

"Said the spider to the fly," she said.

He smiled, a plan forming in his mind. He could not afford to knock himself out in the sack as he had the previous afternoon. Well, he thought, today she would work for it. She would do it with pleasure—enough pleasure for both of them.

They went to the elevator.

"I saw Peter today," she said.

"And?"

"He's leaving, I think. He seemed very angry." She did not appear concerned, but it was clear what she was leading up to. Peter had brought her here; now who would take her away?

ODDS ON

"Jenny," he said, "I think we shouldn't allow this to go too far. When I leave here, I'm scheduled to go to Rome on business."

"That's all right. I wouldn't bother you, and I have plenty of money of my own. Really, I wouldn't be a bother."

"We'll both have to consider it," he said doubtfully. Rome was going to be a busy time for him. It would be inconvenient to have to disguise his activities from her, and there was always the chance that she would penetrate his disguise. His masquerade as a computer expert was, after all, shallow.

"Please take me with you," she said.

"We'll discuss it."

They entered his room, and she sat down on the bed. He went into the bathroom and took a hot shower. When he came out, she was still sitting there, with a funny look on her face.

"Something the matter?"

"I was just wondering . . . no, nothing wrong." She stood, and walked toward him, running her arms around his neck. "Help me out of this thing, would you?"

He reached behind her, and unfastened the snap to her halter. She shrugged it away, and dropped it to the floor. Her breasts stood firm and magnificent. She pressed them against his chest.

"The job's only half done."

His hands went down to her brief triangle, and in a moment, she was naked. She stepped back and walked around him, enjoying his eyes as they took in her breasts, her small waist, and the glorious hips. Above each buttock was a small indentation, like a dimple; he had not noticed that before.

She lay on the bed and stretched. "We can try some variations," she said, "if you're interested." She looked at his body. "I see you're interested."

She was right, Jencks thought, as he lay alongside her. He was very, very interested.

———

Miguel turned the key in the lock. Nothing happened. Son of a bitch, he thought. He withdrew the key, examined it, and tried another. This time he heard the mechanism click. The door swung open.

That was the second time he had used the wrong key. Mistakes like that, which left you fumbling in the hallway outside somebody else's door, were dangerous. He would have to watch it.

He turned his attention to the room, which smelled strongly of Chanel No. 5. Mr. and Mrs. LaBarre were here; he was the gaunt one with the hook nose, and she was the witch who insisted on wearing a bikini even though her fat, flabby body bulged disgustingly over her suit. The vanity of women, he thought. He looked at each piece of furniture in turn—the table, the dresser, the beds—memorizing the objects on them, and their positions. When he was satisfied, he began his search.

Outside, thunder rolled ominously. It startled and disturbed him. That storm had been brewing all day. He hoped it wouldn't break just yet, driving everyone inside to their rooms. He still had lots of work before dinner.

NIGHT,
JUNE TWENTY-FIRST

After dinner, Jencks excused himself, pleading fatigue, and left Jenny in the reading room, thumbing through French fashion magazines. He went out to the lobby.

"Enjoy your swim, Mr. Jencks?" It was the receptionist. She was looking quite radiant. Something going on with that girl, he thought.

He stepped into the elevator, and pushed the fourth floor button. Fortunately, there was no elevator boy on duty. As he was carried up, he withdrew a key from his pocket and inserted it in the elevator lock. When the box stopped at the fourth floor, he opened the door and looked into the hallway. Nobody in sight. He turned the key in the lock, shutting off the elevator. Then he bent the tab of the key, breaking it off and leaving the tongue in the lock. Removing a small, battery-powered heating coil from his pocket, he pressed it to the lock. When he withdrew it, he could see the metal of the key, melted inside the mechanism. The key had been made of Wood's metal, an alloy of tin and lead with an extremely low melting point. It was the same metal the French used to cap their wine bottles.

ODDS ON

Satisfied that the elevator would remain inoperable for at least two days, he walked quickly down the stairs to the second floor and entered his room to change clothes. The elevator jamming was not an essential part of the scheme; he had thought of it as a sort of petty annoyance which he knew would add greatly to the confusion later that night.

It was now 9:30.

He dressed slowly, giving meticulous attention to details. The tuxedo he put on would not have surprised anyone who did not know Jencks well. It was black, not blue, of custom tailoring, with a slight, almost indiscernible looseness around the left shoulder, and pointed lapels which were rather broader than was the current fashion. Behind one lapel, if anyone cared to check, was a small safety pin. His shoes were not pumps but black wing tips, highly polished, and undistinguished except for their soles, which were rubber, not leather.

Into his hip pocket he stuffed a pair of thin black nylon gloves, and a rather unusual black hood, also of nylon, with two holes for the eyes. Together, they made a small bundle no larger than a pocket handkerchief. He went to his suitcase and found his penlight, which he placed inside his breast pocket. He had no handkerchief.

He surveyed himself in the mirror and was satisfied with the result. He adjusted his bow tie and looked quickly around the room, making a final check.

His eyes stopped at the desk. Lying alongside the Reina engraved stationery and the blotter was a blasting cap, dull black with a silver tip. Damn! How long had that been lying there? How could he have forgotten it? He had taken along enough caps for his explosives.

He sat on the bed to think things out, and finally remembered that Miguel had brought an extra cap, "just in case." That explained it, but he was still unhappy. Jenny had spent nearly three hours in the room with him. Had she noticed it? It seemed unlikely—she would have said something, made some comment, asked a question.

He let out a long sigh, and cursed his own stupidity. That little slip could have been disastrous, and there was too much at stake to make an error now. He looked at his watch again—9:50. In three hours, it would all be over.

———

Bryan sat in a booth in the men's room which adjoined the nightclub. Carefully, he set the timer mechanism in the pack of Chesterfields. It was the work of a few moments, then he dropped it in his pocket, flushed the toilet, and went out to wash his hands. He gave the attendant, an old man who appeared supported by his starched uniform, five pesetas.

He went outside and returned to his corner table. A flamenco guitarist was seated on the low stage, fingers flying and face dripping sweat in the glare of the spotlight. Bryan ignored the show; his attention was held by the woman who was coming over to his table.

"Hello," Annette said. "I hope you don't mind my crashing your party."

"I'm pleased," he said, forcing a smile. "It wasn't a very lively party. But aren't you worried about being seen with a guest?" He kept his voice light, hiding his concern. Sometime soon he would have to get rid of her, at least for a few minutes. He checked his watch—10:30. He didn't want to keep the incendiary in his pocket more than an hour. It was not that he didn't trust the timer, exactly; he just had a vision of it going off with an explosive *whump!*, and turning him into a human torch.

"I'm feeling indiscreet tonight," Annette said, "and anyway, it's a very dark table."

"What will you drink?"

"Anything," she said, lighting a cigarette. The sight of the flame made him nervous.

"Champagne," he decided. He would give her lots of champagne, and pray her bladder was small.

She smiled. "It *is* a party."

He called for the wine list, and ordered a good Spanish vintage.

"Isn't that rather expensive?"

"I'm in a mood to celebrate."

She shifted in her chair, and he heard her cross her nylon-sheathed legs. Annette was wearing a chiffon print blouse, with ruffles at the neck and cuff, and a black silk skirt. Looking at her, he felt a momentary pang of desire. It was the tension and excitement, he knew, of the robbery. He was keyed up, full of nervous energy, almost drowned in his own adrenaline. It wasn't like the old days, when he could have worked his way through a job like this with scarcely a quick heartbeat. He sighed.

"Is something wrong?" she asked.

"No. Flamenco music always makes me sad."

She looked across to the guitarist, as if seeing him for the first time. "It's terribly difficult, I'm told. There are only a few remaining masters, and the art is dying out. An apprenticeship takes years, and when you're finally through, you're still nothing but a cheap performer in a nightclub."

The waiter brought the champagne, and uncorked it with a satisfying pop. They sipped it. "Dry enough for you?"

ODDS ON

"Fine."

"Who's minding the store?"

"The desk? One of the girls. Normally Mr. Bonnard would do it, but he's working in his office."

"Not a very pleasant way to spend Saturday night." Bryan was not worried; the fire would draw him out.

"You said you were in a mood to celebrate," Annette said.

"I am," Bryan said. "This is a special day for me."

"Oh?"

"My birthday."

"Congratulations." She raised her glass in a toast, and drained it. He refilled it.

That's a good girl, he thought, as he watched her bring the glass to her lips again. Drink up, drink up.

———

Looking elegant and unconcerned, Jencks stepped outside into the damp night air and surveyed the pool. It was lighted, and looked inviting, but he was alone; thunder rolled, and he saw the first brief slash of lightning flicker across the sky. He walked to the seaward side of the hotel, to the saltwater pool. There he stopped, took out a cigarette, and flicked his lighter. The flame shot up; startled, he shut it again. He tried a second time, but once again the flame leapt alarmingly high. On the third attempt, he lit the cigarette, and puffed for a moment, looking out at the sea. A careful observer would have noticed that he was not inhaling.

Offshore, in a boat that rocked and tossed in the rising wind, a man known only as Barry observed the Reina through binoculars. He was accustomed to the ocean, and so was able to compensate for the movements of his ship and keep his eyes

213

trained on the hotel. He saw the three brief flares, and checked his watch—11:30. That was the final signal, the last contact he would have before he drew close to the pier at 12:50 to receive the package.

As Barry watched, the first heavy drops of water splattered down. It was going to be a hell of a storm, he thought. He went forward to get his slicker. It was a black slicker; Jencks had specified that. He seemed to think of everything.

———

Feeling tired and depressed, Miguel closed the door softly behind him. He immediately recognized the occupant of this room by its contents—five suitcases, all large, all partially unpacked, an immense heap of bananas, and a vast shelf of cosmetics and powders along one dresser. Must be the little English lady with the nice smile and the hash for sale. Sweet old crook—she'd wanted a fortune for the stuff.

He smiled and went to work. She was bound to have jewels here somewhere.

———

Annette giggled foolishly as the waiter brought the fourth bottle of champagne. "You're trying to get me drunk," she said, in a voice so slurred he could barely understand it

"Not true," he said. He tried to estimate the volume she had drunk in the last hour. At the very least, it was approaching two and a half liters. What was the matter with her? She was like a veteran pub crawler, totally hardened to the call of nature.

The cork popped, interrupting the song of a mediocre singer who was pressing her breasts into the microphone on stage.

ODDS ON

"Cheers," he said, raising his glass.

Annette raised hers and gulped it down greedily.

"Ummmm," she said, closing her eyes. "Ummmm."

He refilled her glass. It seemed he had spent the whole evening refilling her glass.

"Again?" She regarded the bubbles thoughtfully, and bent down to listen to them. "They're saying something," she said.

"What are they saying?"

"That you're a wicked man who wants to get little girls drunk."

"Never. Cheers."

Again, they raised their glasses; again, she downed hers in a series of noisy swallows.

"I've had a lot," she said.

"Yes?" he asked, hopefully.

"So you better give me more."

He smiled weakly. "With pleasure." Bryan was acutely aware of the Chesterfields in his pocket. It was now almost midnight. He had to get rid of the thing, and soon.

"Nice champagne," Annette said, "very, very nice. But I have something to tell you."

He looked over at her. She was swaying back and forth on her chair.

"It's time," she said. "Where is it?"

"To the left, through the red door."

Without another word, she got up and walked off. He heaved a sigh of relief, reached into his pocket and tossed the Chesterfields into the corner. It landed next to the draperies with a dull thud. Nobody looked over; nobody heard. The singer was singing something about wet Paris streets. She seemed sad.

Bryan hoped Miguel would get to Jencks with the news;

it was distressing, something he was not sure about. Well, no matter. The operation would be completed now, no matter what. He couldn't worry about little things.

He checked his watch again. It was midnight. In less than an hour, it would be all over.

SUNDAY MORNING, JUNE TWENTY-SECOND (12:00-1:00 A.M.)

At 12:35, Jencks walked out of the reading room, where he had been glancing through month-old issues of *Life* and *Look*. As he entered the lobby, he met Miguel.

"Look," Miguel said, "I've got to talk to you."

"Not here," Jencks hissed. "Not now."

"Listen, it's—"

"Save it. Get back to work."

He walked to the door, and stood with the doorman. They talked for several minutes about the rain, which was now falling in heavy sheets. The wind was high, and the doorman said that the sea was acting up; the skiff might tear loose from the mooring. The doorman had heard Mr. Bonnard, the manager, send someone to check on it.

Anyway, it was the doorman's opinion that the entire hotel might as well wash away in the storm. With all due respect to the clients, it wasn't worth a damn. Did Mr. Jencks know that the elevator was broken again? Jencks said he'd heard about it. Well, the doorman knew that it had broken down three times before in the past year. Junk, that was what the Reina was. Shoddy from start to finish. With all due respect, sir.

When Jencks left the man, he was still ranting. A taxi was just pulling up into the traffic circle.

He walked across the lobby to the phone booth and stepped inside. The light went on as he shut the door. He reached up and unscrewed the bulb, throwing the booth into darkness. He folded the lapels of his jacket over, covering his white shirt, and clipped them shut with the safety pin. Then he brought out his hood and pulled it over his head; finally, he slipped on his thin black gloves. He was now dressed entirely in black. He sat patiently, waiting. He did not look at his watch—there was no need to.

———

Jean-Paul, sitting alone at the nightclub bar with his Cutty Sark and water, listened absently to the fat horse onstage mumbling her bad French. Suddenly, there was a loud *whoosh* as if a window had blown open. He looked over and saw that one wall of the nightclub was a sheet of flame. People were leaping up from their tables; chairs scraped and were knocked back; women screamed.

He grabbed a passing waiter. "Where's the fire extinguisher?" The waiter was shocked, almost speechless. His lips moved but nothing came out. Jean-Paul shook him. "Where is it?"

"There," he finally managed to say, "by the toilets."

The room was a madhouse. The singer, like an old trouper, insisted on continuing her song, but nobody was calmed by her efforts. A woman fainted. People ran everywhere. Somebody smashed a window in an effort to escape, but that only made

ODDS ON

it worse—a strong wind fanned the flames, which now curled around the ceiling.

Jean-Paul jumped off his stool and pushed through the chaos of furniture and people. It was slow business, but he kept his eyes fixed on the red cylinder hanging next to the bathroom door. Why hadn't the staff already gotten to it? Black smoke stung his eyes; his shoes crunched on broken glass.

At that moment, he saw Mr. Bonnard burst into the room, knocking people aside with amazing strength and remarkable lack of tact. He was shouting something to the headwaiter, who seemed suddenly to come to his senses and run for the extinguisher.

At that moment, all the lights in the room went out.

———

Jencks stepped out of the phone booth and pressed his back to the wall. It was pitch black in the lobby; the girl behind the desk was screaming hysterically. He would have to hurry. At any minute, she would come to her senses and strike a match.

He took seven measured steps straight ahead, turned a careful right angle, and paced off three more strides. Stretching his hand forward, he touched a wall. People, running and shouting, brushed against him. He smelled heavy, sooty smoke.

He moved cautiously along the wall. There were more people in the lobby now. Several collided with him, but continued on. There was so much confusion, none of them would remember later. He felt the edge of a closed door, and ran his hand up and down, feeling for the knob. No knob. Must be the wrong side—yes, he felt the hinges.

The door was three feet wide. One pace. He felt another

crack, and then his hand gripped the knob. Mr. Bonnard's office. Locked.

He reached in his pocket and withdrew the key. A moment later he was inside, the door shut behind him. Only now did he dare flick on his pencil flashlight. Its narrow beam illuminated the clutter of letters and forms he had seen that morning. A half-eaten sandwich lay alongside.

He moved around behind the desk and opened the closet door. Then he heard a key scratching in the lock. Quickly, he stepped into the closet, held his breath, and prayed.

The door opened. Mr. Bonnard entered, breathing heavily, a candle in his hand. The yellow flicker dimly lit the room. Outside, he could hear screams and running feet. Mr. Bonnard was alone, swearing softly to himself in German between gasping breaths.

Mr. Bonnard went to his desk and began rummaging through all the drawers. Jencks watched tensely; the closet door was ajar, and although he was dressed in black, Mr. Bonnard had only to look closely and Jencks would be seen.

Mr. Bonnard continued to mutter, to rummage. He was forced to work one-handed, the other gripped the candle. Finally, he gave a little grunt of satisfaction and produced two flashlights. He checked them quickly. One worked, the other didn't. He threw the faulty one back in the drawer and straightened up to go.

He hesitated for a moment, casting the beam of the flashlight around the room, frowning suspiciously. Then, abruptly, he left, shutting the door behind him.

Like a shadow, Jencks stepped out and bent to the safe. His fingers ran over the crackle-gray surface of the metal. He twirled the dial expertly.

Outside, he heard Mr. Bonnard bellowing like a wounded

ODDS ON

buffalo. He paid no attention; his attention was centered on his fingertips, spinning the dial gently. Right, then left . . . right, finally left . . . The heavy door swung open.

Eagerly, he flashed his light inside.

He could not believe his eyes.

———

The cab driver slammed his doors and shoved the car into first gear. He roared off, around the circle and across the bridge. It was a snap, he thought: the easiest 5,000 pesetas he had ever made.

———

Barry, drawing his boat up to the water-skiing dock, saw all the lights in the hotel go out at once. He swore softly. He should have known—a robbery. The big time. He had been a fool to take on this job for only two grand. He could have gotten twice as much, three times as much. And he would have deserved it; he had to live in this country, and it was going to be damned tough when the police started snooping around. A little vacation might be in order, perhaps a month or two in Lisbon. He could stay with his aunt.

———

Jencks stared, dumbfounded. He could not believe his eyes. Except for some neatly folded papers of no value, the safe was empty. It was impossible, absolutely impossible. He shined his light into all the corners, and shuffled through the papers.

ODDS ON

Nothing.

Shaken, he closed the door and stepped back. His mind told him he had to keep moving, had to stay with the schedule or everything would be lost. Automatically, he walked to the door, turned off his flashlight, and stepped into the hall.

The smell of smoke was very strong, now. People were gasping and coughing; their voices had undertones of fright. He worked his way back along the wall, and bumped into Bryan.

"Got it?" Jencks asked. There was only one answer that he could think of—nobody bothered with the safe, but kept their money and jewels in their rooms.

"No," Bryan said.

Jencks stiffened. "Why not?"

"Because there was nothing to get. Miguel tried to tell you. We searched the rooms and came up with practically nothing—maybe two hundred dollars in checks and bills, no more. We thought it must all be in the hotel safe."

Jencks said nothing. His mind was working furiously, blocking out the noise and chaos around him.

"Was it?" Bryan asked.

"No," Jencks said. "The safe was empty."

"*Empty!*"

"Shut up," Jencks growled. "Let me think this out. Just shut up for a minute."

"The schedule—"

"Screw the schedule."

Bryan stood patiently, listening to the people running past him and the drumming of the rain outside. The storm had reached a feverish pitch. He didn't understand what was happening, but he knew Jencks would figure it out sooner than he could hope to.

ODDS ON

When he finally spoke, Jencks's voice was low, with a tone of awe that was almost admiration. "Somebody's beaten us to it," he said at last. "We've been robbed!"

There was a muffled rumble, like thunder, but the two men knew better. The bridge had just blown.

MORNING, JUNE TWENTY-SECOND (1:00 A.M.-12:00 NOON)

The doorman had seen it happen. Right before his very eyes, the far end of the bridge had bucked up, twisted, and plunged down out of sight. His status as the only eyewitness made him the center of attention of a large crowd which had gathered in the rain and howling wind to look at the wreckage of girders and struts. The people were soaked and dripping, hair plastered to their faces, but they talked with excitement and nervous animation. It was like a lawn party, the doorman thought with mild amusement. He had expected something like this to happen before long. The whole hotel was so shoddily built. He had a brother who worked construction in Zaragoza, and his brother had pronounced the Reina badly built. That was enough for the doorman.

Mr. Bonnard was questioning him, shaking his finger at him in the rain. Mr. Bonnard looked ridiculous, with his thin wispy hair hanging down into his eyes. The doorman suppressed a smile.

"And that's all you saw?"

"That's all," the doorman said.

ODDS ON

Mr. Bonnard nodded, shivered, and went inside. Slowly, the crowd became bored with the wrecked bridge, and began to feel the downpour and the chilly wind. People turned into the lobby in groups of two and three. It was then that the doorman remembered the taxicab; the doors slamming in the rain, the car roaring across the bridge shortly before it collapsed.

But he forgot it a moment later, when Mr. Bonnard called him in to help set candles around the hotel. As the manager said, they would not be needing a doorman that night.

———

Annette was at the desk, talking to the worried guests. The entire lobby was illuminated by candles, which gave it a strangely funereal aspect. The clients were unhappy. They wanted to know *why*—why the elevator didn't work, why the lights had gone out, why the bridge had collapsed. What did the hotel intend to do about it? Annette assured them that adequate compensation would be made, that they would be ferried to the mainland by boat in the morning, that there was nothing to fear, that everything was under control. She announced that the hotel's auxiliary generator would soon begin supplying electricity, and that yes, they would be able to have their boiled eggs and toast in the morning. Yes, madam. Certainly. Yes sir, sorry sir, of course, sir. The questions continued, the complaints were endless. It was a nightmare.

She had lost track of Bryan at the nightclub, in the confusion of the fire. The fire seemed manageable when she left, but the lobby was filled with smoke, and she wondered. A little lady with quivering jowls was asking her about bananas—bananas! She answered politely, muttering to herself. Another man pushed to the front; Annette informed him that every effort would be

ODDS ON

made to see that he made his air connection at Barcelona in the morning. Now a woman, who wanted to see the manager. That was not possible. Yes, of course she could have more blankets for her bed. The chambermaid would see to it.

And so it went, on into the morning until she lost her ability to smile, and her voice grew hoarse.

———

Peter stared drunkenly at his glass window-wall, streaked with water which lashed it and drenched the balcony. It was a miserable night and a miserable life. He had taken the washed-out bridge as the final omen that everything was wrong, that everything was conspiring against him.

He picked up the empty shell of his suitcase and tossed it on the bed. He would leave her, God damn her. That's all, just leave. He staggered into the bathroom to collect his shaving gear. He paused as he picked up his razor blades, briefly composing a suicide note in his mind. But no, it wasn't worth it. She wasn't worth it. She would just shrug it off.

He threw the shaving kit into the suitcase. Another thought occurred to him—he couldn't get his XKE off the island, with the bridge blown. And he certainly *couldn't go without it.* He would have to wait until the bridge was rebuilt.

How long would *that* take? He went to the closet and brought out his clothes, throwing them haphazardly on the bed.

Maybe not so long. They could throw up a temporary affair, just to get the cars off. Then he would drive back to the Riviera, and stay in St. Tropez. Hot girls were a dime a dozen, wandering around the port, lying on the beaches. He'd show up in the Jag and knock them dead. He'd make four girls a night—five, even. Jenny could go to hell. There were other girls in the world.

ODDS ON

He would have a good time, eating *bouillabaisse* and fingering chicks under the table with his free hand. He needed a little action. Spain was the wrong country—too reserved, too formal, and inhibited. He'd go back to France, where the girls knew what it was all about.

Feeling slightly better, he undressed and climbed into bed.

———

Miss Shaw fretted. This was all most inconvenient, it really was. Completely unexpected and possibly quite serious. There was bound to be a lot of official rigmarole, and if it made the papers in Brighton—and she was sure it would—her sister would be terribly upset. And there was no way to communicate, to send a telegram, to reassure her. They were stranded, for God only knew *how* long.

And, of course, the police. They must be taken into account. She got up and took the rest of the stuff from her purse, and meticulously flushed it down the toilet. It made her feel a little more peaceful. She wouldn't look well in jail; her health would suffer terribly.

That dreadful bridge. There was no getting around it; it was a damnable nuisance. She raised her small fist and shook it at the storm beating against her window. Thunder, rumbling and imperturbable, replied.

———

The bedroom was dark.

"Oh," Cynthia said. "That's good."

Jean-Paul, still smelling of the smoky fire, was reaching into her, tickling her, probing her, heating her. He was good, but

she admitted slight disappointment. It had been better with *kef*.
Next time, they'd do it with *kef* again, and they would really
have a session. The storm and the wind howled outside. She
began to feel deep stirrings. This wasn't going to be so disappointing, after all.

———

Jencks sat at his desk, his room lit by flickering candlelight,
and struggled to understand. For the last hour, he had been in
a state of shock; all his plans, his careful preparations, had been
foiled. It was not easy to accept, to admit, and he considered
every other possibility first.

The computer had been wrong. But no, that was ridiculous. Perhaps it was capable of a minor error, the result of
misprogramming, but a major catastrophe of this magnitude
was unthinkable.

Bryan and Miguel were holding out on him. That, too, was
ridiculous. Only Jencks knew how to unload the stuff quickly
and safely enough to make it worth their while. He was in sole
possession of that information, and without it, the robbery was
pointless. Besides, the safe had been empty. Neither of them
could have robbed the safe.

Who had? The whole thing sounded to Jencks like an inside
job. Maybe it was Bonnard himself—he had been acting pretty
nervous lately. Maybe that girl at the desk. Maybe an enterpris-
ing and quick-witted member of the staff.

He dismissed each of these possibilities in turn. The planning and timing required for an operation of this size made any
amateur effort unlikely. This was a professional piece of work,
and he would have to approach it in that light.

Miguel burst into the room. He said one word: "Brady."

ODDS ON

"Perhaps," Jencks said.

"What do you mean, 'perhaps'? Who else could it be?"

"That's the question," Jencks said, shaking his head. He had a headache; he went to the bathroom and groped for aspirins in the dark. When he came out, he found Bryan sitting on the bed, looking very tired.

"I dumped the gear," Jencks said. "The flashlight, the rubber sacs, the gloves—everything. By now it's washed out to sea. We're clear."

"So's that bastard Brady," Miguel said. "I could kill him. I'd snap his fat neck like—"

"Just a minute," Jencks said. "Don't jump to conclusions."

"For Christ's sake—"

"Quiet," Jencks said. "Suck your thumb."

Miguel lapsed into wounded silence. Jencks stood and paced up and down the room, forcing his mind to work logically.

"Brady didn't do it," Bryan said quietly.

"How do you know?"

"I ran into Mrs. Cleeves in the middle of the afternoon. She told me she was feeling much better—she had just deposited her jewels in the hotel safe."

That meant the safe had been opened after Brady had gone. In a way, it didn't matter—Brady couldn't have pulled the job alone. He wasn't necessarily in the clear, but he wasn't directly implicated.

"What time did you see Mrs. Cleeves?"

Bryan shrugged. "Tea time. Around four, I'd say."

It was unlikely that anyone would check out of the hotel after four on a Saturday afternoon. Which meant the robbers were still here. He turned to Bryan.

"Describe a room. Any room, just a typical room you searched today."

229

ODDS ON

"Well, there isn't much to say. I'd go in, memorize things, and begin to look for—"

"Did the rooms have anything in common?"

Bryan looked helpless. He couldn't explain it to Jencks. Only a man who has examined one hotel room after another could understand it—the way each room reflected the personality of its occupants, despite the uniformity of furniture and decor. Some rooms were messy, some neat; some smelled of sweat, some perfume, some were antiseptic and neutral; some had the unmistakable stamp of French fastidiousness, some of Italian flair. But each room, in its own way, was unique.

"They weren't disordered, ruffled?"

"Didn't seem to be."

"No signs of a search at all?"

"None."

Jencks stopped pacing and sat down again. He irritably rapped a pencil against the arm of his chair. He was nervous, damned nervous; usually, he would fight to control his tension, to hide it. Tonight he couldn't care less.

"Are you sure you searched thoroughly?"

"Son of a bitch," Miguel exploded. "Of course we're sure. The first few rooms, maybe, I was a little casual. I expected it to be easy. Later on, when I still wasn't coming up with anything, I gave them a real once-over. Everything but pulling out the drawers to see if money was taped to the back. There just wasn't anything to find."

"All right," Jencks said. "Don't take it personally."

"How the hell am I supposed to take it?"

"We've had a big day," Jencks said. "I'm sorry."

Miguel laughed bitterly, and pulled a flask out of his hip pocket. He downed a swig and passed it to Bryan, who gulped noisily and held it out to Jencks.

ODDS ON

"What is it?"

"Tequila," Miguel said. "Imported."

Jencks took the flask and knocked back a mouthful. It burned harshly and warmed his stomach.

"Better with lemon and salt," Miguel said, "but we gotta improvise."

Once again, Jencks thought over the events of the day. He was beginning to feel groggy from the effort, like a man viewing the same film over and over. He forced himself to concentrate. He saw himself jam the elevator, talk to the doorman, light his cigarette three times, enter the phone booth, cross the lobby in darkness, open the safe . . .

"Dinnertime," Jencks said. "They must have done it at dinnertime, around seven or eight. I considered doing it that way myself. It would have saved using all the explosives and bothering with the lights and fires. It's a much more elegant solution, but risky. It means you have to get into the office in full view of anyone who might be in the corridors and out again without being seen. It means you had to take a great chance, because Bonnard often has dinner in his office."

"Somebody obviously took the chance," Miguel said.

There was a long, depressed silence.

"Look," Jencks said. "It seems clear that this robbery was almost a mirror image of the one we planned. Did you see anyone unusual in the halls while you were searching the rooms? Somebody else who might be searching, too?"

"Hell no," Bryan said. "I never went into a room if there was a soul in sight." Miguel nodded.

Dead end, Jencks thought. Right smack up against a dead end. No clues, no leads. How had they done it? Who could have gotten into Bonnard's office during dinner? Who could have

231

searched the rooms? Chambermaids? Repairmen? He shook his head. It must have been done by some group of guests like themselves.

"I'm sure they're still here," Jencks said.

Bryan nodded. "I think so, too."

"They're still here, and they can't get away—because we blew up the bridge." Jencks laughed. "They're trapped here, just like everybody else. And I'll give you odds the stuff is still here with them."

He tapped his chair again with the pencil.

"For Christ's sake," Miguel said. "I'm tired."

Jencks put the pencil down.

"Nobody knows," Bryan said, "that there's been a robbery. Not yet. The management thinks the bridge was destroyed by the storm. That means we are the only ones who know that a robbery has been committed."

"Let's try to build up a composite picture of the thieves," Jencks said. "Try to figure out what they must be like."

He frowned, thinking that if he could feed facts into the computer, the machine would come up with a composite picture of the criminals. How fast? Forty seconds, maybe.

"We've been calling them *them*," Bryan said, "and I think that's probably true."

"They can't be too old," Miguel said. "It's hard work, searching all those rooms."

"That's a start," Jencks said. "More than one, and not too old. Let's say there are three, just like us."

"I don't think there are any groups of three at the hotel," Bryan said, "Except for a few families with kids."

"Nobody would ever think of us as a group of three, either," Jencks pointed out, but he could already see Bryan's point. The idea of building up a picture of the robbers was doomed.

ODDS ON

"Let's try something else," he said. "Three people. What do they do?"

"Just what we did," Miguel said. "Nose around and talk to people. Pry."

"And whom do you remember doing that?"

"Brady," Miguel said.

It all seemed to come back to Brady, Jencks had to admit. And there it ended. Brady was gone, neat as a whistle. He couldn't have pulled the robbery.

"Who else?"

Bryan shrugged. "Nobody. Everybody. You know how it is—when you're talking to someone, you're so busy thinking ahead, trying to figure out how to slip in the next question, you don't pay much attention to what they're saying to you. And you prime the pump with some information about yourself. I've probably told a dozen people my room number."

Jencks knew he had done the same. One of those dozen people now held the answer—and the money. He thought about the people he had met and came up with nothing. He glanced at his watch.

"It's nearly four," he said. "I think we'd better break for the night and meet tomorrow morning. At the pool, around ten. We might as well forget about appearances; there isn't time to be fancy. Okay?"

The two men stood. They were exhausted and trying to smile. They left, leaving Jencks to stare alone into the rumbling night. Lightning crackled briefly. Otherwise it was dark.

———

After breakfast, Peter went to the underground garage, which was cut into the rock beneath the hotel. It was a cheerless, vast cavern of gray concrete, smelling of oil and exhaust fumes. The cars were parked in neat rows, illuminated by overhead fluorescent lights. Thank God, he thought, they had gotten the electricity going. This place would be a dungeon without it.

To one side was a glass-walled attendant's booth and a gasoline pump. The attendant, wearing spotless white coveralls, came up to Peter.

"Señor?"

"I want to see my car."

The attendant shook his head, not understanding. Idiot Spaniard. Peter dangled the keys to his Jaguar in front of the man's face. Recognition flickered across the dark features. Then the man shook his head again and motioned outside.

"Why not? You can't just throw me out."

"Puenta, puenta," the man said. He made a motion with his hand to indicate that the bridge had collapsed.

"I know, I know. I'm not going anywhere. I just want to see my car, to look at it. It's right over there. Okay?"

Confused by the babble of words, the man shrugged and walked off. Peter squeezed past the other cars until he came to his own. It was beautiful, he thought, running his fingers over the sleek curve of the front bumper. Beautiful and graceful and sexy. It made him feel sexy, just to drive it. He had been worried about it, absurdly fearful that it would be damaged during the storm.

He walked around and slipped behind the wheel. The attendant paid no attention to him as he held the polished wood rim in his fingers. He turned the wheel and heard the squeak of rubber on the concrete. The car responded so eagerly. Like a perfect woman, an ideal mistress. And it was his, all his.

Whistling, he climbed out and returned to the hotel.

ODDS ON

Mr. Bonnard stood with Annette at the edge of the island, looking down at the collapsed bridge. The storm had blown out to sea in the early hours of the morning and now, in the clear light of day, the bridge looked, if possible, worse than it had the night before. Partially submerged, it was a tangled gray mass of bent girders and twisted struts; it looked as if it had been wrenched from its foundations by the hand of a giant.

"What do you think?" Annette asked, lighting a cigarette.

"I don't know what to think. We were assured that there wasn't a storm in the world that could do this, but I'm not an engineer. I just don't know."

"Can we ferry people across by boat?"

"I think so. I sent Juan over in the boat two hours ago. He's going to walk to Playa del Rio and call the police from there." Playa del Rio was a little town on the coast, at the mouth of a river. It was the nearest town to the Reina, but it was still four kilometers away over very rough terrain.

"How soon can we get cars to the mainland?"

"It looks too far for a temporary bridge," Mr. Bonnard said, squinting at the gap. "Maybe the police will have an idea—a derrick or some such. In any event, it will be expensive. We'll have insurance people around our necks for the next three months." Mr. Bonnard shuddered at the thought of Cranz, the dapper and obnoxious little investigator from Bern who had visited the hotel when it had first opened. Cranz and his associates would make life miserable for Mr. Bonnard.

Annette took a deep breath. "I'd better get back to the desk and face the angry hordes. What can I tell them?"

"Help is on the way," he said, brisk and businesslike. "We expect to begin ferrying people to the mainland shortly after lunch. Damage claims can be forwarded to Hotelsa, Madrid. I suppose we may have a few lawsuits as well." He sighed. "Such a difficult thing."

Jenny Cameron, looking fresh and youthful in a navy-blue jumper, came up just as they were turning back to the hotel. Her eyes widened when she saw the wreckage of the bridge.

"How did it happen?"

Mr. Bonnard, not wanting to give the impression of uncertainty, said, "Blew down in the storm. We suspect wave action weakened the concrete supports."

"It's really a shame," Jenny said, trying to sound concerned.

"We are doing everything possible to restore a normal situation, I assure you," he said, a trifle pompously. Mr. Bonnard always retreated into stuffy formality when he felt he had no other alternatives.

"I'm glad to hear that," Jenny said.

Annette and the manager left her looking down at the bridge. She had a faint and enigmatic smile on her face. She seemed almost pleased about the wreckage.

———

Irritably, Jencks looked at his watch. It was after ten, and neither of the others had showed up yet. Discipline was shot to hell, he thought. It would never have happened the day before. Across the pool, he saw Jenny, who waved and seemed about to come over. He shook his head and frowned; she shrugged and walked off. It was a remarkably docile display, he thought. He must have trained her better than he had thought.

It gave him little comfort. Jencks had slept the sleep of a tormented man, and he felt grumpy and miserable this morning. The clear, bright sunshine only seemed to accentuate and underline his state of mind, which was black and gloomy. He

ODDS ON

could think of only one good thing—from his point of view—which had happened the day before, and that was the storm. From snatches of conversation he'd overheard at breakfast, it appeared that most people, including the hotel staff, believed the bridge had collapsed as a result of the storm. An expert, Jencks knew, would see in a minute that this was not so, but experts would not arrive for a day or two. Until then, nobody was suspicious, including the real robbers.

That was their only advantage.

He examined the other people sitting around the pool. Some he had never seen before—the weekend visitors from Barcelona, he guessed. Any of them might have pulled the robbery, particularly that grim-looking couple several yards away. He looked mean, darkly handsome and somewhat crude; she had a highly polished, glossy elegance which Jencks guessed disguised an ignoble background. But it was impossible to say, to be sure, to find even a foundation for suspicion. Just because a man looked like a thief didn't mean anything; Jencks prided himself on the fact that he looked like anything *but* a thief.

Who else didn't look like a thief? The Warrens, from someplace in Ohio. Their brat was screaming and splashing in the water now, attracting as much attention as he could. Mrs. Warren had a pasty face and a skinny, birdlike body. Her voice was shrill with displeasure as she cawed at little Herbie. Little Herbie pointedly spit a mouthful of water in her direction. Mr. Warren, who was plump and rumpled looking in his baggy business suits, shook a warning finger at Herbie and said something about paying attention to your mother. Herbie laughed and splashed more water.

Then there was Miss Shaw, sitting in a canvas chair, a pile of bananas at her side, a book in her lap. Jencks could not imagine a more eccentric old woman, but she was charming in her nineteenth-century way. She looked up at Herbie and wrinkled her nose in disapproval. Jencks felt the same way. Little Herbie ought to be strangled.

The Italian architect appeared. He was accompanied by the dark-haired girl with the hourglass body and the beautiful eyes. Jencks had liked the couple instinctively, though rumor was that they were having their troubles. "Not married, you know," Mrs. Aldrich had hissed into his ear, her voice sounding like seltzer water jetting from a bottle. Jencks didn't care. He thought they were an attractive pair.

Could they have done it? It seemed unlikely, but that in itself was a reason for suspicion.

"Morning," Miguel said, dropping into a chair.

"Well, at least you didn't say *good* morning. Where's Bryan?"

"I don't know; I haven't seen him. Sorry I'm late, but I over-slept. I heard some funny things this morning. You know, nobody thinks the bridge was blown up—they blame it on the storm." He chuckled. "That's our luck. We don't even get *credit* for anything."

Jencks let the remark drop. "Any ideas?"

"Not one. I've been hashing it over all morning, and nothing's turned up. And I'm getting tired of giving sneaky looks to everyone around me. There are more people than I have sneaky looks for."

"I admire your talent for levity."

"Christ, there are times when all you can do is laugh."

Bryan came up.

"You're late," Jencks snapped. "Nearly half an hour."

"It was worth it," Bryan said, sitting down.

"What was?" Jencks said, forgetting his anger, not daring to hope.

"Have you observed the hotel routine?" Bryan asked.

ODDS ON

"I have, I suppose because I've talked so much with the girl. They do things very smoothly here, mostly because they can hire all the staff they need at low Spanish wages. In the mornings, the maids come in to clean out the rooms, stripping the linen from the beds of people that are leaving, and—"

"Get to the point."

Bryan smiled, obviously unwilling to relinquish a moment of triumph.

"And tidying up in rooms where guests are staying another night. They arrange things on the dressers, change towels in the bathrooms, and empty the wastebaskets. They empty them into large canvas bags, like mailbags, that the boys later come around to collect. Have you seen them?"

"Yes," Miguel said. "They're green. Light green."

"That's it," Bryan said. "I was walking along, on my way down here, and I noticed something in one of them. It was in the middle, buried among a heap of discarded letters, cigarette butts, and empty bottles. This." He reached into his pocket for a crumpled photograph of the interior of a hotel room.

"Polaroid," Jencks said, looking at the serrated edge of the print. "A Polaroid picture of a hotel room."

"Sixty seconds," Bryan said, beaming.

"The picture was taken from a position just inside the door," Jencks said, examining it again. "And then discarded. Why?"

"You can ask the same question about all these."

Bryan produced three more pictures from his pocket. Each showed a different hotel room; each had been crumpled and thrown away. "I was thinking of what you said last night, about the operation being a mirror image of our own. Well, these are—"

"Flash cards!" Jencks said, "They didn't use flash cards. They didn't rely on memory. The came into a room, photographed it, and searched while the picture was developing. Later, they

ODDS ON

could compare the room to the picture and see if anything was out of place. That's brilliant."

"Know anybody with a Polaroid camera?" Bryan asked.

Miguel, who had listened in silence, now said, "I do."

The others looked at him expectantly.

"The oversexed girl on the third floor who calls herself Cynthia."

"Cynthia?" Bryan asked. "You know her?"

"Yes," Miguel said. "I slept with her."

"It figures," Bryan said.

"How do you know her?" Jencks asked Bryan, fighting to control the excitement in his voice.

"She came up to me a couple of days ago. Made a little play, wiggled her hips. We talked a bit; I wasn't interested. Do you know her, Steve?"

"She pulled the same thing with me," Jencks said.

"Aha!" Miguel pronounced, as if he just had an epiphany.

Jencks's eyes narrowed. "What did you talk about?"

"We didn't talk," Miguel said. "We just—"

"Not you. Bryan."

Bryan shrugged. "All sort of minor things. I don't really remember; she was swinging that body back and forth under my nose."

"She pumped me," Jencks said. "I didn't think much of it at the time, but it all comes back now."

"She pumped me, too," Miguel said, laughing coarsely.

Jencks had a strong urge to punch Miguel in the face, but said only, "I think we'd better visit Cynthia, as a group of mutual friends."

Together, they got up and went into the Reina.

ODDS ON

Cynthia looked up, startled, as the key was inserted into the lock, and the door swung open. Three men walked into the room.

She had been caught dressing and wore only a cashmere sweater which reached her waist. Instinctively, she pulled it down so it covered her crotch, but her buttocks were bare behind.

"Nice legs," Miguel snickered, shutting the door. "You should see what she can do with them, too."

Jencks sniffed the air. "What's that smell?"

Miguel recognized it. "*Kef,*" he said, looking at Cynthia with new interest.

"What?"

"*Kef.* Marijuana. She's been smoking it."

Cynthia drew back, still holding her sweater down with one hand. "No."

"They get very suspicious when they're high," Miguel explained. "What shall we do with her?"

"You may think," Cynthia purred, "that the three of you are too much. You're not. I can take you on, you'll see." The hand holding her sweater began to caress her loins.

"She's high, all right," Miguel said. "Let me handle this."

There was an edge to his voice which disturbed Jencks. "I'll take care of it," Jencks said.

"Let me," Miguel insisted softly. "It will be my pleasure." He walked up to Cynthia and held her face in his hands.

Jencks was about to step forward, but Bryan caught him and shook his head. Jencks hesitated, then relaxed against a wall.

"Cynthia," Miguel said softly, stroking her cheek. "Do you remember me?"

"Yes," she said, her voice dreamy.

"Cynthia, we want to take some pictures. Where is your camera?"

ODDS ON

"I don't have any camera." She pouted and shook her head in an exaggerated, almost drunken way.

"Cynthia."

She stopped shaking her head and looked at him.

"Yes?"

"I don't want to hurt you."

Her laugh, high and lilting, broke the stillness of the room. "You can't. I can take all of you, I told you before."

"I'm not talking about that, Cynthia." The threat was very clear in his voice now, but she did not respond to it.

"No camera."

"Where is it?"

"I never had any camera."

"I saw it, a Polaroid camera. In your room, remember, Cynthia?"

"No camera."

She felt his hand stroking her cheek. It felt good, but his voice was funny. It was alternately loud and soft, like a radio being turned high and low in succession. If he wanted sex, it was all right with her, but he didn't seem interested. All this talk about the camera, with his voice shouting, then soft, shouting, then soft.

"Cynthia, I'm going to hurt you."

She laughed again and released her sweater which snuggled back up around her waist. She could feel it clinging around her, like hands.

A tingle ran through her. A small brush fire was burning, in a deserted field, an abandoned wheat field, a field of olive trees, a grove of bright red cherries . . .

Miguel was leaning over her, his breath smelling of tobacco and coffee. It washed over her face like a wave.

"Cynthia. If it hurts too much, tell me, and I'll stop."

His voice came from an echo chamber, a large dark room where sound returned to haunt you. "Tell me and I'll stop," she heard again. "Tell me and I'll stop . . . tell me and I'll stop . . . tell me and I'll stop . . ."

"Do you think this is wise?" one of the men said. "Think this is wise . . . this is wise . . . this is wise . . ."

"Let me handle it," Miguel said. She felt his hand lift her sweater. Cold air touched her stomach and breasts. Miguel was panting. His fingers ran over her body, comforting her. It was going to be sex. Everything was sex in the end. In the end. She laughed.

He slapped her, each finger stinging her cheek. Her eyes closed. Fear grabbed her as an eagle plucks up a lamb, carrying it into the air, away from the ground, far from safety.

His hands caressed her kneecap, then pinched. It was not a hard pinch, but gentle, almost loving. He began to pinch more, moving his hand up her leg. The pinches were harder. His hand moved to the inside of her thigh. It was tender there, and the pinches hurt, little pricks of pain that rippled like a stone falling into water. His hand moved up. He was hurting her more. Soon it would hurt very much.

"The camera, where is it?"

The voice was dead. She hardly heard him. She was concentrating on the pain, which nipped at her. It was an animal, biting her and growling as it moved up her body. It had no right to be there. It was obscene, it was terrible, it was terrifying.

His hands no longer caused distinct moments of hurt. It was all blended now, each new pinch inseparable from the last. The pain spiraled. And suddenly, it died. Things were gentle, peaceful, and relaxed; his hand was tender as it stroked her legs and lips. She was ready for him. His fingers were drowning in her. They were feeling her small spots, searching for the little place.

ODDS ON

She could tell it was there, a little hill in the golden wheat field. He could find it, and she would enjoy his discovery.

A streak of pleasure shot past her eyeballs, like a comet. Sparks of desire scattered. He had found the place and was teasing it. The backs of her knees were wobbly and loose. She wanted him. He was being so exquisite, she had to have him. She felt helpless, held down like a butterfly waiting for the shock of ether to knock it out. Another lash of excitement, then another. She moaned.

And suddenly she felt pain that was excruciating. He was pinching her again, and it was unbelievable. Nothing could hurt so much. Another hand was at her breasts, pinching there, too. Two centers of pain radiated in her, each agonizing, but one dominated, sending out pulses of pent-up screams.

"The camera," his voice said, panting in her face. "Where is the camera?"

Her neck tensed with a new jolt of pain. "No camera," she said. Didn't he know she didn't want to talk about a camera? Cameras didn't interest her.

The hand was gentle again. Gasping for breath, her bruised nipples heaving, she received the new wave of pleasure. It was incredible, the combination. The pleasure was less bearable than the pain. She almost longed to be hurt again. She saw a house flooded, then pounded by rain, then flooded again by warm, swirling waters. It was in a steaming jungle. Vines hung from the trees, and there were many slim saplings standing straight and resilient.

"Please take me," she said. Her mouth was dry. She was having trouble breathing.

"The camera. Just tell us about the camera."

His voice was dry, too, flaking and cracking like an old painted sign.

ODDS ON

"Take me."

"You must learn to answer the question." Though he was panting loudly, like a steam engine chugging, she heard his words. And suddenly, pain shot through her, from far away to up close, bursting inside her. She bit her lips. She could not take much more of it. The pain stopped, and she bathed in pleasure, but it was not a restful thing. This time he was building her, preparing her for the heights of love. It was wonderful, what he was doing.

He stopped. She moaned.

She had to have a man, she had to take it in her, to be able to press herself down on it, to scratch the maddening itch.

"Please. Oh, please." She was writhing, gasping.

"Tell me."

"No."

"Tell me, or I'll leave."

She hesitated. To convince her, to tip the balance, he touched her again with the delicate stroke, the brush, the delicate brush on the painter's canvas. "Jean-Paul has it," she said, still gasping.

"Jean-Paul?"

"Jean-Paul Morand," said one of the men. His voice was gruff, like gravel being dumped from a truck. "I know who he is. A tough-looking customer."

Miguel said, "It was you and Jean-Paul?"

"You and Jean-Paul . . . you and Jean-Paul . . ." The voice reverberated, repeated, asked again.

"Yes. We did it. Now *please*."

"Where is the stuff?" Miguel asked.

"Jean-Paul," she repeated. "Jean-Paul."

"I've heard enough," said another voice. She opened her eyes, saw light and the three faces. Two were calm; one was sweating. She reached for Miguel.

245

ODDS ON

"Don't leave me, not now."

He turned to the others. The ugly man jerked his thumb toward the door. He looked disgusted.

"I don't really believe in torture," Miguel said to her. "But I'm afraid this time is an exception. Later."

He got up. He was leaving. She wanted to scream. Panic. What were they going to do? She was so hot, so wet. She was still trembling from him. He was leaving her, they were all leaving. Footsteps moved to the door, and then she heard it slam.

She was alone. She burst into hysterical tears.

———

Bryan stopped at the desk, carrying one of his own sweaters in his hand. "Sorry," he said to Annette. "One of the guests left this at the pool a few minutes ago. Fellow named Morand. I thought I'd drop it by his room."

"We can send it up with the boy," Annette said.

"No bother," Bryan replied smoothly. "I'm on my way upstairs anyway. What's his room?"

"214," Annette said, consulting her chart.

"Thanks very much," Bryan smiled.

———

He met Jencks on the first floor. "214," he said. The two men went up one flight and turned down the corridor. The maids were just finishing with the last of the rooms.

"Where's Miguel?"

"He went to get his gun."

"His gun! I told him specifically—"

"I know, I know. But perhaps it's just as well."

ODDS ON

They stopped at Jean-Paul's door.

"Wait for Miguel?" Bryan asked.

Jencks shook his head. He didn't like guns and would use one only as a last resort. He knocked on the door.

"Who is it?" a muffled voice asked. It did not sound fearful, or even interested, just preoccupied.

"*Femme de chambre*," Jencks said, in a high voice.

"*Un moment*," came the reply. Footsteps approached.

The door opened and they had a glimpse of Jean-Paul's face, covered with shaving lather. With brutal force, Jencks slammed the door wide, pinning Jean-Paul's arm against the wall. They entered and threw him down on the bed. He sat there, astonished, and looked at them.

"The cameras," Jencks said.

Jean-Paul stood threateningly, and Bryan hit him once in the stomach, quite hard. The Frenchman crumpled, holding his gut. He got lather on his knees.

"No games," Jencks said. "We're not in the mood. Where are the cameras?"

"*Je ne parle pas Anglais*," Jean-Paul muttered.

Bryan grabbed him by the wrist and elbow, straightened his arm and flung Jean-Paul against the wall. He slapped hard against the plaster, face first. Bryan caught him as he fell, and turned him to face Jencks. There was a little U of lather on the wall.

"Be careful," Jencks said to Jean-Paul. "You can get killed, if you're not careful."

Jean-Paul was barely conscious. Bryan had to prop him up against the wall.

Without another word, Jencks turned and began to search the room. He flung open the closet doors and rummaged among the clothing. Then he checked all the dresser drawers. Behind him, he heard a sigh and looked over to see Bryan dropping Jean-Paul to the bed.

"Out like a light," Bryan said.

"You weren't exactly gentle."

"I'm crying."

Bryan joined the search. Together, they looked under the beds, behind the furniture, in the bathroom. Jencks found Jean-Paul's suitcase locked; he spent several minutes jimmying it open with a pocketknife. It was empty.

"Son of a bitch," Bryan said.

Jencks looked up to see Jean-Paul standing by the door. Neither of them had noticed him get up; they had been absorbed in their inspection. Jean-Paul opened the door, and Bryan dived for him. Jean-Paul kicked; the Englishman grunted and fell to his knees. By then Jencks was on his feet, but Jean-Paul was outside, slamming the door behind him. Jencks heard running feet in the corridor. Roughly he pushed Bryan out of his way and went out into the hall. It was empty, but at the far end, around the corner, he heard running, and saw a passing shadow.

He sprinted down the hall. Behind him, Bryan staggered to his feet and called, "I'm coming."

Jencks rounded the corner and followed the sound of footsteps up the broad, circular stair. Up to the third floor, then the fourth. Above him, he continued to hear running feet. The fifth floor. Still the feet. Jean-Paul was going to the roof.

As he reached the top floor, Jencks heard a door slam. Jean-Paul would be outside now, hiding somewhere on the flat, broad roof of the hotel, a surface which was unbroken except for a half-dozen chimneys and ventilator shafts. He came to the door and looked through the small square window.

ODDS ON

The roof was covered in black tar paper and gravel; heat waves shimmered up, blurring the shapes of the white rectangles that pierced the roof at various places. He did not see his man.

Jencks hesitated. Was Jean-Paul armed? It seemed unlikely, but you could never be sure. Jencks himself had only a pen-knife, and it was hardly a serviceable weapon. One flight below, he heard Bryan approaching. He looked down the stairwell, and saw the black-and-white checked floor of the lobby, five floors down. Nobody in sight; apparently running men did not attract much attention. Perhaps the staff had too many other things to worry about.

Bryan arrived puffing. "Is he out there?"

"Yes. There's no other way for him to get down. This is the only door."

"Then we've got him," Bryan said. He looked out the window. "Any idea where he is?"

"No. I'm going out there, to see if I can flush him out. You stay here—he isn't expecting you—and make sure he doesn't get by." Jencks frowned. "Be as rough as you want. He won't be holding back any punches."

Bryan nodded. Jencks opened the door and walked out to the roof. He shut the door behind him.

The first thing he noticed was the wind, which was strong and gusty, blowing over his face, rippling his clothes. Then he felt the noonday sun, hot on the back of his neck. Except for the wind and the dim whirr of a generator, it was very quiet. His feet crunched on the gravel. He bent down and slipped off his shoes. When he stepped forward on stocking feet, he made less noise but his footsteps were still far from silent. He moved toward the first chimney.

It was a broad, white rectangle, larger than a home

249

refrigerator, and afforded plenty of protection for a man. He moved close and worked his way around to the far side.

Nobody there.

Breathing a deep sigh, he fought back his tension. He had to stay cool. He went to the next chimney. This one was silently belching black smoke. Half-crouched, he walked around it.

Nobody there.

He was going for the third chimney when he heard a grunt behind him. Looking back, he saw Jean-Paul struggling with Bryan at the door. He ran to them just as the Frenchman delivered a telling blow to Bryan's jaw. For a moment, Jencks feared Jean-Paul would escape again. But then Miguel was blocking the passage, throwing two quick jabs at Jean-Paul's nose. Jean-Paul's head jerked back twice.

Jean-Paul toppled, rolled onto his stomach, and scrambled to his feet. He ran straight into Jencks, who hit him very hard. Jean-Paul sank to the ground, gasping. Blood ran from his nose and mouth; one eye was already swollen and closed. Jencks grabbed his hair, hauled his head up, and looked into the exhausted face.

"It's a long drop off this roof," Jencks said conversationally. "Come and see."

He dragged Jean-Paul by the collar to the edge of the tar paper and held his head over the side. Together, they stared down one hundred feet to the blue, clear rectangle of the pool. It said "Hotel Reina" on the bottom, in black tile. Nobody was swimming; various people were seated around the water, just as they had been when Jencks, Bryan, and Miguel had gone to Cynthia's room.

"Care to take a plunge? You're all hot and sweaty." Jencks pushed the limp body forward. "Do you a world of good."

Jean-Paul, still gasping for breath, looked down, then up at Jencks. He hesitated. Jencks pushed him further.

ODDS ON

"All right," Jean-Paul said. "I'll tell you. Get me back."

Jencks did not move. "I don't believe you, and I find you tiresome."

Closer to the edge.

"Jesus! I'll tell you. You've got to believe me." The face was now white, the eyes wide with fear.

With apparent reluctance, Jencks hauled him away from the edge.

"The man is named Brady. He has the money. He—"

Roughly, Jencks dragged him back to the edge of the roof. "Not very good," he said. "You'll have to do much better than that." He slammed Jean-Paul's chin down on the concrete lip, then pulled it back. "Try again."

"Miss Shaw," Jean-Paul said, blood running down his chin. "It was Miss Shaw. She planned the whole thing."

In sudden anger, Jencks punched him again and shoved him aside. He looked down at the pool. Of course! It was brilliant, truly inspired! Brady and Cynthia scouted, Jean-Paul did the dirty work, and the mastermind sat quietly by, selling dope and eating bananas.

As he watched, he picked out the little bundle that was Miss Shaw, seated next to a table strewn with banana peels. A waiter came up to her bearing a message on a silver tray. Miss Shaw took the message, read it, and looked quickly around. Then she got out of her chair and bustled inside.

It was time to get moving.

He ran back to the door, grabbing his shoes as he went. The gravel cut into his feet, but he didn't care.

Miguel was helping Bryan up. "Find out?"

"I'll say. You won't believe it. The person who planned it all was Miss Shaw."

"Miss Shaw!"

ODDS ON

Jencks nodded. "Take care of Bryan. I'll handle Grandma myself."

"Want the gun?" Miguel held it out.

"No. I won't need it."

He ran downstairs.

It made sense, he thought, at least in retrospect. This project required brains, the kind of brains that Brady didn't have and Jean-Paul could never aspire to. It required planning and coolness that had to come from someone else. Miss Shaw was perfect. He remembered how cunningly she had delved into his background, as she played the amusing, eccentric English maiden aunt. He should have suspected at the time. No characterization that perfect could be genuine.

She was a fox.

He reached the third floor and ran to her room. He inserted the correct key into the lock and flung the door wide. Miss Shaw was standing in front of him, relaxed and calm. In one hand, she held a small suitcase.

In the other hand, she held a gun.

AFTERNOON,
JUNE TWENTY-SECOND

"Young man, I must tell you that you are very impertinent."

"Cut it out," Jencks said.

"Are you a policeman?"

"No." He looked at the gun. Somehow, he had to distract her, to make her look away. But the gun was fixed on him; her grip was steady. There were no tremors, no quaverings of age. Miss Shaw was in her element now, with a silver-plated pistol in her dainty, wrinkled fingers.

"One of us, are you?" Her eyebrows went up. "Fancy that. I would never have expected it, here of all places. The hotel clientele is usually so *reliable*. This really is quite a surprise. Would you be terribly hurt if I asked you to step into the bathroom?"

Silently, he did as he was told.

"That's my man. It was so sweet of Cynthia to send a message down to me, after you and your friends . . . visited her. She's a loyal girl, a real dear. I'm going to leave you now and lock the hall door behind me. I really would rather you didn't come bursting out of the bath while I'm locking up. I'm not young and I'm easily startled. Do we understand each other?"

ODDS ON

"Perfectly." Jencks suppressed a smile. Here, at last, was one place where his superior preparation and planning paid off. Obviously Miss Shaw did not know that doors locked from the outside could be opened from the inside merely by turning the knob.

"I'll just trot downstairs to the desk and announce that I found a man in my room, searching it. Soon enough, the guests will all discover that they've been robbed—and who's to blame? That villainous fellow they caught in Miss Shaw's room. You'll have a devil of a time with the police, I can tell you. They're downright *nasty,* I hear."

Jencks tried to look furious.

"Do shut the door, like a decent chap. Very nice of you. Good day, Mr. Jencks."

He waited until he heard the key turn in the lock and then stepped out into the bedroom. She had rumpled the room, leaving clothes scattered and drawers ajar before going. That was a nice touch; Jencks felt a certain kinship with this woman. He would have done the same, in her place. He frowned—he would also have left the gun as incriminating evidence. Looking across the room, he saw it placed discreetly on the dresser. Tricky old fox! He listened at the door to her retreating footsteps, then opened it.

She was heading for the stairs. He chased after her and caught up with her halfway between the second and third floor. She seemed surprised but not at all upset; she raised the umbrella she was carrying like a rapier and jabbed at him with it.

The tip, silver and sharp, glinted in the sun which streamed down from the skylight. He edged forward; she drove him back with darting lunges, always keeping her umbrella between himself and her suitcase full of jewels. Her jowls quivered with

ODDS ON

exertion, but she did not drop her guard. Once she hissed, "You really are an *impossible* man," but otherwise their struggle was conducted in silence.

Up and down the broad marble stairs they moved, he attacking, she repelling him. His eyes remained fixed on the point of the umbrella. It was sharp enough to go right through his stomach. She moved it expertly, flicking back and forth, always controlled, always balanced. Soon he was sweating, tired; at length he stopped and leaned against the bannister.

"I suppose you have that tipped with some South American poison?"

"Dear boy, your imagination is simply *incredible*."

The battle was resumed. She forced him back by slow degrees; he recovered and began to drive her back. They seesawed back and forth for several more minutes, until finally he caught her off guard. He slapped the umbrella aside and threw himself on her. She really was a light and wispy thing, despite her dumpling appearance, and she fell easily. As she did, she flung the suitcase over the stair rail.

Horrified, Jencks released her and looked down.

She scrambled to her feet and watched alongside him.

The suitcase fell.

It seemed to move slowly at first, gathering speed as it went.

"Oh dear," she said.

It hit the marble floor with a crash and sprang open, its collection of necklaces, rings, cash, traveler's checks, and watches spilling out. They rolled, clattered, and bounced across the black-and-white surface.

Jencks stepped back from the railing, unable to look any longer.

"You're white as a ghost, young man," Miss Shaw said.

"How could you do it?"

255

ODDS ON

"Oh, nonsense. I won't listen to such rot. Come along with me, and we'll have a nice spot of banana liqueur."

"I would have split it with you, divided it in some way . . ."

"Be careful," she said, slipping her arm in his. "You'll become overexcited."

Together, they descended to the bar. Jencks went along unsteady and silent; he no longer knew where he was or what he was doing.

"Cheer up," Miss Shaw said, patting, his arm in a motherly way. "You've had a bit of a shock, that's all. When one gets to be my age, one learns to take these things with aplomb—and a glass or two. You'll feel better in a jiffy, I assure you."

———

Annette stared dumbfounded at the floor. It made no sense at all; it was beyond comprehension. People were gathering to see what the noise had been; she heard a crunch and looked over to see an embarrassed man remove his foot from what had once been a watch. Now there was shouting. The house detectives arrived, pushing people back, clearing away the space beneath the stairs. Several guests who were trying to pocket diamond rings had their hands slapped.

Slowly, it came to her. The hotel had been robbed. It didn't seem possible—there had been no complaints, not even a rumor—and yet there was the evidence, all over the floor.

Mr. Bonnard hurried up, in great agitation. His eyes were bulging, his lips trembled. "There's been a robbery!" he said. "Why wasn't I informed?"

Annette ignored the question. "Have you checked the hotel safe?"

ODDS ON

"Oh my God. Oh. The safe. No." He scurried off again, back to his office. She came around the desk and tiptoed among the jewels to the guests and began asking them to please return to the dining room, that everything was under control, that there was no problem at all. With her back to the glittering mass, she felt ridiculous.

"That's my ring," shrieked a woman. "I know it. My ring! I've been robbed. Give me my ring back. Give it back."

The hotel detectives pushed, firmly. The crowd did not yield.

"Robbery! Robbery!" The shout was now nearly a chant.

Mr. Bonnard came up again. "Robbed," he said, in an awed voice. "Cleaned out. We've been robbed!"

"Better make a speech," Annette advised. "You're the manager."

Mr. Bonnard nodded, swallowed, and stepped back. He clapped his hands for silence.

"My friends, please—"

"Robbery! Thieves!"

A man's voice said, not loud but very distinctly, "I knew we shouldn't have come to Spain, Harriet."

"Please, please," Mr. Bonnard begged, holding up his hands.

A resentful silence fell over the crowd.

"I must beg you to return to the dining room. There has been a robbery of the hotel, but the material has apparently been—ah—returned. These gentlemen restraining you are the house detectives, and I can assure you that we of the staff have this situation firmly in hand." His face, he knew, betrayed him, but he continued on. "The police are due to arrive at any minute. They will deal with the recovery of this material, upon suitable identification of ownership. In the meantime, I must ask you to *please step back!* Otherwise, the police will have no

257

ODDS ON

choice but to proceed with the unpleasant business of searching every guest as he leaves the hotel."

The crowd faltered, grumbled, and receded.

"When are the police coming?" Annette whispered.

"Who knows?" Mr. Bonnard said, miserably. "Soon, I hope." He noted with satisfaction that the crowd was breaking up, dissolving into little knots of discussion. A few more words should return things to normal. Feeling more confident, Mr. Bonnard cleared his throat.

———

It was half an hour later and the bar was quiet. Jencks was drinking his third glass of banana liqueur and smoking his tenth straight cigarette.

"This really is a coincidence," Miss Shaw said happily, as if they were old friends who had just run into each other again.

Jencks nodded glumly and puffed at the cigarette. It wasn't very strong. He looked at the pack—Camels. He sighed, called the waiter over.

"Which are strong cigarettes?" he asked Miss Shaw.

"Try Gitanes," she advised. "I understand they will grow hair on your lungs."

The waiter brought a pack, and Jencks gulped the searing smoke hungrily.

"I didn't know you smoked," she said.

"I'm just beginning," Jencks said. "It seems like an appropriate time to take up a new vice." He looked at her curiously. "Did you use a computer, too?"

"Gracious no," she said. "I wouldn't think of such a thing. But you did? How clever of you. I knew you were clever the minute I set eyes on you. But no, I don't have much faith in these new things—computers and jets and such. Cars are a different matter; I'm dreadfully fond of cars. But not much else. I prefer to work things out for myself.

Jencks nodded automatically. He would have nodded, in precisely the same numb way, had she announced that she was the reincarnation of Queen Victoria.

"I suppose you blew up the bridge, fixed the elevator, and did all those other atrocious things."

He nodded.

"And the fire in the nightclub?"

He nodded.

"Such a lot of trouble," Miss Shaw said, "for a simple little robbery. I suppose that's why you Americans are preeminent in the business world. You bludgeon everyone. Really a tactless plan, if you don't mind my saying so."

"It would have worked," Jencks said sadly.

"Of course it would have worked. There's no denying that. But it does seem a bit much, all those diversions. And besides, it's terribly inconvenient for the guests. We have to think of them too, don't we?"

He sipped his liqueur.

"You seem to like it," Miss Shaw said. "That's nice. But you must remember always to specify Bols banana liqueur. The Dutch make the finest by far. It's much superior to Marie Brizard and all the others."

Jencks nodded, set down his empty glass, and motioned to the waiter for another.

"Tell me," he said. "Is this kind of thing just a hobby, or are you in the business?"

"Well, I'll be perfectly frank, Mr. Jencks."

"Call me Steve. You might as well."

"I'll be perfectly frank, Steve. When one gets to be my age, the little comforts of life are very important—much more important than they are when you're younger. So periodically, I . . . contrive to keep my bank balance healthy. Generally, I make my forays into the exciting life twice a year. Sometimes more, sometimes less. Depending."

"Be my partner," he said, on an impulse.

She smiled, genuinely amused. "That's very kind of you. I should be delighted, should our paths cross in the future."

"Let's see that they do."

Miss Shaw considered him for a moment, then dug into her purse and produced an engraved card.

"My address," she said. "I'm away from Brighton a good deal of the time—for my health—but I have excellent forwarding arrangements, and letters never fail to reach me. Will I hear from you?"

"You will," Jencks said, pocketing the card.

"Delightful," she said. "And now I'd like one more glass before lunch."

———

As the *crème caramel* arrived, Peter said, "I'm serious. This is absolutely your last chance."

Jenny finished her wine and looked at him steadily. "I know that."

"And you have nothing more to say?"

"No."

"May I ask," Peter said, "how you intend to get around for the rest of the summer, when my car and I are gone?"

"I'll think of something."

"It's that man, isn't it?" he said accusingly. "That boxer. You're going off with him."

ODDS ON

"Yes," Jenny said, taking a bite of the *crème* and thinking of St. Peter's. It would be hot in Rome, but she wouldn't mind. They'd find an air-conditioned hotel.

"Well, I have news for you," Peter said. "When he leaves here, he'll go alone. He won't give you the time of day."

"What makes you think so?"

"I know his type, that's all."

"Peter, you're so astute. It constantly amazes me."

"Go on, laugh. Just wait and see if I'm right. You'll find it isn't so funny." He stood up from the table, not touching his dessert. "But if you ever want to look me up. I'll be in St. Tropez. It's a small town, and—"

"I've been in St. Tropez before, Peter."

He looked at her, puzzled and annoyed. "You really think he's going to take you with him, don't you?"

"Yes," she said, "I really do." She reached over, and took his dessert. Very slowly, she began to eat it. In her mind, she clearly saw the high skeleton of an oil rig, and she heard the clatter and shouts of the drilling team.

———

"How do you feel?" Jencks asked.

"Like I've fallen down an elevator shaft. But I'll live." Bryan shifted in his bed and winced. There was a large bruise on his forehead, and one eye was a puffed purple-red.

"Steak's good for it," Jencks said.

"I asked, and they brought me a little thing so thin you could almost see through it. I'm afraid I'll just have to make do."

"Are you going back to London?"

"Not immediately."

ODDS ON

Jencks's eyebrows went up.

"It's a pleasant place," Bryan said. "I think I may stay on for a while." He paused. "Well, what's the odd look for?"

"Nothing, nothing."

"I have a friend," Bryan said slowly, "in Lyons. He's been after me for years to join his export firm. He does most of his business in southern France, and I spent a lot of time there, during the war."

"You're not going back to London?"

"I don't know. It depends."

Jencks did not ask on what it depended. He held out his hand. "She's a nice girl."

"And what does *that* mean?"

"Nothing, nothing." They shook hands. "Let me know how it turns out."

"I will. Cheers, Steve."

"Good luck, Bryan."

As Jencks went out, the receptionist came up and knocked on Bryan's door.

She came very quietly inside. "Well, you look a sight."

"I fell down the stairs," Bryan said.

"Right on your eye, I suppose."

"Point of honor, you see."

"Whose honor?"

Bryan shrugged. "Mine. Yours."

"You ought to stay on a few extra days until you look more presentable."

"I intend to." He smiled.

"Very long?" She smiled back.

He shrugged. He did not know what he felt about this girl; as he looked at her he thought again of Jane, but she was a faded image, like a movie he had seen in his youth. He was tired of his old life; there was no more kick in the suspense, only nagging fear. Somehow, Jane belonged to an existence he was shedding—she was a part of it, integral to it, cold and hard in her own way, part of the total pattern.

"Tell me," he said. "Have you spent much time in southern France?"

———

"Oh, you poor thing," Cynthia said, painting Jean-Paul's cheeks with Merthiolate. She smiled to herself. It made him look like a clown, those two pink circles. Jean-Paul winced. "Does it hurt very much?"

"No," he said, "only when I—"

"Never mind," she said smoothly. "You'll feel better in a day or two. Would you like a cold compress for your head?"

He nodded weakly. She brought one to him and placed it over his forehead. He really did look terrible; he had ugly marks and scrapes all over his body and a nasty gash on his chin. Too bad, she thought, but then Miguel was better in bed anyway. Miguel had that little extra something.

"Aunt Elizabeth will be here to see you soon," she said.

He watched her go to the door. "Leaving?"

"Yes," she said. "I have to—pack."

"*À bientôt.*"

"*À bientôt,* Jean-Paul."

She walked quickly down the hall to her own room.

"Baby," Miguel said, as she entered. "Where have you been?" What a body, he thought, what a body this chick had. It was like a rock-and-roll song, whenever she took a step. It pounded in your head, each little movement, every tiny twitch.

"Nursing," Cynthia said. She stretched. The *kef* had worn

off days ago, it seemed. She was down, way down, and she wanted to get high again.

"I'll bet you're a good nurse."

"It's not really my line."

"What's your line?"

"Pleasure, pure pleasure." She looked around the room for her cigarettes. "Let's get blocked."

"You got the stuff?"

"More than enough." She passed him a cigarette, which looked ordinary enough except that the end had been twisted shut. "I want to get very, very high. And then I want to make obscene love."

"I'm with you," he said, lighting the cigarettes. He drew the smoke into his lungs and held it as long as he could. He disliked the smell of *kef,* and always had. But after all, the smell wasn't the important thing.

"We should start some kind of regular arrangement together," he suggested, grinning broadly.

"Maybe. You'll have to prove yourself first."

"Give me half a chance."

"I'll give you half a dozen chances," she said, inhaling deeply.

Later, when they had each smoked two cigarettes, and time jerked and flowed in strange patterns, she began to undress.

"Chance number one?" he asked.

"Coming up," she said.

———

After leaving Bryan, Jencks looked for Miguel, but didn't find him. It wasn't difficult to figure out why, and so he had gone down to the bar for another banana liqueur. He was developing quite a taste for them. He ordered this one on the rocks, just to see how it would go down. The bartender looked at him as if he were crazy. Well, Jencks thought, lighting a cigarette, perhaps he was.

"Steve," Jenny said. "I've been looking for you."

She was wearing her navy-blue jumper, which softened the outlines of her body, making her appear younger, more girlish.

"Drink?" he asked, indicating his own.

"What is it?"

"Banana liqueur on the rocks. An experiment, in its own little way."

"Better get me a bourbon and water."

He did, and they moved from the bar to a table.

"I wanted to talk to you," she said, "about Rome."

"I wanted to talk to you, too," he said, slowly. He wondered how to put it. She was obviously counting on the trip, if only to escape from the pimple-faced kid. But she was looking at him with an expression of such open innocence that words didn't come. Finally, he said, "I'm not going to Rome."

"I expected that."

He was surprised. "You did? Why?"

"Because it all fell through."

"What? What are you talking about?" Her voice had been calm, but it sent shivers down his spine.

"All your plans."

"Jenny," he said, "say what you mean."

"Out of curiosity, where are you going now?"

"I haven't decided," he said.

"I don't believe it."

"Well actually," he admitted, "I was thinking of the Canary Islands. Las Palmas, maybe."

"Just a vacation?" Her voice had a slight, insinuating edge which he caught. Again, shivers.

ODDS ON

"Yes, of course. I need a rest."

"I know you do."

"Jenny, stop talking in riddles."

"I don't know exactly how to explain it," she said. "Did I ever tell you what business my father was in?"

"Yes. Oil, if I remember."

"That's right. Ever since I was a kid," she ignored his smile, "I've been hanging around rigs and drilling operations. I've seen all phases of it and seen all the tools of the trade."

"What you mean," he said dryly, "is that you know a blasting cap when you see it."

"Nice job on the bridge," Jenny said. "It was very professional. How did you detonate it? Radio?"

"As a matter of fact, I considered that, but rejected it in favor of—" He stopped himself. What was he saying?

She smiled. "Take me with you, please."

"It's blackmail!"

"That's the wrong way to look at it. I'd be a perfect companion, attractive, pleasant, undemanding—except in certain areas—and agreeable. And I would never tell."

"Tell what?"

"It was wonderful of you to give it all back, Steve. I don't know why you did it in the first place, but I'm glad you have a conscience."

He put his head in his hands and groaned.

"Take me with you."

"And where would it all end?" he asked. "I think you're being foolish not to consider that."

"I have, and I don't care where it ends. Just so it doesn't end now."

He looked into her soft blue eyes, saw the long lashes, the blond hair, the dimples, and the full lips. Her face was innocent, but she hadn't lost an exciting touch of fire. She was the girl for him; she knew it. They both knew it. For the time being, it was perfect. And she was right—it didn't matter where it ended. That was one thing he had learned during the past week—you could never be sure of the finish. Despite the best of preparations, the conclusion always remained in doubt.

"All right," he said. "Las Palmas it is. We leave tomorrow at nine o'clock."

She smiled—a happy, radiant smile. "I've already packed."